D0916344

NAUGHTY
Little Angel

By J. TREMBLE

A Life Changing Book *in conjunction with* Power Play Media
Published by Life Changing Books
P. O. Box 423 Brandywine, MD 20613

This novel is a work of fiction. Any references to real people, events, establishments, or locales are intended only to give the fiction a sense of reality and authenticity. Other names, characters, and incidents occurring in the work are either the product of the author's imagination or are used fictitiously, as are those fictionalized events and incidents that involve real persons. Any character that happens to share the name of a person who is an acquaintance of the author, past or present, is purely coincidental and is in no way intended to be an actual account involving that person.

Library of Congress Cataloging-in-Publication Data;

www. lifechangingbooks. net

13 Digit: 978-1-934230-88-6
10 Digit: 1-934230-88-X
Copyright ® 2008

All rights reserved, including the rights to reproduce this book or portions thereof in any form whatsoever.

ALSO BY J. TREMBLE

Secrets of a Housewife

More Secrets More Lies

DEDICATION

I'd like to dedicate this novel
to the loving memory of my father
William C. Johnson
I miss you!

This novel is also dedicated to all the little girls, no matter their ages, who still believe that an asset is their body. May you understand that you are meant for so much more, you are meant for greatness. Never allow anyone – family, friend or foe, to stop you from being the most amazing creation that God has made. Enjoy!

ACKNOWLEDGEMENTS

It took a wonderful group of people to make *Naughty Little Angel* come to life, so here I go…

To my wife: I look at you and wonder, what did I ever do to deserve such a woman like you to love me as much as you do? I can only thank God because the answer escapes me. I've never met another woman that can compare to you. You are an amazing wife, mother, lover, teacher, nurse, cook, accountant and entrepreneur (just to name a few of the titles you hold) that I could ever ask for. Thank you for staying up late to read my rough drafts, for being honest with the parts you hate, allowing me to travel to promote my work and not spending all my royalty checks (smile). I can't wait to grow old with you. You are my everything.

To my mother: The last few years have been a major test of your strength and willpower. The tremendous way that you have continued to be a beacon of light in the lives of others, especially when the pain is unbearable, reinforces why you are my one and only role model. I strive to live each hour trying to better myself and become the man that will never disappoint you. I thank you for everything you've done, you do and will continue to do. I just want you to know that my words could never give justice to what you mean to me.

To all my loved ones: I thank God for providing all the amazing people in my live to help and support my endeavors. I love you Mi-Mi for the editing and proofreading that you do even when you're too tired. To my children for allowing me to bring pencil and paper to their activities just in case I get the urge to write. Thank you for understanding that daddy loves you even though I'm off in fairy tale land. I must thank all my family members who spread the word about my books like their life depends on it. Please, keep promoting!!

I want to thank three of the greatest women in the world. Cynthia, Barbara and Jacque for the many hours you've spent typing my work from my notebook paper. It takes a wonderful person to read my handwriting and figure out what words I wrote, meant to write or just tried to write. My novels would only be thoughts on paper if it weren't for you ladies.

I have to give a special shout out to my two top salesmen. Damon and Curry - nobody can compare to you guys. Thank you for the long road trips, the long hours in the stores, and the many books you sell. I love hanging out with you guys at book signings. The both of you are wild. No matter where we go or the type of people who walk past my table, you sell books like nobody else. If there is anything that you need, just ask and it's done. My niggas for life.

Thank you to all my friends and co-workers. Thank you for all the time you allow me to disturb you just to lend me an ear, to listen to my ramblings, or just for showing me support. You guys are truly priceless. Let me roll call: Michelle, Kinesha, Cameron, Wallace, Clark, Moore, Brooks, Blakney, Coates, Battle, Shellie, K. Davis, Ms. Lewis, Mellen, Gudger, Muse, Mayhew, Ms. Harris, L. Davis, Gathers, Lomax, Kelly, Erika, N'Cho, Cox, Griffin, the entire lunch room staff and all my other BSMS family.

I would like to thank all the guys from the flag football league that help promote my books. Big ups to: Rough Riders, We Are One, HUH, Invaders, True Players, Fairmont Falcons, BET, Young Guns, UT and the other teams playing hard on Sunday mornings across the Metro Area. Special shout outs, Gerald, Snack, Derrick, Kurt, Big Ray, Little Ray, Mac, Charmin, Charlie, Stanley, Jamaal, No-No, Tony, Paul, Tu, TO, Rudy, Marlin, Wayne, Marcus and all the new and old guys.

To my Publisher: Azarel, author (*A Life to Remember*, *Bruised*, *Bruised 2*, and *Daddy's House*) and the Director of Op, Leslie Allen. I would be here forever if I wrote down all the great things about the two of you to express my feelings for all the support, time and hard work you put into my books, but I'll start by just saying thank you. I'm truly grateful for everything you do.

To my LCB family: Danette Majette (*I Shoulda Seen It Comin'* and *Deep*), Tonya Ridley (*The Takeover* and *Talk of the Town*) Tiphani (*The Millionaire Mistress* and *Still a Mistress*), Mike G (*Young Assassin*), Mike Warren (*A Private Affair*), Tyrone Wallace (*Double Life* and *Nothin' Personal*), Ericka Williams (*All that Glitters*), and all the new authors on the roster, I wish the best for all of you. Keep putting out those hits!!! Nakea Murray, you know you are the best. Thanks for making it possible for me to stay on my grind. To Kathleen Jackson, thanks for editing my book. Latahsa Hughes, thanks for catching that crucial mistake.

Lastly, I would like to thank all my fellow authors out there on the grind, the stores that support and promote us all, the distributors, vendors (especially NYC and Philly) and last but certainly not least…the readers. If it weren't for you, none of us would be where we are today. Thank you from the bottom of my heart for making Secrets of a Housewife and More Secrets More Lies a huge success.

Yours Truly,
J. Tremble
King of Erotica

NAUGHTY
Little Angel

CHAPTER 1

"Come on girl, show me your skills. Suck every inch of this dick," Antoine hissed, forcing his co-worker's head downward.

Natasha began to twirl and wiggle her tongue around his hardening penis. A smile appeared as he admired the exotic dance that was taking place between her mouth and his shaft. Although she tried her best to please him, Antoine could tell Natasha was having a hard time sucking his entire dick. Fortunately for him, he'd been blessed with a massive tool, which he was extremely proud of.

"Don't hurt yourself with that big thing, baby," he said in a cocky tone, as he removed his hand from her head, so she wouldn't choke. The last thing he needed was a girl with another set of swollen tonsils.

As Natasha continued to massage a portion of his shaft with her warm, moist mouth, Antoine admired her amazing figure. He especially liked the way her ass smiled at him every time she walked by during the day.

Natasha was the gorgeous new temporary receptionist at the Miami Physical Therapy & Rehab Center, a place Antoine worked since graduating with a master's degree in physical therapy from Florida A&M University. He was also a certified personal trainer with an elite clientele that mostly consisted of women, and his private sessions were a big hit around town. Because of his strong passion for females, Antoine knew he either had to become a trainer or an ob-gyn in order to be around women everyday. However, after thinking about it, he decided not to become a pussy doctor. Even though he loved women, he didn't want to be around them when their kitties were on the war path.

After meeting Natasha, Antoine knew it was only a matter of time before he would be tapping that ass. It didn't even matter that she was ten years, his senior. Age was never a factor, when it came to hitting on a woman. As long as she had a pussy, he was down.

She's only been at the center for a month, and I already got her ass on her knees, he thought. Seconds later, the sounds of Natasha gagging, immediately made Antoine look down at his new lover.

"That's enough for now, baby," he said, pulling his dick away from her dripping mouth. "Don't worry. You'll learn how to handle this beast later on." As Natasha stood up, he grabbed her hand and directed her toward the weight bench. "Lay back," he instructed.

Like a good student, Natasha instantly did as she was told. Antoine looked at her, like a fresh piece of meat, before he began playing with her throbbing vagina through her blue Nike bike shorts. He realized how wet Natasha was when her juices began to show through her shorts. She obviously wasn't wearing any panties. His tongue slid across his lips as the urge to taste every ounce of her almost made him explode with anticipation.

Damn, I'm glad she asked me to check out the pain in her lower back earlier today. Even though, Antoine knew that was just an excuse to get closer to him after work, he was more than pleased to take Natasha up on her offer. Besides, they had been flirting with each other every day since she started, so he knew she was ready. The sweet smell of her pussy held him captive as his face drew closer to her jewel. However, before making another move, he looked around the rehab center just to make sure they were still alone. Antoine was the head therapist and closed the facility everyday, but the crazy janitor, Miguel had a set of keys and was known to use the gym equipment before his shift started.

After making sure everything was okay, Antoine turned back toward Natasha. "Take 'em off," he ordered, pointing to her shorts.

Her hands moved swiftly as she pulled off the tight spandex material and exposed her overflowing pussy. Without any more hesitation, Antoine lifted up her legs and dunked his entire face into her treasure.

Natasha let out a slight moan as his nose pressed back and fourth against her clit. Her thighs began to vibrate as the tingling sensations raced up and down her back. Before long, she had reached a climax and her warm fluids squirted into Antoine's unsuspecting mouth. He swallowed her special treat and continued to suck on her clitoris until his jaws felt sore. Seconds later, Natasha pushed him away and sat up on the bench. He watched as she stood up and motioned for him to follow her with a wave of her hand.

Following behind her like a trained puppy, Antoine loved how Natasha's small waist sat on top of her big round ass. As he began to take his clothes off, he also noticed several tiger paw tattoos that walked up the back of her right leg. She paused when they reached the rowing machine.

After motioning for Antoine to sit on the cold leather seat, Natasha threw her left leg over him and slid her dripping pussy down his throbbing pole. He buried his face in her 36C breasts as she sped up the tempo. *She rides horses well*, he thought.

His rock hard shaft banged against her inner walls with massive force. She leaned her torso back against the machine and opened her juicy tunnel, so every inch of him would be submerged. His large hands clamped onto the hand-rails in order to keep up with her pace. After finding the perfect rhythm, Antoine placed his hands around Natasha's waist and moved her up and down at a rapid pace. Even though she was on top, she was no longer in control.

Natasha began to rub his head frantically. His soft curly hair slid through her fingers as his dick pressed against all the right spots. His shaft was so far inside, she felt as if the tip was tapping against her chest.

"This dick is so good," she shouted.

The sound of Natasha talking dirty made Antoine pull her waist up and down with even more force. "You like this shit, huh?" he responded.

"Yes, baby, work this pussy! Work it, baby! This pussy is yours." She kept blurting out phrase after phrase.

Damn, this soon? I know my dick is good, but I didn't expect her to give up pussy ownership this early?

A few seconds later, her legs began to shake like she was having a seizure, and her walls began to tighten. He knew exactly what that meant.

"I'm cuming, too girl. Get ready!" he commanded.

"Oh God, don't stop! It feels so good," she blurted out. "It's your pussy, it's your pussy!"

Almost instantaneously, they both reached a climax and exploded into each other while moaning at the same time. Instantly, Antoine closed his eyes and tried to catch his breath. *This was one hell of a workout. Her pussy is better than I thought it would be.*

As Natasha slowly rose to her feet, her kitty released sections of his dick, starting with the head, then the middle and finally the base. She used both hands to push her long black hair off her face. Her caramel skin glowed as drops of sweat ran down her cheeks.

"I thought I might feel bad about having sex with you," she finally said.

Antoine flashed his sexy smile. "Well, do you?"

She hesitated for a moment. "Not really. But don't think I'm stupid either. I know your reputation around the center."

"My reputation? What are you talking about?" he asked, trying to act innocent.

"No need to play games. I know you've slept with several of your clients along with a few other therapists around here."

Wow, good news travels fast. "Well if that's the case, I hope I've lived up to all the stories," Antoine replied with another smile.

"Actually the women didn't do you justice," Natasha said, turning around. She walked back to the weight bench as Antoine followed closely behind. "I need to freshen up," she said, walking into the ladies bathroom.

"Don't keep me waiting," he shouted as she left the room.

Antoine smiled when he walked past the full length mirrors to gather his clothes. He was proud of the thick muscles on his six foot frame, and the six pack that lined his stomach didn't hurt either. However, when he leaned closer to the mirror, he noticed a mark on his neck. Apparently Natasha had left several scratches on his smooth honey dipped skin. He instantly became annoyed.

"I can't believe this shit. How in the hell am I supposed to pick up other bitches like this?" he asked himself.

Antoine sat on the weight bench fully dressed, staring at Natasha when she exited the bathroom. He continued to admire

17

her body as she slowly walked across the floor. He stood when she held out her arms for a good-bye hug, and smiled when the scent of her J'adore perfume filled his nose. She rubbed her hands up and down his rock hard body until she felt a tingling feeling coming over her again. Quickly, she released him.

"I hope you don't have a man at home," he said.

"Why? What difference would it make now?"

"Actually, it doesn't make any difference to me, but I don't think he would be overly pleased if you came home smelling like another dude."

Natasha rubbed his arm up and down. "I don't have a man, baby. But, if we keep spending time together like this, then I wouldn't mind offering you that position."

Antoine looked like he'd seen a ghost. Every time a woman even mentioned anything about being in a relationship, he immediately felt dizzy. "Umm, actually I don't think it would be a good idea if we saw each other again, especially since we work together."

Natasha put her hands of her hips and frowned. "What? It didn't matter if we worked together when you had your dick up in me. But now that the fun is over, you wanna try and play me?"

"Listen, calm your lil' ass down before you get embarrassed up in here. I don't have to explain shit to you. Besides, I thought you knew all about my reputation." Natasha didn't respond. "But, if you need me to check out your back pain again then let me know."

If looks could kill, he would be dead instantly. Natasha looked at him with an evil stare as she clenched her jaw. "I need to go," she said, walking toward the front of the center.

Shit, let me follow her ass before she grabs a gun or something.

When they reached the waiting area, Antoine unlocked the front door, then held out his arms. "Can we still be friends?" He poked his bottom lip out like a sad child.

"Fuck that, this shit ain't over motherfucka!" Natasha yelled as she stormed out the door.

Antoine shook his head as she walked toward her car. "See this is why I fuck 'em then leave 'em. Women are too fucking emotional and crazy."

Just as he was about to turn around, he saw the janitor, Miguel pulling up into the parking lot. Once Miguel loaded all his cleaning materials inside his cart, he finally made his way into the building.

"Hola, Mr. Moore. I didn't know you were working late sir," Miguel stated after Antoine greeted him.

"Yeah, I had a late session with one of my clients," Antoine replied with his famous smile. He then turned around and walked into the office that all the therapists shared to grab his backpack. After looking in his appointment book, he walked back to the waiting area.

"I'm out of here, Miguel," he said. "Oh, before I forget, the weight bench and the row machine are gonna need a little extra cleaning tonight. That's where my client and I put in most of the work."

"No problem, senor. Have a good evening."

"Actually, Miguel I already have."

        ชǝ   ชǝ   ชǝ

Twenty-five minutes later, Antoine pulled into the Lincoln Residences subdivision and up to his brand new 3300 square foot single family home. As he walked past the freshly cut grass, he felt proud to be able to afford the beautiful home in Coconut

Grove, and provide a nice environment for his sixteen year old daughter, Angel. *It's nothing like being a good father*, he thought as he stuck his key into the gold plated doorknob.

When he walked into the house, Angel was washing a glass in the kitchen sink, and bobbing her head to a Rihanna song that blasted through her iPOD speaker. Antoine went straight to the refrigerator and picked up a can of Red Bull, which he rubbed across his head before downing it. When Angel noticed her father enter the room, she turned the music down, and looked at him with a blank expression. Even though she was used to his lack of affection by now, a hug would've been nice after calling him with the news that she'd gotten her scholarship to Howard University.

"What's up, baby girl?"

"What's that smell?" Angel asked when she walked past him. "It smells like two day old fish."

Antoine laughed. "*That* is the smell of something wonderful. It's the smell of a special gift that only a woman can give."

She shook her head. "I guess you convinced another one of your flunkies to sleep with you, huh?" Angel asked.

"What can I say? Baby girl, you must know by now that I love women and they love me," Antoine said jokingly.

"Whatever. Daddy, are we still going out tomorrow night to celebrate me getting the scholarship?" Angel asked.

"I wouldn't miss it," he replied, leaving the kitchen.

"Well, don't bring any of those women. It's just supposed to be me and you!" Angel yelled.

"Yeah, yeah."

Seconds later, the phone rang, which instantly made Angel nervous. She moved her head from left to right, trying to find one of the cordless handsets, but didn't see one.

"Shit," Angel said quietly, before she ran from the kitchen to grab another phone before her father picked up. But unfortunately for her, she was too slow. By the time, she reached the living room, Antoine was already speaking into the receiver.

"Hello."

"May I speak to my Angel?" a deep voice said through the phone.

Antoine's face frowned. "Your Angel? Nigga, it's ten o'clock. She can't have phone calls after nine. Who is this?"

"Well, tell her Wink called then," the deep voice replied.

"Wink! What the hell kind of name is Wink?"

Before the deep voice could respond, Angel pulled out the phone cord on the wall, disconnecting the call. "It's a nickname. You don't have to embarrass me like that. I'm about to graduate, and I still can't have phone calls after nine. There are six graders who can have phone calls later than I can. Besides, I need my own line."

"Why, so you can sit around and talk to these dumb ass boys? No...I don't think so. I just told you two days ago that nobody should be calling my house after nine," Antoine replied. "Hold up, that was a different boy anyway. The other day it was someone named Bones. Damn, do you know anybody with a real name?"

"Fine. Well when my cell phone is fixed, then they can just call me on that."

"Angel, if you keep being disrespectful, I won't get the damn phone fixed."

"I bet if I was one of your *women*, you would get the phone fixed." Angel pouted as she stomped up the steps to her room.

He laughed when he heard her bedroom door slam. *Little do you know baby girl, I don't buy women shit.* However, his smiled quickly faded. *Angel better not be doing grown up things. I would hate to kill her and some little punk ass dude. I'm the only one who better be fucking up in this house.*

Antoine wondered for the hundredth time since Angel turned into a teenager, if it was time to have that talk. He really wasn't ready to think about his daughter having sex. Besides, he couldn't have done it if he tried. For some reason, Antoine felt that a woman could get through to her better than he could. But the question was, which one of his female friends would be good enough to handle the job? No one came to mind as he finally went to his room to clean off the sweet smell of Natasha's pussy off his body.

CHAPTER 2

It took several circles around the congested downtown area before Antoine finally found a parking space. Bayside Marketplace was always packed, and even though he would've rather been throwing back Hennessy shots in South Beach, the night was about Angel, so he had to bite the bullet. After escorting his daughter into the restaurant, a young hostess escorted them to a table near the back. A table choice that Antoine was happy with. This way he could watch everyone, especially Miami's beautiful women. He hoped like hell there would be some single ladies floating around.

As they sat down, Antoine took out his wallet and fumbled around for a few seconds before placing it back in his pocket. "Shit, I can't believe this," he stated.

Angel's honey colored eyes widened. "What? Oh no, please don't tell me you forget your money. What about paying with a credit card?"

"No, it's not that. I left my business cards in the car. You know I need to give those out to a couple of beautiful females. I'm sure I'll meet some tonight."

Angel let out a huge sigh. "Dad, I would appreciate it if this dinner was about me."

"It is baby girl, but how do you expect me to keep you in all those Juicy sweat-suits you like, if I don't get more clients?"

Before Angel could respond, someone walked up to the table. "Good evening. Welcome to Bubba Gump Shrimp. My name is Kimberly and I'll be your waitress this evening. Can I take your drink order while you look at the menu?"

Antoine looked up and instantly realized how stunning Kimberly was. As he checked out her entire package, he noticed she was thick from top to bottom, especially in the bottom area. He gave her half of a smile when he took the menu.

"Well if this little lady was old enough, I would tell you to bring us two of your best drinks, so we could celebrate."

"Oh, what's the special occasion, if you don't mind me asking," Kimberly said, moving her eyes to stare back at Antoine.

"Tonight we are celebrating my Angel getting into college."

Kimberly smiled. "Oh, that's wonderful. Congratulations, Angel."

Angel knew her father well, and could tell what was going on between the two of them. For her, this was just another day with another woman.

"Thanks," Angel answered with a hint of anger in her voice. She knew Kimberly could care less about her future.

"You're so pretty," Kimberly said to Angel admiring her beautiful golden skin tone. "I can definitely see the resemblance between you two," she continued with a huge smile.

"I'm sorry Kimberly. You have a very pretty smile. I was just wondering, how many times do you hear that a night?" Antoine asked.

Here we go, Angel thought.

"Thank you. I don't hear it at all around here. Most men stare at other places. The other ones just have weak pick up lines that I easily ignore." With a touch of blush on her cheeks, she went in for the kill. "I don't see a ring. Will your wife be joining you tonight?"

"I'm not married. I'm a single father taking care of my daughter," he replied, using Angel to get him some bonus points.

Angel cleared her throat to get Kimberly's attention. "Can I get a Jenny's Favorite Smoothie please?"

Kimberly never took her eyes off of Antoine. "I'll bring you something special from the bar," she said to Antoine before writing down Angel's order then walking away.

"I can't believe you're trying to pick up the waitress on my big night out," Angel complained in a harsh tone.

"I can't help it if she finds me attractive. Did you forget how you used to break the ice with women for me when you were a little girl?"

"No, and I don't want to."

As Antoine sat and watched his beautiful daughter pout, memories of when Angel's mother, Mariah practically left her on his doorstep twelve years ago, started to cloud his mind. Although he knew his old college sweet heart, Mariah had decided to keep the baby they'd conceived while in undergrad, Antoine thought he'd made it clear once Angel was born, that he didn't want anything to do with her. Obviously, Mariah had decided to respect his wishes for the first five years of Angel's life, but somehow changed her mind.

The only thing she managed to say before leaving her daughter that day was, "You may not have wanted her before, but she's all yours now, asshole."

Speechless, all he could do was watch as Mariah turned around, got in the car with another man and left. Antoine remembered how Angel never cried or ran after her mother, but only stared up at him and smiled, exposing two missing front teeth. It was a hell of a way to meet his daughter.

"So you don't even care that I'm upset?" Angel asked, interrupting his thoughts.

Antoine cleared his throat. "Of course I do, baby girl." He paused for a moment before continuing. "Let me ask you something. I know we've tried to talk about this before, but you always want to change the subject. How did you feel, when your mother left you with me?"

Why did he have to bring this up while I'm trying to have a good time? He sure does know how to spoil a mood. Plus he's always ignoring me.

"Abandoned of course. I guess she didn't want me anymore. Just like you didn't want me when I was born." Antoine eyes bucked. "Yeah…she used to tell me that all the time."

Antoine was at a loss for words. He paused for a few seconds to try and get his thoughts together. "I did want you. But your mother wouldn't allow me to be in your life at first," he lied. He couldn't bear to tell her the truth.

"Honestly, I don't believe you. If you wanted to be part of my life, you would've fought for me. I mean, look at all the women you've allowed to keep me once I started living with you."

Antoine began to go back down memory lane, thinking about how Angel's arrival in his life was sudden and unexpected, and how challenging the transition was. He'd never been responsible for taking care of anything his entire life, not even a plant, so gaining a daughter overnight was a bit rough. *Damn, I do remember all the times I had to take her to work with me in the beginning because school wasn't in at the time.*

He remembered how all the male therapists in the center looked at him like they didn't want to be in his shoes, but the reactions from the women were totally opposite. They all seemed to think Antoine was the greatest father in the world by taking care of his daughter by himself, and before long they were standing in line to be of some assistance. Antoine left work with several numbers from women volunteering to help take care of him and Angel that day. As time went on, he soon realized that being a single father wasn't going to be so bad after all. Angel was a 'pussy magnet' and that seemed to work better than his best pick up lines any day.

"What are you gonna eat?" Angel asked.

"So, let me ask you another question. How do you feel knowing that your mother has two other kids now, and still doesn't want to spend time with you?" Antoine asked, ignoring her question.

I wish he would stop with all the questions. He's ruining my night with this Dr. Phil shit. "It's her loss the way I see it. Besides, I don't wanna be around somebody who acts like I don't even exist."

At that moment, Antoine felt bad for his daughter. He couldn't even imagine how it felt to have someone not care about him. He began to think about how he'd decided to contact Mariah a year ago after seeing her on television as she and two small children cheered from the stands at a football game. Antoine couldn't believe his eyes, when the words, *Mariah Lewis-Wright wife of Dwayne Wright* popped up on the screen. It was at that moment, he knew she was now married to the highly respected quarterback for the Miami Dolphins, and by the look on her face, she was quite happy. Rage was the only thing that came to mind as he watched her wave to the camera like she'd won the Miss America contest. He couldn't believe that she was living the good life while he struggled to raise their first born.

After contemplating for a few days, he finally decided to pull a few strings, and managed to find out what gym Mariah attended from another trainer. Once Antoine got up the nerve to make the surprise visit, he walked in with complete confidence that she would fall into his arms, and immediately ask to be back in Angel's life. However, he was wrong. Mariah cursed Antoine out in seven different languages, and told him that she didn't want anything to do with either one of them. Despite her request, Antoine tried several more times to talk to Mariah, but nothing worked. She eventually hired two bodyguards, and threatened to get a restraining order. It was at that moment when Antoine decided that enough was enough. It was time to fight back.

"Here you go," Kimberly said, putting down the drinks and bringing his thoughts back to the present once again. She brought Antoine a Sex On The Beach. "Are you ready to place your order?"

"Yes, I'll take the Shrimp New Orleans for my dinner," Angel answered.

"And what can I get for you, sir?" Kimberly asked.

"I really would like you on a platter," Antoine boldly stated.

Kimberly glanced over at him as if she couldn't believe he was saying that in front of his daughter. Antoine softly rubbed her hand as he returned the menu to her. Angel became visibly annoyed.

"My father is experiencing erectile dysfunction. I wouldn't waste my time if I were you," she snapped handing back her menu. "Just order him the same thing I got."

Kimberly's facial expression went into shock. Antoine looked at Angel with disbelief. He didn't say anything for a moment, just sat there as Kimberly turned around and walked away.

"Why in the hell would you say something like that?"

"Because tonight is supposed to be about me. Why does everyone else get your attention except me? Do you think you can get your hormones under control so we can enjoy a night out like a family?" Angel pleaded.

"I'm sorry. I promise, I'll be on my best behavior. You're the only woman who will get my attention for the rest of the night."

Even though the celebration started off rocky, Antoine kept his word for the remainder of the dinner. He also managed to ignore all of Kimberly's flirting, which was painfully hard. Every time she would come to the table, he would act like something was in his eye or go to the bathroom. He even went outside to get some fresh air a few times, just so he wouldn't let his daughter down. After waiting for Angel to finish her Chocolate Cookie Sundae, Antoine quickly signed the credit card slip when he saw Kimberly with another customer, then he and Angel left. He was more than happy that Kimberly had already placed the bill on the table. The last thing he needed was more temptation with Angel clocking his every move.

However, as soon as they got to the car, Antoine conveniently forgot his receipt and ran back into the restaurant to get it. All Angel could do was shake her head because she knew exactly what he was up to.

"This is ridiculous," she said to herself.

As soon as Antoine walked back into the restaurant, he immediately spotted Kimberly over by the bar. "Hey gorgeous," he said, walking up to her. "You know I couldn't leave without saying goodbye."

"Oh, I thought you were gone already. Thanks for the nice tip."

"You were worth it." Antoine licked his lips. "Let me give you something else," he said, slipping his business card into Kimberly's hand. "Call me sometime. My cell number is on there too."

Kimberly smiled. "You're a therapist, huh?"

"Yeah, and I'm also a personal trainer."

29

"Well, I'm sure there's a part of my body that needs to be worked on."

Antoine liked her style. She didn't play hard to get, and women like that always turned him on. He gently kissed the back of her hand before making his way back outside.

He could see the look of disappointment in Angel's eyes through the window as he walked to the car and got in. He knew he had broken his promise like so many other times before. They rode home in complete silence.

ھ   ھ   ھ

"Dad, do you love me?" Angel asked, as soon as they walked in the house.

Antoine was shocked. She hadn't said one word to him since they'd left the restaurant. "What kind of question is that? Of course I love you. You're my daughter. Why would you ask such a crazy question?"

"I know you love me because I'm your daughter, but I wonder if that's the only reason you love me…because you have to."

"I love you for being my daughter and just for being you," Antoine said, rubbing his temples. He could feel a slight headache coming on. It's what normally happened when he and Angel had conversations like this. "Listen baby girl, I lied to you earlier in the restaurant. When your mother told me she was pregnant with you, I told her to get an abortion. Then when she decided to have you anyway, I was furious because at the time I didn't want any kids. So yes, I did tell her that I didn't want anything to do with you. But I just want you to know, that was a long time ago. I was young. It has nothing to do with the way I feel about you now."

Angel shook her head. "I'm glad you decided to finally be truthful, but I still think you love women more than me. I mean,

I asked you not to give anyone else my attention for just one night, and you couldn't even do it."

Antoine held a smirk on his face. "Technically the night was over."

"How can you sit here and make jokes like that?"

"What do you want me to say, Angel? This is how I make a living. I flirt with women with the hope that they'll become clients, or so they can refer my services to other people. Don't you like all the nice things I buy you? Don't you like this big brand new house you live in?" Angel sucked her teeth. "Well, I can't get all those things if I don't work."

"You always use that excuse. It worked when I was younger, but I'm older now. I know that you sleep with most of your clients, so is that still business? You need to come up with a better reason," Angel said, walking up the steps.

"You know sometimes I think you're confused, because the last time I checked, you were my daughter and not my damn wife. Like I told you before, I don't have to explain myself to you!"

"I guess you won't be getting the father of the year award!" Angel shouted back, before slamming her bedroom door.

Man, this parenting shit, is for the fucking birds, Antoine thought as he walked into the kitchen and fixed a shot of Hennessy. After downing the warm liquid, he took two more shots. He hoped the alcohol would make him forget about the entire incident, but he was wrong. *Damn, maybe I should've put her ass up for adoption when her mother rolled out because I'm not trying to deal with this shit.*

CHAPTER 3

Three days went by with Angel giving Antoine the silent treatment the entire time, but he didn't mind. He was used to women being mad at him all the time, so his daughter was no exception. He walked into an empty house after work that evening, which was quite surprising, being that, Angel was normally at home. Becoming concerned, he quickly walked into the kitchen and grabbed one of the cordless phones, to see if she'd at least left a voicemail on the house phone because she hadn't called his cell.

"I've gotta remember to get her cell phone fixed," he said, picking up the silver handset. However, before he had a chance to hit the talk button, he saw a white piece of paper taped to the refrigerator. Walking over to see what it was, he instantly let out a sigh of relief as he read the torn piece of notebook paper.

Dad, I'm going over my friend Brandi's house to study.
If my cell phone was working, I could have called (hint… hint). I'll be back before nine.
Angel

"That's my girl," Antoine said to himself. "Always in those books." He balled the paper up and threw it in the trash before grabbing the phone again. This time, he was able to check the voicemail, which said, "You have seven new messages." Curious to see who wanted to get in touch with him so badly, he hit the button for the messages to begin.

3:00 p. m. — *Hello Mr. Moore. My name is Gerald Livingston, and I'm an agent for several NFL players. A few of my players are in need of a good trainer and my new client, Jonathan Smith recommended you. If you have any openings in your schedule for three new clients contact me at 305-555-6913.*

3:47 p.m. —*What's up baby? This is Deanna. I've been calling you for weeks now. Why haven't you called me back? I really need to see you because I got one hell of an itch that needs to be scratched. Please don't keep that big thing away from me too much longer. Call me.*

The next four messages were from little boys trying to reach Angel. Each one sounded older than the one before, so Antoine immediately hit the number three, and erased them all. *I'm getting real tired of these lil' niggas.*

4:22 p.m. — *You no good son of a bitch. I can't believe you're doing this. I just got papers in the mail about you wanting me to pay you for back child support. Are you fucking serious? Child support? What the fuck is this all about, Antoine? I can't believe after all this time you wanna do some dumb shit like this. I mean how old is Angel now, sixteen…seventeen? That means you would only be entitled to the money for a year or less than that, stupid ass. Oh, wait a minute…now I know what this is about. You hate the fact that I've moved on with my life. With my man and my kids. The kids that I love and adore…the kids that I want. You're just jealous because my man is paid, and you have to rub dicks for a living. Bitch, you won't be getting a fucking dime from me. Besides, my husband isn't gonna use his NFL checks to pay for a child that's not his. It takes all he has just to keep me happy. You better hope he doesn't find out about this shit, because if he does, trust me I'm gonna fuck you up so bad. I can't believe you brought this ghetto ass drama into my life...CLICK.*

Antoine listened to Mariah's message a few more times before a smile crept up on his face. He knew taking Mariah to court for child support was crazy and far fetched, but it was the only thing he could think of to get back at her. Hell, he'd been taking care of Angel for twelve years now, and even though Mariah's money wasn't needed, her pain was. She'd completely stop loving her own flesh and blood, so now it was payback time. However, he couldn't let Angel in on it just yet. She'd gone through enough, so he didn't want to add to her frustration with all the new drama.

Twenty minutes later, Antoine went into the small gym that he'd installed in his home to work out all the frustration that was built up. He turned the radio to 99. 1 and began to beat the heavy bag hanging from the ceiling as Lil' Wayne came blasting through the speakers. During his workouts, he loved to listen to rap, but normally his favorite grooves were slow sexy jams, especially when he was with his women. Antoine was starting to get into a nice groove, when he heard the sound of a car pulling up into the driveway.

"Hold up, I know this ain't one of my chicks coming over uninvited," he mumbled to himself. "They know the damn rules." When he looked out the window, he saw a brand new silver Lexus GS 350 with chrome wheels parked out front. "Who the fuck is that? None of my bitches have rides like that."

Before he could figure who the unfamiliar car belonged to, Angel stepped out wearing a short black skirt, a tight baby-doll t-shirt and four inch heels. Antoine was in complete shock. Even though he thought the sixty-one degree temperature was nice for a late March evening, that didn't mean she should've been in that skimpy-ass attire. Before she closed the door, he tried to see who was driving, but the tinted windows made it impossible. As the car drove off, he watched as his daughter stopped in the middle of the driveway and pulled out a pair of jeans from her book bag, slipped them on under her skirt, then switched her stilettos for a pair of Nikes. The fact that she'd put so much thought into her devious little plan, made Antoine even more furious. Angel was putting her key in the door when Antoine swung it open.

"Who in the hell was that?" he shouted.

Angel sucked her teeth. "Please don't overreact, it was only a friend."

"What type of little boy has a forty-five thousand dollar car?"

If only you knew me, you would know that I don't fuck with little boys, she thought. Angel laughed.

"What's so damn funny?" Antoine asked, as she walked past him into the house.

"Dad calm down. Brandi's brother gave me a ride home after we finished studying. It's their father's car." Angel lied with a straight face.

"So, where was Brandi, when her brother was doing all of this?"

"She was in the car with us." Angel lied again.

"So, if you were just studying, what's the purpose of the short-ass skirt and the prostitute shoes?"

Angel seemed caught off guard. "Umm...we had to dress up like our favorite celebrity at school today, and I was Tina Turner. I know taking the shoes off in the front yard seems odd, but I knew you would be pissed if you saw me in that type of stuff."

Antoine looked at his daughter suspiciously. He knew she was lying. "You better hope I don't find out you're playing games, lil' girl. Besides, you're about to get me upset like your damn mother did today."

"Like my mother. What does she have to do with this conversation?"

"Look, just go to your room. It's nothing that concerns you."

Angel looked at her father, who was sweating like a nervous groom, and decided not to press the issue any further. She watched as he slowly walked back into the gym. Moments later, she heard him banging away on the bag like a mad man. *What ever my no good mother did, must've been something major. I've never heard him hit the bag like that,* Angel thought. *Oh well, better her than me.*

Antoine continued to pound the leather until both of his hands were sore, and after working out for another hour, he finally decided to call it a night. When he went upstairs, he peeked in on Angel before continuing to his bedroom, which is something he hadn't done in years. He wanted to make sure she hadn't jumped out the window, and then tell him she decided to practice being Superman for career day. He still couldn't believe she'd actually sat in his face and lied about who she was with earlier. At that point, Antoine knew he was gonna have to watch her a little bit closer from now on.

Angel looked so beautiful as she slept in her pink satin pajamas. However, the more Antoine looked at his daughter he quickly became upset. He hadn't realized before how shapely her figure had become. Her thick thighs and big perky breasts were starting to resemble a full grown woman. It was also at that moment, when he could see how much of Mariah's Cuban heritage was in Angel's face, which pissed him off as well. He didn't need anything to remind him of Mariah's crazy ass.

All night he stared up at his ceiling trying to decide how to handle Mariah, and the crazy shit she might pull. Even in college, she was known to do crazy things when she didn't get

36

her way, so he knew he had to be prepared. *Let the drama begin,* he thought.

๛   ๛   ๛

The next morning, the Miami sky was covered by dark grey clouds when Antoine walked out his front door, which immediately put him in a somber mood. But he knew he had to get himself together because he had a morning therapy session with a voluptuous civil attorney named, Bianca Robbins, and he always made sure his clients got their monies worth.

Minutes later, when Antoine walked into the rehab center, Bianca was already waiting for him. After greeting his client, he asked her to give him a few more minutes to get himself together, then walked in the back toward the therapist office. Once in the large space that smelled like Ben Gay and rubbing alcohol, he put down his backpack, looked at himself in the mirror for a few seconds and finally headed back out to the waiting area. However, before he could reach his destination, he was greeted by Natasha, who looked like she had a serious attitude.

"Good morning beautiful," Antoine said.

"My name is Natasha, and I would appreciate it if you only called me that, asshole," she replied, looking up at his tall frame. She also couldn't help but look at the muscles that bulged out from Antoine's black wife beater.

He displayed a slight grin. "Oh, so I can't call you beautiful, but you can call me asshole? Who in the fuck put piss in your coffee this morning?"

"Look, I advise you not to have your clients waiting like that anymore. I already informed Dr. Wolenski, and he's not happy."

"Why the fuck would you do some shit like that? Ms. Robbins has only been waiting for about five minutes at the most,"

37

Antoine replied looking at his Suunto Titanium sports watch. He made a mental note to go in his boss' office to plead his case before the day was over.

"I don't give a damn if it's only a minute. Our clients pay a lot of money for our services, so they don't need to wait."

"Girl, you're just the damn receptionist, and a temporary one at that. Your ass has only been here for about a month, so don't be throwing no threats at me like that. Besides, I'm the head therapist around here. Don't fuck with me," Antoine belted as he brushed past her and into the waiting area.

"We'll see how long you stay the fucking head therapist," Natasha added.

≈   ≈   ≈

An hour into the session, Bianca could tell that Antoine was very withdrawn, and finally decided to say something.

"What's on your mind?" she asked.

Antoine shook his head. "Just got a few problems at home, but nothing I want to talk about."

"Well, you need to figure out something. You're really not paying me any attention today. I almost dropped the bar on my chest." She squeezed her breast together. "You wouldn't want me to hurt these would you?"

The way her nipples poked through her shirt, Antoine knew Bianca was in her wanna-be-fucked mode. Ever since she'd walked through the center's door a year ago, they'd been fucking in the parking lot after almost every session.

He looked around the room to make sure no one was listening. "Of course, I wouldn't want anything to happen to my babies, and if the three of you believe I've been neglecting you all, then tell me how I can make it up. I'll do anything."

She smiled. "Oh, I can think of a whole lot for you to do."

"How about a one-on-one session?"

Bianca instantly blushed. "You just said the magic words, but I don't want any parking lot action today."

"So, what about your place. That way I can get ten times freakier than my usual act."

"Sounds like what the doctor ordered," she purred.

"Cool, I'll meet you there."

Minutes later, Antoine walked back to the therapist office, and grabbed his backpack before walking back to the front desk. As soon as he saw the crazed look on Natasha's face, he hated the fact that he had to deal with her.

"I just got a call from my daughter's school. She doesn't feel very well, so I need to go pick her up and take her home."

She looked at him and rolled her eyes. "So, what about your other appointments? You're booked solid today. I'm sure your other female clients will be disappointed," she replied in a sarcastic tone.

"I'll try to come back this evening. In the meantime, just give my appointments to the other therapists. You can handle that, can't you? Just tell Dr. Wolenski I had a family emergency if he asks." He could feel Natasha's eyes burning a hole in his back when he turned around and walked away.

ॐ ॐ ॐ

The drive to Bianca's two bedroom condo in North Miami Beach was quick. When Antoine arrived at the eighteen story building, and was buzzed inside, he could feel his dick getting harder by the second. By the time he reached her front door, he was harder than a five day old bagel. All Antoine could think about as he knocked on her door was how he couldn't wait to get inside of her. Seconds later as she opened the door, he rushed inside and immediately ordered Bianca on her knees.

After slamming the door shut, she didn't waste any time and quickly obliged. It wasn't long before she faced his throbbing penis. Her tongue slid slowly over the outline of her mouth, and she snatched his shorts down. He smiled as she twirled her long tongue around the tip of his dick.

"I always love how you smell after our workouts. All I could think about today was how good your dick was gonna taste," she admitted.

"Well now is your chance to find out," Antoine replied.

Bianca grabbed his dick and invited every inch into her mouth. The quick jerks of her tight jaws quickly made his eyes roll back into his head. She grabbed his thighs to hold his shaking body still. Every movement her tongue and lips made were done with purpose.

Antoine admired her attention to every detail as she sucked his dick with passion. It made him chuckle watching her head move like a bobble head toy. He put his hands on her shoulder to acknowledge she was making him light headed. Antoine knew if she kept that pace he would be ready to explode in her mouth sooner than he wanted, so he pulled her up by her arms.

"I want to feel this dick inside of you before I cum," he said.

Bianca flashed a sexy smile. "I can't wait to feel that big dick inside of me either." She directed him to her master suite before laying on the queen sized bed and striping down to her birthday suit. She looked up at Antoine. "I want you to fuck me like never before."

"Oh in that case, let me bring out the heavy artillery," he replied. Antoine looked around the room and saw a light green towel laying on the chaise beside her bed, then spotted a pair of scissors on her dresser. After walking over to retrieve both items, he cut the towel into several long strips, and proceeded to tie all four of her limbs to each bed post. He then left the room to find items he could incorporate in their sex session.

Bianca became excited as she playfully tugged at the strips. She could hear Antoine closing cabinets, fumbling through the refrigerator and pushing buttons on the stereo in the living room. However, a slight feeling of concern came over her when she saw Antoine enter the room with two plastic grocery bags filled with all sorts of stuff.

"In order to fuck you like never before, I gotta make sure I do things to you that nobody else has," Antoine whispered into her ear before dropping the bags.

"Shit. You've never done anything like this before. I knew your ass was freaky."

Antoine decided to begin with a little body art. He took out a can of whip cream along with some cheese dip. Bianca's body shook when the whip cream made contact with her body. He outlined her two perky breasts to resemble the number eight, and filled in the circles with the dip. He then grabbed a little plastic container that held chunks of pineapples and placed one on each nipple. Throwing the can of whip cream and cheese dip into one of the bags, Antoine then pulled out a bottle of Hershey's Chocolate syrup. He used the syrup to outline her naval. Bianca smiled when she saw him bend over to go through another bag, and then emerged wearing a shower cap, painters mask and long yellow rubber gloves.

"I'm your doctor, Mr. Pleasure. It's time for your physical." Antoine pulled out a flashlight and a Tampax Pearl.

"Oh my God! What are you getting ready to do?" Bianca asked. She was beginning to think that she'd bit off more than she could chew.

41

"I'm gonna have to use my medical tool to examine you a little closer." He snickered slightly.

Before she could respond, Antoine leaned in with the tampon, and began to rub it against her clit. As she became wet, he held out his tongue and licked her dripping pussy a few times. "This is very strange," he said.

"What's wrong, Doctor Pleasure?" she asked getting into the role.

"It doesn't look like this tool is big enough to examine you," he replied, referring to the tampon.

"Please exam me," she begged.

He grabbed his erect dick and shouted, "I must use this larger tool to save your life!"

"Yes, doctor. You know what's best. Use the big tool to fill my aching body. Save my life!" Bianca screamed.

Antoine jumped between her legs and pushed her thighs apart. He then positioned her body and rammed his dick inside her wet pussy. She let out a loud moan. He circled his hips faster and faster until her pussy was on fire. Bianca was ready to cum and Antoine felt it. Her pussy began to tighten, so he pounded her spot until it exploded.

"Yes! Yes! Now that's what the doctor ordered."

"Doctor? Who's the doctor?" Antoine said, pulling his dick out.

Bianca looked confused. "I thought you were the doctor," she answered.

"Oh fresh fish, you're in trouble now."

"Fresh fish…. what are you talking about?"

Antoine stood up and snatched off the shower cap and mask. "You're the new inmate up in this penitentiary and my bitch, fresh fish. Have you been giving this pussy away?"

"No baby, I wouldn't ever give it to anybody but you," she panted, getting into the role again.

Antoine untied her left leg then rolled her sideways and smacked her ass with the cold metal spatula. "Whose ass is this, fresh fish?"

"It's your ass!" she shouted.

Antoine smacked her ass a few more times, leaving little red circles all over her butt cheeks. "I'm gonna toss your salad, and if I taste anything funny, I'm going to whip that ass!" Antoine was getting ready to dive in head first, when he heard his cell phone ringing.

Shit, whoever that is has to wait, he thought as he opened Bianca's ass cheeks a little wider. However, as soon as the phone stopped ringing, it started back up again. At that point, Antoine started thinking about his job, and how it could've been his boss. He released Bianca's butt and walked over to his shorts that were on the floor. Even though he loved pussy, now wasn't a good time to get fired over it. He reached in his pocket and glanced at the flashing number and realized it was Angel.

"What's up, baby girl?" He was so concerned that something could've been wrong, that he didn't even bother to ask what she was doing at home when she should've been in school.

"Dad, you need to come home right now!" Angel yelled through the receiver.

"Why, what's wrong?"

"Someone has spray painted our house with all sorts of crazy stuff."

Antoine couldn't believe what he'd just heard. "What? I'm on my way," he replied, closing his cell phone.

He turned and locked eyes with Bianca. He could see the disappointment on her face that he had to cut their session short. "Baby, I'm sorry but…"

Bianca cut him off. "You go handle your business. We can finish this another time."

"Think of your wildest fantasy, and I promise to make it a reality," Antoine said, as he kissed her forehead. He quickly put his clothes back on then ran for the door.

"Antoine, wait!"

He ran back to the room, hoping that what she wanted was important enough to stop him from leaving. "Yeah."

"Can you at least untie one of my arms? I can't stay like this forever." They both laughed as he went to untie her. "When are you gonna come back to put out the fire you started?" Bianca asked in sexy tone.

Antoine looked at her like he was irritated. "Didn't you see that I was just in a rush to get out of here? Please don't make this about your needs right now."

"Look, I refuse to keep doing this shit. We can't keep having sex without it ever going anywhere!"

"Why not?" Antoine responded as he gave a slight smirk and left the room.

All he could hear was Bianca yelling, "Asshole," as he walked out the front door.

CHAPTER 4

Antoine made it home in less than twenty minutes. He couldn't believe his eyes as his Cadillac Escalade screeched to a halt. Someone had spray painted Male Whore, and No Good Nigga on the front door, almost every window and even his driveway in jet black paint. Out of all the things someone could've messed with, trashing the home that he'd worked so hard for was unacceptable. Antoine's temper rose to his boiling point.

"Look at this shit!" he shouted, getting out his car. Antoine immediately started sweating from the eighty-four degree weather.

"Let the police handle this," one of his nosey neighbors replied as she walked her miniature yorkie along the sidewalk. "They know we don't tolerate this sort of stuff in this neighborhood." She looked at the house in disgust.

"If I find out who did this, the police won't be able to help them." Antoine began to think about who could've done such a thing, and then it hit him. With the countless number of women, he'd dogged over the years, it could've been any one of them out for revenge. When he began to go down a mental list of women he abruptly stopped at Mariah. *I know her ass probably did this*, he thought. *She's probably trying to get back at me for the whole child support thing*. As he continued to think about his crazy former lover, Angel walked out the house.

45

"Dad do you see this?" Angel asked.

"Why the hell are you at home in the middle of the day?"

Angel looked at the neighbor, who decided to walk away on that note. "If you would've asked me, what was wrong instead of yelling at me, I would've told you that I left school early because I was sick."

He wasn't sure if his daughter was lying and didn't want to take any chances. "So, if you're sick why didn't the school call me?"

"If you check the voicemail, you'll see that they did." Angel turned around and walked back toward the house, but quickly stopped. She looked up at her father's tall frame. "Don't get mad at me because one of your women messed the house up. Learn how to keep them in check."

"What…" It was the only word Antoine could get out as he watched his smart mouth daughter walk back into the house. He wanted to catch up with Angel and knock her ass into the middle of next week, but didn't have time to be in court for child abuse. After looking at the house for a few more seconds, he got into his car and headed for Home Depot.

It took him half the night getting the paint off the windows. He also ended up having to repaint the door and strip the driveway. Mariah's crazy behavior had placed this game on another level. At day break, he was going to the court building to file a restraining order. If she wanted to play rough, then he was the perfect opponent.

ॐ ॐ ॐ

The next morning, Antoine was waiting for one of the clerks at the courthouse to call his number when his cell phone rang. He didn't recognize the number and thought about letting the call go to the voicemail. Besides, the dirty looks from the old white woman behind the desk when his phone kept ringing was also making him uncomfortable. However, he decided to answer anyway.

"This is Antoine."

"Good morning Mr. Moore. This is Gerald Livingston. Sorry to call you so early. Is this a bad time?"

Antoine looked at the old women, who continued to give him nasty looks. "No sir, not at all. I got your message yesterday, and was getting ready to call you back."

"Really…well that's why I'm calling. I have a player in real need of a trainer. Do you think you can see him today?"

"Right now I'm taking care of some personal business, but I'll be done in about an hour or two."

"My client was hoping for at least a one o'clock appointment."

"That'll be perfect. Just make sure he brings his medical history. I need to see any information about his prior treatments. I'm a firm believer of not repeating things that might've already been tried and were unsuccessful," Antoine said cautiously.

"When I bring my client over to his appointment, I'll have the necessary forms," Mr. Livingston assured.

"Number twenty-one," the old woman said.

A guy sitting next to Antoine tapped his shoulder. "Hey man, you're number twenty-one. The lady is ready for you."

"Thanks main man."

"No, thank you, Mr. Moore," Mr. Livingston said, thinking Antoine was talking to him.

Antoine didn't bother correcting him as he began to walk toward the old woman.

"You have to turn your phone off sir," she ordered. "Didn't you see all the signs when you came in?"

Antoine nodded his head and held up a finger. "Mr. Livingston, I have to go into this meeting. I'll meet you and your client at the Miami Rehab Center at one."

"Wait, you didn't give me an address, Mr. Moore?"

"Sir, what did I just say?" the annoying woman asked.

"Oh, the center is on Biscayne Boulevard in Miami Shores. Next to the Country Club," Antoine said, before hanging up his phone. He walked back up to the old woman. "Sorry about that."

"I shouldn't even serve you since you totally disregarded the court rules."

Damn lady lighten up. I can't help it if your man ain't pleasing you at night.

After learning that he should've gone through a lawyer to file the restraining order, the old woman finally processed the paperwork after an hour of flirting and lying about Mariah constantly harassing him. Even though he could only get a temporary restraining order that was better than nothing. Antoine knew Mariah was going to have a heart attack after being served the papers, and he couldn't wait.

He rushed home and gathered his equipment for the scheduled session, then arrived at the center thirty minutes later. After being threatened by Natasha a few times when he first walked in, he began working out in order to look totally fit when Mr. Livingston and his client showed up. Antoine had just finished his second set of abdominal crunches and toe touches when he noticed a guy in a grey suit standing next to rookie sensation Michael Epps.

That has to be Mr. Livingston, he thought. Antoine walked over to the two men. "Uh, Mr. Livingston?"

"How are you Mr. Moore?" Mr. Livingston replied as the two shook hands. "I'm sure you know Michael Epps."

Antoine smiled. "Of course I do. The records don't stand a chance with you in the league. I'm sure the Dolphins are proud to have you on the team."

"Man, I hope you're right," Michael responded, shaking his hand.

Damn, I wish I could get some information out of him about Mariah and her bitch-ass husband Dwayne. "What do you need to work out?" Antoine asked.

Michael grabbed his left inner thigh. "I pulled my groin during practice last week, and it's really bothering me."

"Is the pain consistent or does it fade in and out?"

"Shit, it's a constant pain. It's waking me up in the middle of the night and everything."

"We'll start off with a good massage, then I'll start some electric shock therapy to ease the tension deep inside your muscle. Why don't you go change, and I'll meet you back here when you're ready." Antoine pointed to one of the private rooms.

When Michael walked away, Mr. Livingston pulled out a few forms. "Here's the medical history you requested."

"Thanks," Antoine responded taking the forms. "Now all Michael and I need to do is sign a contract for the rehab center, which I'll have the receptionist bring to us in a few minutes, and then we're all set."

"Great. Hey since you're highly recommended in the league, why haven't you started your own company yet?"

"Well, the rehab center has treated me so well, it's been hard for me to leave. However, that day is coming soon. I've even chosen a name for it already…Five Star Therapy."

Mr. Livingston laughed. "That's kind of catchy. I like it."

Antoine held a huge smile after his first session with Michael was over. He knew it was only a matter of time before his name would be ringing throughout the league, and Five Star Therapy would be the hottest ticket in town. He'd worked hard to build up his reputation at being the best at what he did, and now it was about to pay off.

He looked at his watch and realized it was still early. Not wanting to take anymore clients, he decided to call one of his many female companions who would be willing to help him celebrate his victory. Antoine quickly opened his cell phone and went to his contact list, which he called his pussy patrol. This list was filled with women from horny housewives, to ghetto girls who would immediately stop whatever they were doing just for a quickie. Antoine scored on his first call.

"Clear the rest of my schedule," he said to Natasha. He was so glad Dr. Wolenski was out of town for a medical conference. He didn't even wait to hear her bitch and moan before walking out the door.

Minutes later, Antoine pulled up at Ramona's apartment. She was a firefighter for Miami-Dade County, and stayed ready for a booty call, which was his type of woman. As soon as Antoine walked through the door it was on. Ramona was on top of him before the door closed. He spent the next hour trying to make sure Ramona reached repeated orgasms.

They were in the middle of a break when his cell phone went off. After realizing it was Angel's school calling, Antoine quickly sat up to take the call.

"Hello, this is Mr. Moore."

"Mr. Moore, this is Joan Perez. I'm the principal at your daughter's school."

"Good afternoon Mrs. Perez. Is something wrong with Angel?"

"Oh, it's Ms. Perez, actually. Well, there's just no easy way to say this, and I hate to inform you of this over the phone."

"Oh God, what happened!" *Please let Angel be okay.*

"Mr. Moore your daughter was caught with a male student in the boys' locker room by one of our P. E. teachers."

Antoine breathed a slight sigh of relief. "What did she get caught doing?"

"I have her sitting in my office. Maybe it's better for you to hear it from her. Is it possible for you to come to the school right away?"

"I can't wait that long, Ms. Perez. I need to know now. What was she caught doing?"

She hesitated for a moment before continuing. "Mr. Moore, Angel was caught performing oral sex on a male student," she replied softly into the phone like she was trying to weaken the blow.

"What the fuck?" Antoine said, letting out another burst of air. "I'm sorry Miss, excuse my language. Keep her little ass right there. I'm on my way."

CHAPTER 5

It didn't take long before Antoine burst through the large doors of Coral Gables High School. The smell of funky lockers penetrated his nose as he barged down the squeaky hallway at top speed. When he finally reached the front office, he swung the oak door open with a tremendous force. The two secretaries quickly leaned their heads around their Dell computers to see what was going on. However, they had no idea that it was a father ready to break his foot off in his daughter's ass.

Antoine walked over to the counter. "Excuse me, my name is Antoine Moore. I have a meeting with the principal, Ms. Perez concerning my daughter, Angel Moore."

An elderly woman stood from behind her desk. "Yes, Mr. Moore, Ms. Perez is expecting you. Please, right this way."

Antoine followed the older woman to a closed door down the hallway, and then waited as she tapped softly.

"Come in," a woman's voice said from inside the room.

"Excuse me Ms. Perez, Mr. Moore is here to see you."

"Thank you Mrs. Richardson. You can send him in."

As soon as Antoine walked into Ms. Perez's office, he saw a beautiful woman, who appeared to be of Mexican descent sitting behind the desk, and was in complete awe. *Damn, why didn't they have principals as fine as this when I was in school?* He continued to stare at the Eva Longoria looking woman until he managed to snap himself out of his trance. *Come on Antoine,*

52

you're not here for this, he thought. He then looked over at Angel, who was sitting on a couch with her arms folded and a serious attitude to go along with her defensive gesture. Antoine stared at her with disgust as he walked over to Ms. Perez's desk and extended his hand.

The principal stood and accepted the handshake. "I really hate having you come up here for a situation like this. Have a seat." Antoine sat in the black padded chair facing her desk. "Well, Angel do you have anything to say?" Ms. Perez asked.

However, before she could respond, Antoine interrupted. "What in the hell was going through your mind, Angel? Why would you do such a thing!" he shouted.

She didn't say a word. The only response Antoine heard was Angel sucking her teeth.

"Mr. Moore, I have no other choice but to expel Angel. We refuse to tolerate that sort of behavior around here," Ms. Perez said.

"Oh my God! What's gonna happen when she's expelled?"

"Well, I'm afraid Angel will not be able to attend anymore Dade County Schools, and it's so unfortunate because she's one of our brightest students."

Antoine looked at Angel. "Are you listening to the lady? You've thrown your life away by having oral sex with some nasty-ass boy. What were you thinking?" Antoine asked. When she didn't say anything, Antoine became furious. "Answer me!"

"I guess I wasn't thinking," Angel finally replied, although she never looked her father directly in the eye.

"Does her expulsion start right now?" Antoine asked.

"Yes, I'm afraid so," Ms. Perez answered. "Oh, and before I forget, I'm afraid we're gonna have to contact Howard University to let them know what happened here today. Once we do, I'm more than sure Angel will lose her scholarship."

Antoine's stomach felt as though it had fallen into his shoes. "What about the boy? He's being suspended too, right?"

"Oh, of course," Ms. Perez responded.

"Angel, go get your stuff and meet me at the car out front!"

As she stood up and walked out, Antoine thanked Ms. Perez then walked out the office in complete embarrassment. Reality immediately set in. Now he was going to be known as the parent whose child sucks dicks in her spare time.

Minutes passed as Angel took her time clearing out her locker, and headed to the exit doors. She wasn't in any rush to get chewed out or even worse, slapped upside the head. She was also glad that school was over, so she didn't have to answer tons of questions about what happened.

When she finally walked outside, Antoine waited in the car with his head leaned back against the head rest. He didn't even look at Angel when she opened the door and scooted into the passenger seat. He didn't even acknowledge her presence as he started his truck and quickly pulled off.

Minutes later, they were at a light when Antoine decided to finally break the silence. "Why would you do some slutty shit like that?" Angel let out a little sigh. "Oh, don't act like I'm getting on your fucking nerves. You're the one going around sucking on dicks in school."

Little do you know I don't usually fuck with guys my own age, but I had to get my lunch money somehow. Especially since your cheap-ass thinks twenty-five dollars a week is cutting it.

"You're one to talk. Do you know how many times I looked through your cracked door growing up to see women giving you head almost every night?" Angel's voice began to tremble. "I never heard you complaining about them. You sure are a fine example. Do as I say and not as I do. Don't you think I remember listening to you and Terrell talk about all your

54

college stories? You weren't prefect either!" Angel shouted. "Shoot, you were probably in my principal's office trying to see how you're gonna sleep with her!"

Antoine's anger had him whipping in and out of traffic like a Nascar driver. "Don't try to turn this shit around on me."

Despite her trying to play the reverse psychology role, the mention of his best friend, Terrell's name, did bring up memories of his crazy college days. He remembered all the wild parties after each football game like it was yesterday. Being the star, wide receiver and running back for the Florida A&M football team supplied Antoine and Terrell with tons of women. So much, all the girls on campus gave them their own fraternity name… Ho-Phi-Ho. The girls had even taken it a step further and gave Terrell the nickname, Tightness because of his tight ass.

However, it was at one of these legendary parties, that he met crazy-ass Mariah, who was a freshman at the time. Antoine remembered being hypnotized by the way her ass moved as she bounced to the beat of *Jingling Baby* by LL Cool J. However, although it wasn't in his character, this was one woman, Antoine wished he'd passed up.

"I can't believe you're being such a hypocrite. You actually created me in school. At least I'm trying to be smart about the way I roll. The last time I checked, you can't get pregnant from sucking a dick," Angel said, in a sarcastic tone.

"Who the fuck are you talking to like that? I'm not one of your little girlfriends. Have you lost your mind? It is do as I say and not as I do in my house. If you're so damn grown to talk that way and do things your way, then get your own place to live. As long as you're in my house, you will follow my rules. I mean, don't you even care that you're gonna lose your damn scholarship?"

"I don't care about a lot of things anymore. I only care about my happiness right now."

"So sucking a dick is what makes you happy?"

"Doesn't it make you happy when women do it to you?"

Antoine raised his voice. "Angel, why do you keep saying shit like that? Besides, what I do in the privacy of my own bedroom is my business. I'm a grown man. You can't do what I do... you're only seventeen!" Antoine continued to drive like he was crazy. "What's this boy's name you were with anyway? Oh, let me guess...it's probably some crazy shit like Dirt or Pickle."

"What difference does it make what his name is? It's not like he made me do it."

"Because I asked that's why. Besides, I need to find out, so I can go kick his ass like I might do yours."

"Why didn't my mother come back and get me?" she asked sadly, folding her arms.

Her question caught him a little off guard, being that she totally changed the subject. "You know what Angel, I'm sick of you saying that every time you get mad. You know as well as I do that your mother doesn't want anything to do with you or me. Mariah only looks out for Mariah!"

"I guess the apple doesn't fall far from the tree," Angel whispered under her breath.

"Don't say another word. When we get home, take your ass straight to your room and stay away from me. You'll be lucky if you ever see daylight again."

As they continued to drive, Antoine couldn't believe what his precious daughter had done. *I just can't believe she's about to throw everything away she worked so hard for over a fucking dirty-ass dick.*

CHAPTER 6

The next three days, Antoine decided to take some time off of work in order to monitor Angel a little closer since she'd been suspended. During that time, he spent most of his time trying to come up with a plan, but nothing seemed to be working. Antoine knew he couldn't ask Mariah to finally become a mother and talk to their daughter, and he also knew he couldn't be a guard dog forever. Hell, he couldn't even take her to work with him anymore.

Since Angel had practically grown up at the center, most of the staff treated her like a daughter, and thought she was their little princess. However, some of the newer staff members thought she was a video hoochie and always asked her to impersonate Beyonce's famous booty dance, which pissed Antoine off. Regardless of what her role was, Angel was a like a mini-star at the center now, so tagging along with him wasn't going to work. He needed her to be just as miserable as he was. Besides, he hadn't had sex in three days, and it was starting to affect him.

After ignoring all of Natasha's phone calls, Antoine finally decided to answer her last call later that afternoon. He'd grown tired of listening to her threatening calls on his voicemail, and felt it was time to put this madness to an end.

"What?" Antoine answered, in a harsh tone.

"Do you plan on coming in today? I can't keep covering for your dumb-ass."

"What the hell do you mean cover for me? I called in today. That's what the fuck I have leave for."

"I don't give a damn how much leave you got. The walk-in clients keep leaving once they find out you're not here. We're losing money!" Natasha yelled.

Antoine laughed. "We? Natasha that's not your fucking rehab center, and technically you're not even a real damn employee. Why don't you leave me alone? I never had these problems until your ass started. Damn, I liked the other receptionist better…she stayed in her place."

"Well, maybe I would've stayed in my place if you would've stayed out my pussy, asshole!" Before Antoine could respond, she continued. "Look, Michael Epps was here earlier, and even though he didn't have an appointment, he wanted to know if you could squeeze him in. Now, I'm sure Dr. Wolenski wouldn't be happy if he knew you weren't taking care of a client like that."

I can't wait until I start my own shit. "Call Mr. Epps and tell him, I'll be there in an hour," Antoine replied, blowing into the phone.

"No, be here in thirty minutes. I already told Mr. Epps you'd be here by then." CLICK

Antoine was furious. He was getting tired of Natasha and her stupid games. With the problems going on in his personal life, he didn't have time to be dealing with any nonsense at work, especially from a temp. When Antoine finally went upstairs to get ready, he thought he heard talking coming from inside Angel's room as he walked past. Knowing she was on punishment, and shouldn't be on the phone, he quickly opened the door, but when he did, she appeared to be sleeping. After staring at her stiff body for a few more seconds, he closed the door and walked into his bathroom.

Little did he know, as soon as the coast was clear, Angel peeked from under her comforter when she heard Antoine's footsteps disappear down the hall. "Wink, you still there?" she whispered.

"Yeah baby, what you do? It sounded like you put me on mute or some shit," he responded.

"I think my father is getting ready to leave. What are you doing in a half an hour? When he leaves, I'll be here all by myself, with all my sexy shit on."

"Hell, whatever I was doing, there ain't no way I'm passin' up free pussy."

My shit ain't free. Trust me…I'll end up getting something out the deal. "Did I forget to mention that my thongs are sheer?"

"Man, my dick is hard just thinkin' bout that shit."

Angel made a sexy little laugh. "Well good. My free pussy will be waiting then."

After finalizing her plans with Wink, Angel closed the new cell phone that she'd recently gotten from another one of her boyfriends, and placed it under her pillow. Once she heard Antoine walking back toward her room again, she got in position to play sleeping beauty once again. *Thank God for those hardwood floors*, she thought. *I can hear everything.*

"Angel, wake up. I need to talk to you," Antoine said.

Angel pretended to be rolling over as Antoine opened her door. She then yawned and stretched her arms into the air like she'd been sleep for hours.

"Sit up so I can talk to you," he repeated, in a stern voice, before walking into her all white room. Her choice of colors always reminded him of heaven whenever he came in. *I guess her ass really thinks she's an Angel.*

"Dag! What did I do now?" she replied with a huge sigh.

Antoine stood at the foot of her bed and frowned when he looked at the pictures of Boris Kodjoe from *Soul Food* on her wall. "Why can't you like guys your own damn age?" he asked. "Never mind…don't even answer that. Listen little girl, I don't think you understand how mad I am right now. You've put me in a real messed up position. By the way, why are you still asleep in the middle of the day anyway?" Angel replied with another huge yawn. "Are you serious? I know I'm boring you with what I have to say. You know what Angel, you're not too old to get an ass whipping. Do I need to get my belt and come back?"

"Dad, give me a break…I'm just waking up. Then again you know what, I think you need to go ahead and beat me. Get it off your chest."

Antoine looked at her like she was crazy. "Don't push it. Anyway, I'm on my way to the center for an appointment. But I'll be right back, so don't get cute. Your ass is on punishment, so you're not to watch T. V. , or listen to your iPOD. As a matter of fact, don't even breathe until I come back."

Angel gave him a salute. "Yes sir, Captain Moore."

"You're really starting to piss me off. Oh, by the way here's the phone, but you better not use it unless this fucking house is on fire."

He tossed her one of the cordless handsets, grabbed his backpack, then headed out the door. Antoine knew she was going to go against his wishes and use the phone to call one of her little boyfriends. He just hoped that she wasn't smart enough to clear the number. His plans were to hit the redial button as soon as he got home, so he could add more days to her sentence.

Angel peeked through the custom made curtains on her bedroom window as Antoine backed out of the driveway. When he finally pulled off, she quickly jumped onto her bed to call Wink. She decided to call from the house phone in order to cut down on her cell phone minutes. As soon as Angel picked up the handset, she accidentally hit a button and the caller ID log popped onto the screen. Trying to see if any of her lovers had called while she was being detained, Angel scrolled through the calls in anticipation. However, her excitement turned into confusion, when the name *Mariah Wright* showed up on the phone.

"What the fuck did she call here for?" Angel asked out loud. All type of thoughts ran through her mind as she tried to figure out what her mother could've wanted and why her father hadn't even bothered to tell her. She thought about checking the voice mail to see if she'd left a message, but then quickly changed her mind. Angel then thought about calling the number back, but after fumbling around with the receiver for a few minutes, she decided against that as well. She didn't want or need any unnecessary drama at the moment, so she finally decided to call Wink back. He answered on the first ring.

"My dad is gone and I'm getting into the shower. We don't have all day, so hurry up. Oh, and don't park in the driveway or in front of the house."

"I'm on my way. Keep that pussy warm."

∾   ∾   ∾

Angel was spraying on her favorite pink grapefruit body splash when Wink rang the doorbell. He peeked through the glass on the mahogany wooden door and watched as Angel glided down the staircase. He pushed the doorbell again hoping it would make her move a little faster.

Angel unlocked the door, and then ran away. "It's open," she said, walking toward the family room.

Wink twisted the gold knob. He opened the door to see Angel's plump round ass switching from left to right. "Where you goin'?" he asked, as he quickly closed the door and locked it.

"Come find out," Angel replied in a sexy tone.

When Wink walked into the family room, he ran up behind Angel and pinched both butt cheeks. "You really know how to get a nigga ready."

She laughed. "You haven't seen anything yet."

Wink kept one hand on her ass as Angel directed him to sit in her father's favorite chair. When he followed her orders, she closed all the blinds and curtains. Despite the bright sun outside, the room darkened instantly. Wink took off his brand new Jordans, leaned back into the plush cushion and threw his feet up on the matching ottoman. He never took his eyes off Angel, or the white silk robe that revealed her matching bra and thong. He smiled when she turned around and her hard nipples stood at attention.

"It looks like you're cold. Why don't you come over here so I can warm you up?" He tried to use a smooth tone.

Angel slowly sat next to Wink then grabbed his hand. "I wanna feel these fingers all over my body." She placed his hand on her right breast and held it there for a second, then leaned over to kiss him. His thick tongue almost overpowered her mouth. She responded by sucking on his tongue to tease him with her skills.

It wasn't long before Angel felt the juices between her legs start to make its way down her leg. She quickly pushed his right hand down to her heated thighs.

Wink's eyes opened even wider when he felt the dampness of her thong on his fingertips. He began to move three of his fingers back and forth until her cum slowly started to pour out. Wanting to get inside, he slid her thong over, gaining entry for two of his fingers.

Angel's moans grew as he went deeper inside her. However, as her breathing increased, and their playful kisses turned to a passionate embrace, the doorbell rang. Angel's heart began to beat extremely fast. At first she thought it might be her father, but quickly realized he would've just used his key. As the doorbell rang again, she pushed Wink off of her, walked over to the door and looked through the peep hole. Angel became annoyed as she opened the door.

"Can I help you?"

"Hello, my name is Ramona. I'm a friend of Antoine's. Is he home?"

Angel pushed the door open wider to allow the woman to see her sexy outfit. "Why, what do you want with him?"

Ramona looked at Angel up and down, then cleared her throat. "Well, I just wanted to drop off his watch. He left it over my house the other day and I thought he might need it," she said, handing Angel the expensive sports watch. "By the way are you his daughter?"

Angel paused for a second and then smiled. "No, my name is Tawana. I'm Antoine's new woman. I mean you couldn't possibly think you were the only one."

Ramona looked at Angel for the second time. "You're a little young to be his new woman, don't you think? I had no idea he was into jail bait."

"Well I guess he likes his pussy young and wet instead of old and dry. Leave the watch outside," she responded, before slamming the door in Ramona's face.

Angel walked back into the family room to find Wink playing with his dick. She thought of what her father was going to say when one of his many female companions told him about their encounter at the door. She then let out a slight giggle from what their conversation might entail.

"Get your sexy ass over here. I'm supposed to be keeping you company, remember," Wink said, breaking her train of thought.

J. TREMBLE

Angel made her way back over to Wink with a seductive strut. She then crawled onto his lap and rubbed her pelvic area up and down his manhood until she saw his face tightening. *I can't wait to fuck you,* Angel thought as she moved her hips back and forth even faster. Her pussy was on fire, and she couldn't wait until Wink put out the flames. However, little did she know the flames were about to be more than she could handle.

As Antoine pulled back into the driveway, he banged the steering wheel after thinking once again how Natasha called to tell him Michael rescheduled. At that moment, he wondered if he ever had an appointment in the first place. For some reason, Antoine thought Natasha could've been making up the entire thing just to play games. The moment he got out the car and shut the door, he became puzzled after seeing his watch lying on the ground by the front door.

"How the hell did this get out here? I've been looking for this thing," Antoine said to himself as he picked up the watch and wiped the smudges off the face.

Angel and Wink never heard Antoine's key unlocking the front door. As he walked into the house, he immediately heard moans coming from down the hall.

What the fuck is that, Antoine thought. *Angel better not be watching a fucking porno or some shit.* He tiptoed to the family room, and was almost floored when he saw his daughter's half naked body with some nigga in his favorite chair. He was beyond speechless.

CHAPTER 7

"What the fuck is going on in here?" Antoine finally managed to say.

Angel almost broke her neck twisting it around, only to lock eyes with her father. Antoine became enraged when Wink's head emerged from between Angel's breasts, and it instantly set him off. He rushed over to the chair, grabbed Wink by his freshly done cornrows and yanked him to his feet.

"What the fuck are you doing in my house?" Antoine shouted. Wink was so afraid and caught off guard, he didn't respond. Antoine still held Wink's collar with a forceful grip, then decided to let him go. "How old are you?" Antoine asked cracking his knuckles.

"I…I'm twen…ty-three, sir."

"Good, you're old enough for this ass whopping," Antoine responded, as he punched Wink in the stomach. When he fell to the ground, Antoine grabbed his arm and dragged him to the front door. "Motherfucker, do you realize you're messing with a seventeen-year old!"

"Daddy, stop it! You're gonna hurt him!" Angel yelled. She ran up to her father and tried to release his grip, but nothing worked.

When they finally reached the front door, Antoine dropped Wink's arm, and then pushed Angel away when she ran over to console her friend.

"Angel, you better step your lil' ass back or you'll be on the floor with his punk ass." He looked at his daughter's matching pink lingerie and instantly became nauseous.

"Wink, are you okay?" Angel asked, slightly ignoring her father. He didn't respond.

"Get the fuck up!" Antoine ordered. It took a couple of seconds for Wink to comply, but he finally stood up. "Now get out!"

"You can't just put him out like that. He doesn't even have any shoes on," Angel said.

Antoine looked down at Wink's dingy socks then looked at his daughter. "I don't give a fuck if he doesn't have on any shoes or not. Either he can leave willingly or with my foot up his ass. It doesn't matter to me." He opened up the door, and waited for Wink to buck.

Angel looked concerned for her friend as he walked out the door. He took a couple of steps before turning around. "Umm… sir. Those Jordans cost me a lot of money. Do you think I can come back and get 'em?"

Antoine responded by slamming the door in his face. It didn't take long before he was on Angel's ass next. "I see you don't have any respect for yourself or my damn house."

Angel crossed her arms over her chest to finally cover her exposed body. "How can I have respect for anything with all the shit you do?"

Antoine's eyes looked like he was about to have a heart attack. "Don't you ever use that type of language in this house! You know…I'm so sick and tired of you always trying to turn things around and make everything my fault. You need to find a new excuse because that shit is not going to work!"

Mariah could hear the arguing from the sidewalk as she stepped out her snow white Range Rover. *That's probably Antoine and one of his hoe's,* she thought as she walked up to the door. "Well, it doesn't look like he's done too bad for himself," Mariah said, looking at the house. "Shit, who am I kidding? That nigga still didn't do as well as I did." Mariah looked down and admired the six carat radiant cut wedding ring displayed on her finger and smiled. In her eye, she'd definitely hit the jackpot, so she thanked Antoine for fucking up their relationship. She began to bang on the front door repeatedly. "Antoine," she shouted.

As Antoine and Angel continued to argue, he stopped suddenly and looked around the room. The annoying voice that he'd grown to hate sounded like it was in close proximity. *Is this a damn nightmare. I know that ain't Mariah's voice I hear at my door.*

"Antoine, open the fucking door. I need to talk to you!" Mariah shouted.

Great...first Angel's bullshit, now this. He stood in one spot as he tried to figure out the best way to handle the situation. "Angel, go to your room. I need to handle this in private."

She let out a huge sigh. "See, that's your problem. You've let too many of your women come before me over the years." It was obvious Angel had no idea that it was her mother on the other side of the door.

"I'm not gonna tell your ass again. Go to your room!" Antoine shouted. He looked at his daughter in shock as she stood her ground, and refused to budge. She was starting to become extremely disrespectful.

"I hear you moving around in there. Open the fucking door right now. We need to talk!" Mariah continued to shout.

"I swear, if I have to tell you again, it's not gonna be pretty."

Angel watched as Antoine bit the inside of his cheek and could tell this time he meant business. Trying not to piss him off anymore, she finally turned around and headed upstairs.

Antoine walked to the door and opened it slightly. However, he had no idea Mariah was going to burst inside, causing the door to hit him in the face. The entire thing caught him completely off guard.

"You no good son of a bitch, I just got your restraining order in the mail. How dare you file that shit," Mariah said. "Motherfucker you better be glad my husband is busy playing football and doesn't have time to check the mail, because if he had found that paper, it would be over. I mean what the fuck are you trying to prove?"

As Antoine rubbed his head, he couldn't believe they'd delivered the restraining order so quickly. *Wow, I guess me flirting with that old ass lady worked.* He looked at Mariah's petite frame up and down. She was the spitting image of their daughter with her honey roasted skin tone and long dirty blonde hair. Even at thirty-four, she could still pass for a teenager, especially with her shapely figure.

Antoine snapped out of his thoughts. "I don't have time for your bullshit, Mariah. Your daughter is giving me all that I can handle. See…if you were in her life, you would know that I just caught her with one of her lil' boyfriends on my damn favorite chair!"

Mariah laughed. "Serves your punk-ass right. I hope she's driving you crazy."

"What? You need to be a mother for once and have that talk with her, so she knows that men don't like freaks. I mean aren't you tired of laying on your back? You've been doing the shit for years," Antoine said, finally slamming the front door, signaling it was okay for Mariah to stay inside the house for the moment.

"Fuck you Antoine. Have you forgotten that I haven't spoken to her in twelve years? Angel's your problem. Not mine. I could care less who she's fucking. I just want to know about this restraining order."

"So, you don't care that we have a daughter that's probably fucking every boy she comes in contact with?"

"No, not really. Besides, I'm sure she gets it honestly. Don't you fuck every woman that you come in contact with?"

Mariah's comment made Antoine furious. He couldn't believe how she could just turn her back on Angel and turn everything around on him.

"Look...I got the restraining order because you came over here and spray painted my fucking house."

Mariah's face frowned. "What the hell are you talking about? I didn't do shit to your house. You must have me mixed up with one of your bitches! I just found out where you live."

Antoine was sure that Mariah just wanted to play innocent, and he didn't have time for her silly games. "Listen, like I said before...I don't have time for this shit. Angel is getting out of control and I need help. Your help preferably. I mean she's thrown away a scholarship and any hopes of going to Howard University."

"If that's the case, you need to stop this child support shit before it gets out of hand. I mean what would you need money for now since she's not even going to school?" Mariah chimed in.

"Are you listening to yourself? How could you be so damn cruel? I bet you those two big head motherfuckin' kids you got by that football nigga end up going to college."

Before Mariah could respond, she and Antoine heard a crashing sound coming from upstairs. When Antoine looked like he was about to lose it, Mariah ran and got in front of him.

"Wait…let me go talk to her," she said. *Shit maybe if I do this, he'll stop all this nonsense with the child support, and I can get on with my life,* she thought.

"Thanks, I would really appreciate that," Antoine responded. "Maybe she needs a woman's touch right now."

"Believe me, I'm not doing this shit for you, bitch," Mariah said, walking up the steps. Seconds later, Mariah opened Angel's bedroom door to find her breaking trophies and kicking over pieces of furniture. She cleared her throat as she walked in so that Angel wouldn't hit her with any flying objects.

Angel stopped and stared at Mariah. "Who the fuck are you, one of his whores?" She could've cared less if the woman was offended. The last thing she needed right now was some fake-ass pep talk from a stranger.

It was the first time in years that Mariah was at a loss for words. She couldn't believe how beautiful her first born had turned out to be. It was also like looking in a mirror. "Um…I'm you're mother, Angel," she said, in a low tone.

Angel held the sixth grade science fair trophy in her hand tightly, then threw it across the room. Mariah ducked as tiny little pieces of gold metal flew everywhere. "Lady, don't play games with me because I'm not in the mood!"

"I'm serious. I'm your mother, Mariah. Hell, look in the mirror. We look just alike."

Angel stared at Mariah for a few seconds. "Well if you're my mother, I've waited a long time to ask you this question," Angel admitted. "Why did you give me up? What type of mother gives up her child? I need to understand what was going through your mind!" Angel yelled. Tears quickly began to roll down her cheek.

"Look, I didn't come up here to talk to you about that," Mariah responded.

"So why in the hell did you come up here then?"

"I just wanted to see you." Mariah became jealous when she looked at her daughter's big perky breasts. Something she had to pay her plastic surgeon for.

Angel stood in front of Mariah wondering what she was thinking. *I can't believe all she wants to do is look at me like I'm a fish in a fucking bowl*, she thought.

"Listen, I need your help," Mariah finally said. "I guess your father is trying to get back at me for leaving you with him years ago, and he's asking me for back child support. So, when we go to court in a few months, I need you to tell the judge that you don't need any money from me. My husband would be furious if he has to help me pay for a child that's not his."

Angel had no idea what her mother was talking about, and it didn't matter. After being out of each other's lives for twelve years, she couldn't believe this was all she had to say. "Now I can see why I turned out like this. With parents like y'all, who wouldn't be fucked up? Get out my room!" Angel yelled.

No good little bitch, Mariah thought. "Just remember what I said."

Angel threw another trophy toward her mother's backside as the door to her bedroom closed. Mariah thought about going back inside to slap her, but knew it wouldn't help the situation. She looked at Antoine, who sat listening on the middle of the steps, and rolled her eyes.

"Thank you. You were really a big help," he said sarcastically. "You know, you never cease to amaze me."

"Fuck you, Antoine. I hope she drives your dumb-ass crazy," Mariah replied. She quickly ran down the steps and toward the front door. Before long she was outside heading to her car, with Antoine on her heels.

"We'll see how much your husband likes it when he has to come up off that pro ball paper!"

Mariah stopped in her tracks, then turned to push him in the chest. "Fuck that. My man won't be paying shit. His money is my money and nobody else's. You know what, Antoine you ain't no real man."

"I am a man. I've been taking care of our daughter by myself without help from anyone, so don't go there with me. You're just mad because you can't get me to take care of you too."

Mariah laughed in his face "Are you serious? I don't need you to take care of me. You got it twisted. I have a man that makes millions...seven figures to be exact. All you do is rub people's asses all day. So, you can't do shit for me."

"No, sweetheart, you got it twisted. He may have seven figures, but you know I have about twelve inches and that's what I mean by taking care of you. If that wasn't the case, then why are you here yelling and making a scene," Antoine said folding his arms.

"Fuck your big dick ass. This shit ain't nowhere near over. You just opened a can of worms. I know you don't need any fucking money from me. You're just trying to cause problems for me and my family because we're happy and your life sucks having to raise a child you never wanted." Mariah went to push Antoine again, but he blocked her hand.

"Take your psycho-ass home, and don't come around here anymore!"

Staring at each other like lions ready for a serious battle, Mariah finally backed away, turned around, did an about face, and walked to her truck. However, her surrender didn't come without one final move. As Antoine made his way back into the house, he paused when he heard a familiar sound. Without even turning around, he knew it was the sound of Mariah's key scrapping against his car. With all the women Antoine had screwed over, he'd heard that sound more than he could remember.

Seconds later, he heard the sounds of Mariah's heels running to her truck, and then tires peeling off down the street. All he could do was shake his head when he saw the long zigzag pattern digging into his paint.

CHAPTER 8

When Antoine walked back into the house, he realized that nothing good was going to come from confronting Angel anymore for the rest of the day. As angry as he was, the slightest thing was bound to set him off, and possibly have Angel in a coffin. He knew the best thing for both of them was to calm down before he caught a murder charge, and even though it was hard, he left her alone. Antoine walked in the family room, and then picked up his cell phone before taking a seat on his favorite chair. He thought about calling a woman, in his head banger list, so one of them could come over and take away all the stress that had built up. A nice blow job would've hit the spot at a time like this, but he quickly decided against it. He ended up calling his buddy, Terrell and asked him to come over for a drink that evening, and his friend happily accepted the last minute invitation. He and Terrell had been best friends since college, and when Antoine needed somebody to talk to, his frat brother was the one he called on.

When Terrell arrived several hours later, Antoine led him to the family room were he was watching a kickboxing match that he'd recorded a few days earlier. He was desperate to watch some type of violent sport, in order to ease his frustration.

"What's up man, what took you so long?" Antoine asked. He was still sitting in the same spot from earlier. "It's almost ten o'clock." He picked up the glass of Hennessy and Coke then lifted it in the air.

"You got one of those for me?"

Antoine shook his head, and pointed to the glass on the coffee table. "It's been waiting right there for hours. That shit is probably watered down by now."

"Well, the wait is finally over. It doesn't matter if it's watered down or not," Terrell replied, as he picked up the glass. "Here's to a fucked up day for both of us."

"Cheers," Antoine said, throwing back the drink. He looked like he was about to jump off a bridge.

"Man, I haven't seen you like this since that girl gave you Gonorrhea. Is it that bad?" Terrell asked taking a seat on the couch.

"It's worse than what you think."

"Oh, shit what you got this time…Syphilis?"

Antoine shook his head. "Nah, it's worse than that."

Terrell jumped up. "No, man don't tell me…AIDS!"

"No, man you're going too far with this."

As Antoine began to fix another shot, he started telling Terrell the entire story. They had finished a whole bottle of Hennessy by time he reached the end, and had started on a second one. Terrell sat in amazement.

"You know Ant, I think you need to find a real role model for that girl. She needs a mother to teach her how to act like a woman. A woman that men will respect and desire. Now all Angel sees are the sleazy women you fuck and duck."

"Wow! You sound just like Angel right now. Are you saying it's my fault that her self-esteem is all fucked up?" Antoine asked.

Terrell refilled his glass. "You missed the point."

"What's the fucking point then?"

"I think you need to raise your requirements on the type of women you bring around her. Find a woman to settle down with and make an honest man out of yourself," Terrell preached, with a slight grin. He knew he was asking a lot of his friend, but it was worth a shot. Besides, he couldn't be a male whore forever.

Antoine broke out into laughter. He looked at his friend, who constantly reminded him of Denzel Washington. Not only did Terrell have smooth milk chocolate skin, but his sexy smile always seemed to make the panties of every woman he met wetter than a pissy diaper. His cool-ass walk also mimicked the highly acclaimed actor's characteristics.

"Man, are you serious? You know I can't do that. That shit is not in my character."

"Yeah, I know, but if you don't want your daughter to be another fucking Superhead, then you might wanna think about it."

Antoine's smile slowly faded as Terrell's words began to sink in. His friend was right. He didn't want Angel to be known around the city as an easy lay, so he knew something had to be done. The problem was he didn't know what to do or where to begin.

"Oh, by the way, why did you have a bad day?"

Terrell sighed. "You know how it is."

"Know how what is?"

"I got caught cheating again today."

Antoine shook his head back and forth. "See, you need to be more like me. All my women know that I'm not committed to none of their asses. I keep telling you about that shit, Tightness."

Terrell frowned at the sound of his old college nickname. "Shut up, Ant." He stared at the T. V. for a few seconds. "You know what man, I really hate the fact that I let my future wife get away."

"Terrell, please don't start this shit again." Antoine hated the fact that every time Terrell started drinking, he always brought up something about his old college sweetheart.

"Don't start what? I can't help if it I fucked up the best thing that ever happened to me. I mean Nina was my heart…she didn't deserve to be treated like that. She was a good girl."

Antoine shifted in his seat. *I wouldn't be so sure about that, bro.*

While Antoine and Terrell were downstairs drinking and sharing their ideas of correcting the problem, Angel sat in her room thinking about her life. She constantly wiped away tears as the thought of not being loved by either Mariah or Antoine entered her mind. It was painful not being able to have a natural and healthy relationship with the two people who gave her life. She was also envious watching all the parents pick up their kids at her school or cheering them on at football games, with big bright smiles. The only time Angel could remember seeing Antoine come to her school with that same bright smile was whenever one of his female companions stayed over the night before. Since being dropped on Antoine's doorstep, the relationship with both of her parents had been non-existent, and for once in her life Angel decided that she'd gone through enough. If her parents didn't think she was worth loving, she'd find somebody who did.

What is the point of being here, when all he cares about is those bitches anyway? Angel made sure her door was locked then quickly walked over to her closet, got her fuchsia Victoria's Secret overnight bag and stuffed it with as many clothes as she could. She then hurried over to her dresser, threw in a few toiletries, along with her favorite curling iron and brush. After nervously rushing around the room and tossing in a few more items, she finally tossed the bag out her bedroom window and into the bushes. A part of her wanted to leave out the same way, but jumping from a second story window without getting hurt was unlikely. She would just have to take her chances and go out the front door.

Dressed in a black Bebe sweat-suit, Angel grabbed her Juicy purse, and slowly opened up her bedroom door. She stuck her head out and looked from right to left, then stopped to listen out for Antoine. Once she heard him and Terrell downstairs laughing, she finally made her way out the room, and closed the door. She'd even gone a step further and locked the door, knowing it would piss her father off when he finally came to check on her. Taking one step at a time, Angel could tell by the direction of their voices, they were in the family room.

Damn, I hope they're laughing over a bottle of Hennessy as usual, she thought as she kept her eyes in the direction of the family room. Angel knew if Antoine walked toward the staircase, she would have to haul ass back upstairs. Once she reached the bottom, the laughter had turned into arguing, so it was obvious Antoine and Terrell were drunk.

"Good, he's in there with his wife, so now I know he's not coming," she said to herself. Angel often referred to Hennessy as Antoine's wife due to the close bond they shared. A bond that seemed like a consummated marriage.

After walking up to the front door and opening it slightly, Angel looked back one final time, to see if Antoine was coming. When she heard the arguing transform back to laughter, she knew he wasn't going to appear. As crazy as it was, deep down she wanted her father to stop her from running away. To stop her from possibly making a mistake. But once again, he wasn't there when she needed him.

"Bye Dad," Angel said softly, as she closed the door.

She rushed over to the bushes and grabbed her bag before making her way down the street. Once she walked out her development, she pulled out her cell phone from her purse, and called a cab. Angel instructed the cab company to pick her up at the Kwik Stop convenience store that was located a few blocks from her house, and to make it snappy.

After ending her call, once again, she looked back to see if her father was coming. However, the only thing that appeared to be moving in her direction, were the palm trees that swayed briskly from the wind.

Ten minutes later, Angel was stepping inside the cab with no idea of where to go.

"Where to, young lady?" the older white cab driver asked. However, Angel didn't respond. She just sat in the backseat and stared out the window like she was looking for someone. "Hey…did you hear me?" the driver repeated looking through his rearview mirror. "I said where are you going?" Angel still didn't say a word. "Listen, are you on some type of drugs? You're gonna have to get out!"

"Don't fucking yell at me, old man!" she finally said.

"Well, where are you going?"

That's the problem. I haven't figured it out yet. After sitting there for a few more seconds, she finally answered. "Just take me to the bus station. The one on 1st Avenue is fine."

The cab driver finally turned around. "Are you sure you wanna go down there?" Before she could answer, he continued. "Are you in some kind of trouble, young lady?"

"Look, can you just take me where I asked to go. Mind your business, and just drive the damn car!"

The cab driver looked at Angel with concern, but then turned around and finally drove off.

☙ ☙ ☙

Minutes later, Angel stood in front of the Greyhound Bus station in downtown Miami frantically trying to come up with a plan. She watched as homeless men and women walked back and forth in front of her, with some even stopping to ask for spare change. Growing up in a nice neighborhood, the closest filthy person that Angel had ever been around was on T. V. , so she knew being in that part of town was out of her comfort zone. There were all types of crazy people in Miami, but when the sun went down, the real freaks came out.

At that point, she began to ask herself why she'd chosen the bus station in the first place. It wasn't like she had enough money to go anywhere. With the ten dollars that was in her purse, she probably only had enough to get to Fort Lauderdale.

Oh, I'll call Wink, she thought. *I'm sure he'll be happy that I rolled out.* She pulled out her cell phone, and dialed his number, but quickly got his voicemail. "Maybe he's in a bad area," Angel said to herself, as she dialed the number again. Her face frowned when she got the voicemail for the second time.

"Shit!"

At that moment, a strange man walked up to Angel and stared at her like she was a piece of meat. The look from his cold eyes and massive size caused the hair on the back of her neck to stand up. She didn't know what to do.

"Can...I help you with something?"

The man who instantly started to remind her of a mental patient, didn't say anything and continued to stare. A few uncomfortable seconds later, he finally walked away shaking his head. It was at that moment when Angel thought her location may not have been the best choice, and decided to look for a safer place to stand until she could get in touch with Wink.

She turned around and walked up 1st Avenue dragging her duffle bag that seemed to weigh a ton. However, the more she walked, the more Angel heard footsteps walking fast from behind her. Her first instinct was to start running, but she didn't want to waste her energy if it was unnecessary.

Maybe it's just somebody trying to pass me. I am walking a little slow with this bag. When Angel realized the footsteps were right on her heels, she finally turned around to see who it was. She tried to scream when she realized it was the mental patient from the bus station, but it was too late. He grabbed Angel from behind and covered her mouth with his large hands. Even by her kicking and scratching him in his face a few times, the man still managed to drag her into a dark empty parking lot.

Angel tried her best to fight the deranged man off with her bag, as he pulled her down to the ground, and proceeded to grope her body. Tears began to fall as she felt his other hand slide down to her stomach and rest on her pussy. He was big and dirty and smelled like day old garbage, which was enough to make anyone sick. Angel's body wiggled back and forth as she tried to prevent him from untying the string on her sweatpants, but was unsuccessful. It was only a matter of seconds before he managed to pull her pants, along with her panties, down far enough to expose her kitty. She tried desperately to break free when she felt him pulling down his own pants, but nothing worked. He continued to overpower her.

The man was just about to insert his dick when bright head lights flooded the parking lot. Angel could've shouted for joy when the red and blue colored strobe lights from a police car circled the air.

Thank you God, Thank you God, she repeated to herself over and over. However, her silent praises were interrupted when the man quickly inserted one of his fingers inside her pussy and took it out, despite the police presence.

"Freeze, don't move," a voice said over the loud speaker.

When the man jumped to his feet, Angel started screaming. "Help me, please, this man is crazy!"

He hurried to pull up his pants, and when the door to the police cruiser opened, the man took off running. Despite his size, he looked like an Olympic track star as he sprinted in the opposite direction. One of the police officers immediately took chase.

At that moment, the passenger door to the police cruiser opened and another officer exited to give his partner assistance. However, as he started to give chase, Angel's cries stopped him. He quickly walked back over to find her shaking in the prenatal position. She'd already managed to pull her pants back up.

"Did he hurt you?" the officer asked, kneeling down. Angel shook her head up and down as tears flooded her eyes. "Dispatch this is Officer Campbell. I need an ambulance sent to the 1100 block of 1st Avenue. I have a possible rape victim and...," the officer said in his shoulder radio, before Angel interrupted.

"I don't need an ambulance," she said, wiping away tears. "I'll be okay."

"Campbell, are you there?" the dispatch asked.

"I thought you said he hurt you?" Officer Campbell asked.

"He did in a way, but I'll be okay."

"Are you sure?" When Angel shook her head, the officer grabbed his radio again. "Dispatch, cancel that ambulance. The victim appears to be okay."

"10-4...copy that."

"Well even if you don't wanna go to the hospital, I'm still taking you to the station, so you can press charges." The officer helped Angel up, then walked over to grab her bag before walking her to the car. As he began to ask her more questions, surprisingly the other officer walked back to the scene with the perpetrator in handcuffs.

"I can't believe you caught that piece of shit," Officer Campbell said. "How far did he get?"

"About two blocks. The big motherfucker ran out of breath," the other officer responded.

"Fuck you," the crazy man stated. Angel covered her face as soon as she heard his voice. She didn't even want to look at him.

"Put his dumb-ass in the car," Officer Campbell said once he realized Angel was uncomfortable. After watching his partner put the perpetrator in the back of the squad car, he continued with his questions. "What are you doing out here all alone?" he asked Angel, and then pointed to her duffle bag.

"I just got in from out of town, and I was on my way home."

"So, what's your name and how old are you?"

"It's Angel...Angel Moore and I'm seventeen."

"Well miss Angel, we're gonna need your statement, so I'm gonna call for backup, so they can escort you to the station, while I take that piece of shit with me."

Angel nodded her head. "Okay."

Dispatch, I need a backup officer in the 1100 block of 1st Avenue please."

"10-4...copy that."

"What's your mom or dad's number? They need to know what's going on, so they can come pick you up from the station," the officer said.

Angel knew she wasn't about to give them Antoine's number, so she had to come up with something. It wasn't long before she thought about Wink. "My dad's out of town, but you can talk to my big brother. He's old enough to come get me." She knew Wink's voice wouldn't pass for a father.

"I wouldn't be comfortable leaving you in your brother's care. What about your mom?"

Her face frowned. "I don't deal with her."

After thinking about it for a moment, the officer finally wrote down Wink's cell number and began calling. In the meantime, two female officers arrived on the scene to escort Angel to the Central District Police Station.

"I can't reach your brother, is there someone else you want me to call?" Officer Campbell asked, closing his cell phone.

Shit, why isn't Wink answering the damn phone? "Umm...do you mind if I use my phone to try and call my uncle? He doesn't answer strange numbers, so I'm sure he wouldn't answer your call."

After the officer agreed, Angel used her phone to call someone else. A couple minutes later, she hung up with a smile. "My uncle is so glad I'm okay. He's gonna meet me at the station," she told the officer. It didn't phase her one bit that she was throwing out one lie after another.

 ࢠ   ࢠ   ࢠ

After making her statement, Angel was still sitting on the wooden bench at the police station when the double doors opened, and a tall dark skinned man with a shiny baldhead walked up to the information desk.

Angel called for him. "Uncle LD, I'm right here."

The man looked to his right and waved. But before he could speak, a detective walked up to him. "Can I speak with you for a minute?" he asked.

The gentleman followed the officer into his office. They talked for several minutes before the man finally came back out. "Let's go sweetheart," he finally said to Angel.

She played the innocent niece role until they walked out the station, and to his car. Angel then looked around before jumping into his arms and planting a huge kiss on his mouth. The man squeezed her ass before putting her back down.

"Thanks for coming to get me, Poppy. What did the officer say in his office?"

"He told me that you were almost raped and that I should take it easy with you. I was instructed to give you nothing but tender loving care, and that's what I plan to do," he replied slapping her on the ass.

"So, you're taking me to your spot, right?"

"I can't think of a better place, baby."

"Me either, Uncle LD," she responded, in a babyish tone.

"What's with the Uncle LD? What does the LD mean?" he asked.

Angel smiled. "Long dick of course."

As they got in the car, this time Angel didn't look back to see if Antoine was coming to rescue her because in her mind, her man was giving her want she desperately wanted...love.

CHAPTER 9

The minute Antoine opened his eyes the next morning, the room seemed to be spinning out of control. He slowly moved his head and looked around trying to figure out where he was, when he noticed his 60 inch plasma T. V. on the wall. Luckily the television's automatic timer had turned itself off because Antoine hated when his prized possession was left on. At that point it was clear that he was still in the family room, and had obviously been there since the night before. As he sat up on the couch, he gently rubbed his temples, and tried his best to figure out what happened. The last thing he recalled was arguing with Terrell for the fifth time that night, and taking another shot.

As the thought of alcohol entered his mind, he looked at the coffee table, and stared at the three empty bottles of Hennessy along with Terrell, who was stretched out on the floor like a wino. Antoine let out a little chuckle as he began to think about his old college days, and how Terrell always ended up on the floor after one of their parties. Feeling a massive headache and grueling stomach pains coming on, Antoine stood up and slowly made his way toward the master bathroom upstairs. His medicine cabinet was like a local drug store, so he knew he could find something to ease the pain.

Once Antoine reached the top of the stairs, he stopped for a second and looked at Angel's door. A part of him wanted to barge in her room since he hadn't seen or even talked to her in hours, but the effects from his hangover wouldn't allow it.

I'll do it when I get myself together, Antoine thought as he walked past her door and into his room. Once in his bathroom, he searched the cabinet like a crack head looking for a rock, before finally finding an Alka-Seltzer packet. He grabbed a glass off his counter, filled it with water, and then dropped the two tablets inside, hoping it would settle his swirling head.

After drinking the lemon-lime flavored water, Antoine looked at himself in the mirror and shook his head. "Damn, I must be getting old if I can't handle liquor like I used to." He continued to look in the mirror for a few more minutes before thoughts of Angel entered his mind again. He wondered what she'd been up to all night, and if she'd attempted to do anything that would piss him off. He'd been a teenager once, and knew what it was like to be at odds with your parents. Even though he still felt like shit, Antoine decided to go to Angel's room to check on her.

Who knows...maybe if she's up we can try and talk about what happened yesterday. As Antoine approached the door, he began to practice the conversation in his head before grabbing the doorknob. Normally, he would've knocked, but after Angel's incident with Wink, her privacy privileges had been revoked for a while. He immediately became upset when he realized the door was locked.

"Why the fuck is this door locked? Angel, open this door immediately!" Antoine shouted.

There was no response. He began to knock on the door, and soon his knocks turned into banging. Still, there was no response. Antoine's thoughts went wild. *If she has anther motherfucker in my house, he better be dead by the time I get in there.* Without another minute to spare, Antoine used all the strength he had and kicked in the door.

He entered the room like a mad man, only to find, an empty space. The only thing moving were the curtains blowing from the open window. "I can't believe this girl!" he shouted, after checking her bathroom. He then looked in the closet before finally walking over to the window. She was nowhere in sight.

Antoine turned around once he heard Terrell running up the stairs. He could've sworn he even heard him stumble in the process. "What was that noise? It scared the shit out of me?"

"That was me kicking the door in. I think Angel ran away."

Terrell looked surprised. "Don't say that, Ant. Maybe she just stepped out for a second."

Antoine shook his head back and forth. "No, you don't take your toothbrush if you're just stepping out. Even that body lotion shit she wears is gone." He pointed to her dresser then quickly left the room. Terrell was right behind him.

Antoine ran to the house phone and immediately started going through the caller ID. He knew Wink had called the house a few days before, so he hoped he could find the number. After calling two of Angel's other male friends, Antoine finally hit the jackpot on the third try.

"Listen Angel, you better find a way to get my fuckin' shoes back from your pops," Wink said, as soon as he answered.

Antoine knew at that point, his daughter wasn't with him. "Umm…Wink this is Angel's father. So I take it she's not with you."

"Hell no, she ain't wit' me."

"Well do you have any idea where she might be?"

"Why the fuck would I tell your punk ass after you punched me in the stomach. You better be glad I didn't come back and fuck you up!"

"Listen you little motherfucker, don't..." Antoine heard the phone when it clicked. Wink had obviously gained a back bone and hung up. "Shit!" he shouted.

"Calm down, Ant. We'll find her," Terrell assured.

Antoine paced the floor and then began to rub his temples again. "Fuck this, I need to call the police." He picked the phone back up and dialed 911. In his mind, this was an emergency even though it wasn't life threatening. After telling the operator what happened, she finally gave him the number to the South District police station, and within minutes, he was making a missing person's report. Antoine was so relieved when he found out there wasn't a twenty-four waiting period for children under eighteen.

"Okay, Mr. Moore. I'll post this report immediately, so one of our detectives in the criminal investigation unit can get right on it," the officer said.

"Thank you so much," Antoine replied, before hanging up. Terrell could tell that his friend was worried, by the way Antoine continued to pace the room.

Don't worry, Ant. They'll find her," Terrell said, trying his best to sound reassuring. However, Antoine never responded.

An hour later, the house phone rang. Antoine's heart began to beat faster than a speeding car, as he immediately thought it was Angel on the other end. He knew she would come to her senses sooner or later, but he also didn't want to scare her away by going off. He wished Terrell had decided to stay a little longer because at that moment, he could've used some support. Antoine made sure to take several deep breaths before answering, but never managed to look at the caller ID.

"Hello."

"Hello, is this Mr. Antoine Moore?" a man asked.

Antoine seemed a bit disappointed that it wasn't Angel. "Yes, it is. Who is this?"

"Mr. Moore my name is, Detective Gilliam and I'm from the Central District police station. I was just on the phone with another detective from South District, and he informed me about a new missing person's report. Now, this is strange to me because he said the name of the girl was Angel Moore."

"Okay, so what's so strange about that?" Antoine asked. He was obviously becoming irritated and nervous all at the same time.

"Well Mr. Moore, it's strange because I just spoke with your brother LD Moore, in my office last night before he left with Angel."

Antoine's face frowned. "I'm sorry Detective Gilliam, but I think you have me mistaken with someone else," Antoine responded.

"Are you sure because we just released Angel into your brother's custody?"

"Sir, I have no idea what you're talking about. How could you have released my daughter into my brother's custody when I don't have a brother? I don't know who the hell this LD person is. Besides, why was she there in the first place?"

"What's your address?" Detective Gilliam asked.

"It's 2620 Lincoln Avenue, why?"

He could hear the detective shuffling some papers around. "Yeah, that's definitely not the address she gave us. So, your brother wasn't just at the South District police station last night to pick up your seventeen year old daughter, Angel Camille Moore?"

Antoine was now beyond upset. "For the last damn time, I don't have a brother, so the answer to that is no!"

"Mr. Moore, I think you need to come down to the station

because your daughter...." Detective Gilliam paused. "This is something we need to discuss face to face."

❧   ❧   ❧

Angel rolled over to find the California king sized bed empty. The soft Egyptian cotton sheets felt good against her naked body as she continued to toss and turn around the huge bed. Trying to figure out where her man was, she was getting ready to call out his name, until the bedroom door opened, and he walked in with a tray full of food.

"I was just about to wake you. After last night, I thought you might need to regain your strength with something to eat."

Angel sat up in the bed like an excited little kid. "Oh Poppy, you know exactly what to do to put a smile on my face."

"So, what about this?" he said, pulling on his dick. "Does this put a smile on your face?"

Angel laughed. "I have a sore mouth and swollen pussy to show that long thing makes me happy."

Poppy smiled as he placed the tray over Angel's lap. He removed the silver cover to reveal French toast, sausage, bacon, scrambled eggs, and a bowl of grits on the side. Poppy even had a glass of freshly squeezed orange juice to finish it off.

"Something's missing," Angel said, looking over the delightful breakfast.

"What, I think I have more than enough."

"Where is my vase with the rose or tulip? I always see that on T. V. when somebody is getting breakfast in bed. I thought I was supposed to get the five star treatment," Angel said.

"I'm sorry baby. The next time I'll have a dozen of roses. Shit, two dozen."

"The next time? Shouldn't it be all the time? I mean I did run away from home you know, so now we can fuck whenever we want."

I'm not sure if that's gonna work out, lil girl. Poppy sat down at the foot of the bed. "Well let's just take it one day at a time for now."

Angel's face frowned from his strange comment. She thought he would've been happy that she could stay with him now instead of sneaking around like they used to. *I know he loves me, so I'm not sure why he's acting like that. Maybe some of this sweet stuff, will get him back on the right track.*

"How about you climb back into these soft sheets and make them stick to my body with some hot sweaty fucking? Besides, my mouth could use another workout."

Her freaky language was always music to his ears, so Poppy quickly stood up and took off his pajama pants. His dick wasn't hard at first, but by the time he removed the tray from her lap, his manhood was fully erect. When he pulled back the sheets, Angel's fingers were working overtime to get her pussy nice and wet, which instantly made his dick jump.

Damn, maybe I can let her stay around a little while longer, Poppy thought as he climbed on top of Angel. *Besides, my wife is not due back for a couple of days anyway. I should have her ass out by then.*

ᔕ   ᔕ   ᔕ

When Antoine walked into the Central District police station, he was determined to get some answers. He'd never in a million years heard of police fucking up this bad. As he walked up to the information desk, the female desk duty police officer looked at him with suspicion.

"Where can I find Detective Gilliam?" Antoine asked.

The officer continued to look at him strangely before responding. "And you are?"

"It's funny how you all can ask questions now, but didn't bother to ask the asshole who walked out of here with my daughter any. Just tell him it's Antoine Moore."

The female officer didn't hesitate before picking up the phone to let the detective know he had a visitor. "He'll be right out, sir."

"Good," Antoine replied, in a slightly sarcastic tone.

"You know we have guns around here."

Antoine looked at the officer like she had three eyes, but didn't get a chance to respond before the detective walked up. "Can I see some identification sir?"

"Oh, so now you ask for I. D. ?" Antoine asked, reaching into his pocket. He pulled out his wallet, and took out his driver's license before handing it over. "Where's my daughter?"

"I don't know how else to say this, but here we go. Last night your daughter was involved in an attempted rape downtown."

"Angel got raped!" Antoine shouted.

"No sir. It was an attempted rape, but luckily two police officers were in the right place at the right time. They were able to stop the man before he actually raped her."

"Oh my God. Was she okay?"

"Yes, she seemed fine. The officer on the scene even said Angel refused any type of medical assistance. He also said that Angel used her cell phone to call her father, or apparently who he thought was her father."

"This is all crazy. Angel doesn't even have a cell phone."

"Well obviously she did Mr. Moore, because Angel wouldn't allow the officer to call from his phone," Detective Gilliam replied. Antoine lowered his head and shook it back and forth.

"I'm sorry Mr. Moore, but when the gentleman showed up pretending to be her uncle, I just assumed he was."

Antoine's face became hard as stone. "Well I guess your ass shouldn't assume because you gave my child, who was almost raped, to some strange pervert posing to be her damn uncle."

"I'm sorry. Angel had already been through so much. I had no idea that she would have any reason to call that man Uncle LD if it really wasn't her uncle."

"You didn't check his I. D? I mean why would you just let my child leave with some strange man?" Antoine covered his face with both hands.

"Mr. Moore, I have no excuses. I should've checked his identification, but I would've never believed any one would come to a police station to kidnap a child. I never would've expected that."

Antoine sighed. "So, what do we do now?"

"This case has turned another way because now she was actually abducted from the police station by an adult. I'll put this out as a kidnapping immediately," Officer Gilliam answered.

"Well, what should I do?"

"My only suggestion is to go home just in case she shows up. In the meantime, I'll keep you up on everything we're doing on our end. However, I just need you to know that the first forty-eight hours are the most important in locating your daughter, so please do your best and call everyone she knows."

Antoine couldn't believe what was happening as he shook Officer Gilliam's hand and walked out the station. Regardless of how much he tried, it was hard to digest that his seventeen year old daughter was out in the street with some man, and there was nothing he could do about it. His only hope was that she would be okay.

CHAPTER 10

Angel could feel herself being yanked out of the bed before falling onto the floor with a hard thump. The pain that shot down her lower back and into her hip area immediately indicated that this wasn't a dream. As Angel opened her eyes, she looked up to find Poppy standing over her and looking as if he'd seen a ghost. She knew something was wrong.

"What...," was all she managed to get out before Poppy quickly placed his hand over her mouth.

"Shut the fuck up," he whispered. "Now listen, I need you to hurry up and put your shit on, and get the fuck outta here." He began to help her up, as Angel started mumbling something, but Poppy couldn't understand. "Look, you gotta be quiet. Do you understand?"

Even though she didn't, Angel shook her head up and down anyway. She didn't have the slightest idea what was going on, and as soon as Poppy took his hand away, she demanded answers. "What the fuck is going on?" she whispered.

"My wife just pulled up. She must've finished her workshop early. I can't let her find you here, so hurry up and put your shit on, so you can get out," Poppy whispered, as he pushed Angel's clothes and her purse into her arms.

"Your wife! You didn't tell me you had a damn wife," Angel responded. She could barely whisper at this point.

"Look, lil' girl, I didn't tell a lot of shit." He rushed Angel down the stairs and into the kitchen.

She was able to get her thong on, and one arm inside her shirt as he opened the back door and pushed her out. She could see the front door opening as the back door slammed in her face.

Looking around to see if anybody was watching her, Angel quickly hid behind a trash can in the back of Poppy's house, as she quickly put the rest of her clothes on. Luckily it was nightfall, so she may have been hard to make out anyway.

"Shit, my overnight bag," she said. "How am I supposed to get that now? His ass better call me because I need my stuff."

Angel crept beside the house and out onto the sidewalk not to be seen by Poppy's wife, then ran down the street. Her heart began to beat like a race horse as the excitement of almost being caught got her juices flowing between her legs. A small smile appeared on her face, and she began to laugh thinking how wild it would've been if his wife would've come home an hour earlier to find Poppy eating her pussy.

She better be glad he didn't fall asleep from all the fucking like I did.

Angel reached inside her purse to retrieve her cell phone, then dialed Poppy's number, but it went straight to his voice mail. "Shit!" She moved her head back and forth. "I don't even know where I am. Why would he just leave me out here?"

The reality that Poppy had put her out with nowhere to go started to set it, and immediately began to make Angel upset. She started to turn around and go back to his house, but decided against it. For all she knew his wife could've been crazy, and the last thing she needed was extra drama added on to her already drama filled life.

"Maybe I'll just call a cab and go to a hotel. That'll even give Poppy time to call me," Angel said, looking back in her purse.

However, when she looked in her wallet, panic began to overcome her body. All the money she had to her name was three one dollar bills. Barely enough to even get a happy meal.

At that moment, Angel didn't know what to do and began to walk around the neighborhood in a daze. She picked up her phone and tried to call Poppy for the second time, but again it went straight to voicemail. She began to search through her address book looking for someone else to call, but each man she talked to made up excuses like, they couldn't get away or it wasn't a good time as to why they couldn't come get her. Angel started to feel like all the men, who she believed loved her at one point, really didn't.

She continued in her daze like walk until she finally came up to a Metro bus stop, and luckily for her the bus was headed her way. Public transportation seemed to be her only option. Angel stepped on the bus and paid her fare before walking toward the back to take a seat. Having only a dollar left was extremely depressing.

She ended up riding the bus to the end of the line, which was two blocks from South Beach and got off. As she began to walk by all the mouth watering pizza parlors, her stomach started to growl. It was at that moment, when Angel really began to feel homeless because she had no idea when or where her next meal was going to come from.

"Let me try Poppy again," she said, pulling out her phone. However as she dialed the number, the phone kept cutting off. "No, please don't go dead on me!" she yelled to the battery. "What else can go wrong?"

Not knowing what to do, Angel found an empty bench on the sidewalk and sat down before lowering her head. *I'm not going to cry*, she kept thinking to herself as the tears tried their best to make a grand entrance. *Even if I have to fucking panhandle down on South Beach, I'm not going back home.*

"Hey, Sweetie, is everythin' a'ight?" someone asked, interrupting her thoughts.

Angel looked up to find a dark skinned black woman with a long blond weave talking to her from a Hummer. Angel remembered seeing the loud colored yellow truck driving around the block several times when she got off the bus, but didn't make much of it. Looking at the gaudy twenty-four inch rims, the woman seemed a bit too old to have a pimped out ride like that.

"I'm fine."

"Are you all by yo'self on these crazy streets?" the woman asked.

Bitch, you might be crazy. You don't need to know all that. "No, I'm waiting on my friend to pick me up," Angel replied.

"It's not safe to be out here alone, you know. Especially someone as beautiful as you." Angel shook her head in agreement. "Well, I'll sit here for a minute, and wait just to make sure you okay. Do you want to get inside? Normally perverts don't bother women when they wit' someone. My name is Freddie by the way," she said, pushing the passenger door open.

"No, that's okay, I'll be fine."

"Are you sure?"

"Positive." They were both quiet for a moment. "You don't look like a Freddie," Angel responded.

"It's short for Fredricka. Livin' and workin' out here in these streets is hard for a chick wit' a soft name, so I shortened my shit. What's yo' name, beautiful?"

Why in the hell does she keep calling me that? "It's Angel."

Freddie let out a loud laugh. "If you gonna run away from home and stay away, you gotta get a tougher street name. That shit is too biblical."

Angel frowned. "What do you mean run away? I'm waiting on a friend," she repeated.

"Trust me, I'm not the one you need to convince. But I do know a runaway when I see one. Shit, I ran away from home when I was only twelve myself. I even had the same look of confusion on my face. I used to tell the same lies until the street lights came on, and then no one was there to pick my ass up."

Angel turned her head. "Well, I'm not you." She began to reach for her cell phone, but suddenly remembered that she didn't have any power. Her eyes began to water.

"You wanna use my phone Starr?" Freddie asked, extending her hand. The phone was so small, it could almost fit in her palm.

"My name's not Starr. Why would you call me that?" Angel snapped.

"Because it's somethin' about you that has star quality. I mean, it's like a muthafuckin' star has been born."

Angel had no idea what Freddie was talking about. *Now I know her ass is crazy.* "Well Starr sure don't sound like a tough street name to me." Angel stood up and walked over to the truck. At that moment, she decided to take Freddie up on her offer, and use her cell phone, even though she really wasn't sure who to call. It was getting late and she definitely didn't want to hang out in the street all night.

Damn, because everybody is on my speed dial, I can't even think of anybody's number. She played with the buttons on the keypad trying desperately to think of somebody's number by heart, but kept coming up short. The only two numbers she knew like the back of her hand were both attached to Antoine, and there was no way she was gonna call either one of them.

"What's wrong Starr? You don't have anyone to call?" Freddie asked with a slight grin. "You might want to call 'dat friend because they runnin' kinda late. Besides, you wouldn't wanna be out in the streets for the entire night, would you?"

Suddenly Angel began to cry as she reached through the window to give Freddie her phone back, then sat down on the curb and covered her face with both hands.

Freddie got out the truck and walked around to Angel, then began to rub her shoulder. Her tall six foot frame seemed to tower over Angel. "I tell you what…you can post up at my spot if you want, but let me know somethin' quick 'cause I gotta roll out in a sec." Freddie turned around and got back in the truck to wait for Angel's response.

As crazy as it sounded, Angel knew her only options were to go with the stranger, to a shelter, or sleep out on the street. However, it was something about Freddie that started to make her feel a little more comfortable. After contemplating for a few more seconds, Angel slowly rose to her feet, then stepped into the big yellow truck that reminded her of a school bus.

It didn't take long for Freddie to pull away from the curb, and immediately push a button on the steering wheel to play some jazz. Still trying to contemplate about her decision, Angel sat back and closed her eyes, so she could think. Freddie knew Angel wasn't in the mood to talk, so she refrained from trying to start a conversation. As they drove down Washington Avenue the only thing that was heard were the smooth sounds of Miles Davis.

Twenty minutes later, Freddie put the truck in park then took out her keys when they pulled up in front of a run down twelve unit apartment building. Angel looked around nervously as she watched two men fighting across the street. Freddie smiled once Angel began to clinch her purse like a scared white woman.

"Let me guess, you ain't never been to this part of town before?"

"No," Angel replied. "Where are we?"

"You sound like we out of town or some shit. We in Little Haiti."

Angel's eyes got big. "Little Haiti...I've seen so much bad stuff on the news about this neighborhood. Is this where you live?"

"You damn right this where I live. Shit...I wouldn't have it no other way." She watched Angel as she continued to look around. "So, I take it you ain't never been to the hood before. You know...places like Opa Locka or Liberty City?"

"I messed with a few dudes from Overtown before, but they always came to my part of town."

"So where you from anyway, Starr?"

Man I wish she would stop calling me that. She looked at Freddie. "Coconut Grove."

Freddie smiled exposing a shiny gold tooth on the side of her mouth. "Oh, so your mom and pops doin' it big huh?" When Angel sucked her teeth, Freddie could immediately tell that talking about her parents was a touchy subject. "Well none of 'dat don't matter anyway because now you up in my hood."

Angel wanted to laugh at the fact that Freddie reminded her of a broke Mary J. Blige. "I can't believe you park your nice truck around here," Angel said, as she continued to hold her purse with a strong grip."

"I wish a muthafucka would put they hands on my shit! Starr, you'll soon find out, don't nobody fuck wit' me around here. I got mad respect!" She grabbed her black Gucci backpack. "Now, let's go."

Angel jumped out the truck and quickly followed behind Freddie like a lost little puppy. It was at that time when she noticed how big Freddie was in size. She even walked like a dude. Freddie appeared to be at least two hundred pounds. Angel even almost lost her balance and stumbled a few times as she continued to watch the two men throw blows across the street. She couldn't believe that Freddie acted as if nothing was going on.

They walked into the foul smelling building then up to the second floor, before Freddie opened the door. As soon as they stepped inside, the strong smell of weed almost knocked Angel off her feet. She covered her mouth and began to cough lightly then stopped instantly. Angel's eyes almost popped out of her head as she watched a girl suck on one's man's dick while another man fucked her from behind. It was like being in a live porno movie. It was also crazy to see three other girls sitting on the opposite side of the room laughing like hyenas. They seemed to be in their own world.

"What the fuck is goin' on in here?" Freddie shouted. She slammed the door, then walked over toward the porno stars. "How many times do I gotta tell y'all nasty-ass bitches 'dat it ain't gonna be no fuckin' up in my crib!"

The men immediately stopped, and quickly started to put their clothes on. From the way they moved, it was obvious that no one fucked with Freddie.

"Sorry, we didn't mean no disrespect, Freddie. But Lexus told us we could come in here and have some fun," one of the men said.

Freddie stepped to the man like she was a dude herself. "I don't give a fuck who told you 'dat shit, nigga. If you don't get the okay from me, then don't come up in my spot. You got that muthfucka!"

"Yeah," the man replied.

"Now get the fuck out, now!" Freddie walked back to the door and opened it. Both men didn't hesitate following her orders. However, Freddie stopped them just before they walked out. "Wait a minute…did y'all niggas pay any money for that pussy and head job you just got?"

The men looked at each other like they were afraid to answer, then looked back at Freddie. "No," they both answered at the same time.

Freddie looked furious. "Y'all niggas owe me $100.00 a piece, and you better consider that a good-ass discount. I also want my fuckin' money by tomorrow!"

"Bet," one of the guys said before they both walked away.

Angel could tell Freddie was about to go off from the way she slammed the door then turned around to look at Lexus, who had slipped on a long red robe. "How many times have I told y'all to respect my house?" Freddie asked. She then looked at the three girls who'd stopped laughing, but couldn't seem to get rid of their constant giggles. "If y'all three cacklin' hens don't shut the fuck up over there, I'ma give you somethin' to laugh at." She looked back at Lexus. "It's one thing 'dat you was fuckin' up in my crib, but then your dumb-ass is gonna have the nerve to do it for free."

"My bad, Freddie. I guess the weed had me trippin'," Lexus responded.

Surprisingly Freddie looked at Angel, and then seemed to calm down a little bit. "Lexus, all I gotta say is, you better be glad we have company or it wouldn't be good for you right now. But I'm not gonna tell you again. If you wanna keep livin' here…save that shit for the club. Fuckin' is what you get paid for. We not in business to give out free pussy around here." She looked around the room. "Remy, Crystal, Sandi. . . y'all go put your fuckin' clothes on, and get ready for work. And that goes for your stupid-ass too, Lexus. Y'all bitches got ten minutes to get out of here."

The women almost trampled over each other trying to get out the room before Freddie got started again. Slightly uncomfortable, Angel turned her head as Freddie walked up to her. "I'm sorry you had to see that."

Yeah I'm starting to wish that I'd stayed in South Beach and begged for money. "It's cool," Angel lied.

"Well come on, Starr. Let me show you around."

Angel followed Freddie to a small bedroom in the front of the apartment that looked like a college dorm room, from the bunk beds and empty Ramen noodle packages all over the floor. The junkie room, instantly made Angel miss her fresh clean home, but she knew she had to suck it up. At least she had a place to lay her head.

"Hey, you can take the top bunk. I know it may not look it, but it's very comfortable," Freddie assured. "You gonna be sharin' a room wit' Remy, even though she ain't in here right now. They all probably in the other room talkin' 'bout me and shit."

Angel smiled. "Thank you so much. I really don't know what I would've done if I didn't run into you."

"What type of person would I be if I left a beautiful little star like you in a place like that? Especially wit' all those damn weirdos and freaks down there? You just try and get some sleep. The best thing 'bout tomorrow is 'dat you get another chance at doin' it right." Freddie gave her one last smile before closing the door.

Angel slowly walked over to the childlike bed and placed her forehead on the thin blanket. To her surprise, the mattress was thick and firm. She kept wondering what she'd gotten herself into as she briefly closed her eyes.

I hope I didn't make a bad move, Angel continued to think. She turned back around and moved her head from side to side, checking out her new home. However, it didn't take her long to get disgusted again, once she saw two pairs of dirty thongs lying on the floor.

"Damn, this girl is nasty," Angel said, stepping over the leopard print and red lace underwear. She made her way over to the window and anxiously looked out, hoping she could catch another round of the ghetto fight, but the only thing that she saw were the four women from downstairs leaving the building. They were all in high inch stilettos and dressed in tight attire, from booty shorts to mini-skirts, which reminded Angel of the girls in the BET videos. Seconds later there was a knock on the door. "Come in," Angel said.

"Listen, we're gettin' ready to roll. I know the battery is dead on yo' cell phone, so there's a house phone in my room. Now, only go in my room if you need to call me, otherwise stay the hell out," Freddie ordered. "I don't like people snoopin' 'round my shit."

Angel seemed concerned. "You're leaving me here by myself?"

"Trust me...nobody is gonna bother you up in my crib. I already left specific instructions for my people across the street to watch this apartment like two nosey-ass old women. Now you know don't shit get past old folks."

Her comment made Angel smile, which instantly made Freddie light up as well. Angel was even more beautiful when she showed off her perfect set of teeth. "Don't worry, beautiful. I'll be back before you know it." She closed the door before Angel could respond.

Angel was in her new bed sleep when she heard people yelling from outside several hours later. As tired as she was, she tried her best to drown out the sounds, and go back to sleep, but one woman kept getting louder by the second. *Damn, do the people around this neighborhood ever sleep*, Angel thought as she jumped out of bed, and walked to the window. When she looked out and saw that the women yelling was Freddie, her ears immediately tuned in.

"Bitch, do you think you was gonna get away wit' 'dat shit from earlier!" Freddie yelled, snatching Lexus' hair. Angel pressed her face against the window, and watched as Freddie pushed Lexus onto the ground.

"I'm sorry Freddie, but I thought you said everything was cool!" Lexus shouted.

Freddie kicked her in the stomach, "Bitch, you don't fuck in my house unless I say so!" she yelled. "You the type of bitch 'dat will cause me to lose everythin' that I worked for."

Lexus started coughing uncontrollably, then managed to get something out. "I will never do that shit again," she cried out.

The other girls stood and watched as Freddie continued to kick Lexus repeatedly. Angel also watched in amazement from her window. Lexus tried to crawl under a truck that was nearby, but Freddie pulled her back by her leg.

"I own you. Do you understand? Yo' pussy belongs to me. Have you forgotten all the shit I've done for you." Freddie reached down and pulled Lexus up by her neck. "Remember, you still work for me, but you just got yo' ass kicked out my spot." She pushed Lexus away. "Now, go find somewhere to stay and get the fuck out my sight before I kill yo' dumb-ass."

Angel felt for Lexus as she got herself together and slowly walked down the street. Angel was amazed at what she'd just seen. *Damn, now I really hope I didn't make a mistake.*

CHAPTER 11

The next morning, the heat from the bright sun made Angel's living quarters almost unbearable to sleep, so she opened her eyes and jumped out of bed. Angel turned around and expected to see Remy sleeping on the bottom bunk, but she wasn't there. However, the small Daisy Dukes and nasty underwear that were tossed on the floor was evidence that she'd at least been there.

Angel slipped on the same sweatpants that could probably walk on their own from being worn over the past few days, and then went to the kitchen. As thirsty as she was, as soon as Angel spotted a water cooler, she used the plastic cups on the side to get something to drink. But the machine made a loud noise when she pressed the button to release the water.

"What the hell? Who's makin' all that noise?" Freddie yelled from her bedroom. "It's too damn early. Carry yo' ass back to bed!"

Angel was too afraid to even reply after what she'd seen the night before. Trying to tip-toe around the apartment at that point, Angel knew she wasn't going back to her hot-ass room, so she decided to go outside on the balcony and wait for everybody to get up.

The last thing I need right now is to get kicked out like Lexus. When Angel walked outside, she watched four little girls as they were crossing the street. Three of them were dancing to their iPODs, while the other one was talking on her cell phone loud as ever.

Just a week ago, that was me, Angel thought. *Now I'm standing on a stranger's balcony, in a crazy neighborhood with nothing to my name except a dollar and the clothes on my back.* As Angel continued to think, the door behind her opened, and Remy stood in the doorway with a cigarette.

"Hello," Angel said.

"Freddie knew you were the one making that noise in the kitchen a few minutes ago because she's the only person who drinks water out that thing. She wants me to give you some clothes."

As long as you don't try and give me any of that shit on the floor, I'm fine. "How did she know I needed clothes?"

Remy smiled. "Umm…you walked in here with no bags yesterday, and now you have on the same clothes, so it wasn't hard to figure out," she said, patting her ashes on the ground.

"Yeah, I guess you're right. So, can I ask you a question? What time do you all normally get up?"

"We don't usually get up until three or four in the afternoon because we put in late hours around here." Angel shook her head like she understood.

"My name is Remy like the drink. What's yours?" she asked, with a smile.

Remy reminded Angel of a black Barbie doll with her perfect cinnamon complexion, bright grey contact lenses, and a long fake ponytail that almost touched her waist. "Ang…I mean Starr. My name is Starr." Angel didn't feel comfortable letting Remy know too much about her yet.

Remy looked at Angel as if she'd heard the story before, but just with another person. "Well, Starr, you still need to be quiet.

108

The other girls are still asleep. It's the first of the month, so guys wanted to party all night." Remy put the cigarette out, then tossed it over the balcony before walking back into the apartment.

Angel wanted to ask what it was that she and the other girls did, but decided against it as she followed Remy into their bedroom.

"You can look in the closet to find something to wear. Whatever you can fit is yours. I'm getting back in bed, so try not to be too loud," Remy said. "Oh, by the way if you wanna take a shower, washcloths and towels are in the closet beside the bathroom. Hopefully, you can find something clean, because as you can see, we all about getting money 'round here. The hell with cleaning." Remy laughed before pulling the blanket over her head.

Yeah, you all are definitely in need of a maid around this place, Angel thought as she looked around the room. "Thanks for all your help."

After looking in Remy's closet and realizing she had all of the latest designer jeans and shoes, Angel's eyes lit up. There were so many clothes. Most of them still had tags on them and had never been worn. *Damn, this is like going to the mall and having a free shopping spree.*

Luckily, Angel and Remy shared the same size twenty-eight waist, so she ended up picking out a cute pair of True Religion jeans. Angel's breast and feet were slightly smaller than Remy's, so she knew the sexy, cream off the shoulder shirt and Manolo Blahnik peep toe pumps might be a little big, but she didn't care. It felt good to dress in style for a change.

Angel placed her new clothes on the top bunk and admired the shoes for a few seconds before walking to the bathroom to take a shower. Her face frowned when she stopped at the hall closet, and was only able to get a hard towel that felt like a Brillo pad, but no washcloth. It was obvious that she was gonna have to use her hand. Angel shut the closet with a slight attitude, then walked into the bathroom before closing the door. She hadn't even been in the apartment for twenty-four hours, and she was already tired of the nastiness.

It didn't take long for Angel to shed her underwear and three day old clothing, before stepping into the dirty tub. After turning the knob, she placed her entire body under the hot water, which felt delightful against her body. It seemed like she hadn't taken a shower in months. She stood under the water for what seemed like eternity before finally lathering up her body with a bar of Dove soap. She then used the bottles of shampoo and conditioner that were also in the shower to wash her long hair. At that point, Angel wasn't sure when her next bath was going to be, so she made sure to get everything squeaky clean. After rinsing off the last lather of soap, Angel turned the knob to shut off the water. However, she was completely shocked when she opened the shower curtain to find another woman brushing her teeth in the mirror. She was completely naked. Angel quickly closed the curtain and looked around like she was trying to find the woman something to wear.

"Girl, I know you not afraid to come out of the shower," the woman joked.

As Angel was about to respond, Remy showed up at the bathroom door. "Sandi, get your dike-ass out the bathroom so Starr can get out the shower."

"She can still get out. I'm just brushing my teeth. Oh and your dumb-ass should know that I'm bisexual not a dike," Sandi responded.

"I don't care what you are; bisexual, dike, lesbian, whore, whatever. Your ass don't even get up this early, and now you in the bathroom the same time Starr is, brushing your teeth in the nude. Come on now...your game is weak."

"I had no idea we were claiming pets. Are you gonna dry her off too?" Sandi laughed as she left the bathroom.

"Get your Lil' Kim ass up outta here," Remy replied, referring to Sandi's massive boob job.

"Well since y'all bitches wanna continue to be fuckin' loud, let's go get somethin' to eat," Freddie yelled from her room.

"Okay Freddie," Remy answered. "Hey Starr, you can come out now."

Angel stuck her head through the curtain. "Thanks. I'm not used to any of this."

"Well get used to it if you decide to stick around. Listen, I got out of bed to give you this anyway." Remy handed Angel a new toothbrush, and a black thong with the matching bra. "Don't worry, the underwear are brand new," Remy stated. She could sense the concerned look on Angel's face. "Hey, I hope you don't think you have time to do your hair because Freddie is not gonna wait."

Angel shook her head. "No, it's cool. I'll let it air dry. It'll just curl up if I do that."

"Man, it must be nice to have that good shit," Remy said before closing the door.

The women didn't waste any time following Freddie's orders. All of them were up, washed and dressed within the next hour. As they walked out the house, Angel realized how stunning everybody looked, and how each of them was dressed like they had a date. She continued to admire everyone, until she noticed one of the guys from the night before, coming up to them. Angel had to admit, she was extremely nervous because for all she knew, he could've had a gun.

"Well, well, well, look what we have here," Freddie said. "I hope you got my money."

"Yeah, here's the two-hundred we owe you," he replied, handing Freddie the money. "We good now?"

Freddie quickly counted the ten twenty dollar bills. "Oh yeah, but just make sure you follow and respect my fuckin' rules next time, nigga."

"You got it, Freddie 'cuz I don't want no beef wit' you," the guy said walking away.

Getting back to her girls, Freddie formally introduced Angel to Crystal when they all reached the Hummer. "And I guess you met another one of our freaks in the house," Freddie said, pointing to Sandi.

"Yeah we've met, but I hope to get to know Starr a little better," Sandi responded with a wink.

Angel didn't waste anytime climbing into the third row seat of the truck as Freddie unlocked the doors. She wanted to be as far away from Sandi as possible, and was glad when Sandi chose to ride shot gun. *She's beautiful and everything, but I'm addicted to dick, so her ass can cancel whatever plans she got with me,* Angel thought.

As they pulled off and drove down the street, Freddie rolled down the windows and cranked the song *Same Girl*, by Usher and R. Kelly. Angel felt like she was at a club the way the loud base vibrated through her body. Guys in the neighborhood started blowing their horns, trying to get the ladies to pull over, but nothing seemed to work. Besides, between the base and Crystal's loud singing, nobody could hear a thing anyway.

Minutes later, the truck pulled up to the valet parking of the Marriott Doral Golf Resort near the airport. The hotel's, Terrazza Restaurant was known for their delicious lunch buffet, and since Freddie was a big woman, she usually didn't bother with restaurants that only provided one course.

As each lady stepped out, the parking attendant's eyes widened with each pair of long legs. Noticing the attention, the women took sexy strides to illuminate their hour glass shapes as they walked to the restaurant. It was hard for old married white men not to stare when the ladies followed the hostess to their seats.

After settling down and grabbing their first helping of food, Freddie began to share her story with Angel about ending up on the streets. It wasn't long before each woman began to reveal their stories, telling Angel about similar situations. By the third plate of food, Angel started to feel a little more comfortable with her surroundings because as it turned out, each of the women were somewhat just like her.

Eventually, they changed the subject to a more pleasant one, and the laughter got louder as they began ordering a few drinks. Despite the waiter's concern, Freddie even ordered Angel a drink. She was giggling in no time.

"I say we go to the nail shop and get Remy's feet done after this because her heels look like she's been playing in baby powder all day," Crystal announced.

Everyone laughed except Remy.

"Good, we should go there, so maybe one of those chinks can remove Sandi's mustache and fuckin' unibrow," Remy scolded leaning back in her chair.

"Bitches. I can't stand jealous bitches. I'm the baddest one at this table. My style is flawless. I have long thick legs, a firm ass, tight stomach and these big bouncy titties that all the men love." Sandi began to push her breasts up and down.

Yeah, she definitely wants to be Lil' Kim, especially with that reddish color weave she has, Angel thought.

"Bitch, don't try and act like those fake-ass silicone things are real," Remy said.

"I know…I think she actually believes that shit. It still won't make up for your extra male DNA that makes you grow facial hair," Crystal added on.

113

Angel started laughing. She was really starting to enjoy herself and liked having some females to hang out with. Something she rarely did when she was back home with Antoine. For some reason, she felt free...like a grown adult. Out of all the girls, Angel thought Crystal was the one with the most natural beauty. Her light colored skin tone was smooth and seemed free from any blemishes. She was also the only one who didn't have a weave. The long jet black hair that hugged her shoulders seemed to suit her perfectly.

Sandi turned and gave Angel a look of death. "Hold up. I know Miss Thang ain't over there laughing!" Sandi shouted.

"And what if she is?" Freddie finally asked.

Sandi seemed surprised that Freddie was taking up for Angel like that, but knew she had to be careful with how she responded. "Well, I bet all the money I got on me right now that her lil' young ass never even seen a dick, so how the fuck would she know what men like!"

The customers in the restaurant began to look in the ladies direction. Angel was now laughing so hard, she started holding her stomach.

"What? What's so fucking funny?" Sandi asked.

"Shit, it's because of dick that I'm here in the first place," Angel shot back.

"Wow Coconut Grove, I thought you were just mad at yo' parents because they got you a white BMW, and you asked fo' a red one," Freddie said laughing. Remy and Crystal started laughing too, but Sandi never cracked a smile.

"Hell no, I got caught giving head to the captain of the basketball team, so I got kicked out of school. Then my father caught me just before *one* of my dudes went down to eat my pussy at home one day," Angel responded. She took a huge sip of her top shelf margarita.

"Pay up bitch!" Remy shouted to Sandi.

"Girl, fuck you. I was just playing. It wasn't a real bet," Sandi replied. "Her ass probably lying anyway."

Freddie frowned. "Now you know not to play 'dat shit, Sandi. A bet is a fuckin' bet. Reach in yo' purse and pull out all yo' fuckin' money. It ain't her fault 'dat you tried to be cute, and lost. Now pay your bill," Freddie demanded, leaning forward.

"Come on Freddie, I had a real good night last night," Sandi whined.

"Does it look like I give a fuck 'dat you had a good night? Yo' dumb-ass shoulda' thought 'bout that shit before yo' mouth wrote a check that yo' ass couldn't cash. Now don't make me ask you again."

Remy grabbed the fresh fifty and hundred dollar bills as Sandi emptied her purse, and threw the money on the table. "Three thousand, one hundred forty-one…forty-two…forty-three dollars. Damn, your pussy must've been on fire at the club last night," Remy said. "Here you go, Starr." Remy extended her hand.

"I told y'all I was the baddest one at the table," Sandi said, in a low tone.

Angel waved her hand back and forth. "No, I'm fine. I don't want her money."

Sandi's face lit up, and she quickly held out her hand. "Well you heard her…give my shit back."

"Don't give Sandi's ass nothin. Starr you need to take the money. Besides, how else were you gonna pay the bill?" Freddie asked. Angel gave her a confused look. "I'm just playin', but you are gonna use Sandi's shit to pay it now."

After letting out a sigh of relief, Angel reached across the table and took the large stack of bills from Remy. Crystal snickered as Sandi sat back in her chair and pouted. Throughout the remainder of the lunch, everybody kept ordering drinks including Angel as Sandi just looked the other way. The way she bit her lip and shook her leg under the table, it was obvious that she was beyond pissed.

"Starr, yo' folks have probably called the police by now, and are lookin' for you," Freddie said.

Angel lowered her head. "Not my folks, just my dad. I don't deal with my bitch-ass mother," she answered. "What should I do?"

"The street life is hard. You need to make this decision on yo' own. Livin' out here, you might have to do terrible unthinkable things just to survive." Freddie responded.

"Shit, well if this is the street life then I'm cool because I want to live like y'all," Angel said. "I really don't' want to go home."

"I think you need to see the girls at work tonight before you make up your mind." Freddie looked around for the waiter. "Check. Can we get the fuckin' check over here?" She held up her hand in the air and started snapping her fingers.

After Angel paid the bill and left a huge tip, the Hummer partied all the way back to the apartment. As soon as they arrived, Freddie gave Sandi permission to go out on a quick date with a client, while she and Crystal went to their rooms to take a nap. Remy and Angel however, stayed up and laughed about the whole lunch incident, then went to Remy's closet to figure out what Angel was going to wear for her first night out with the girls.

CHAPTER 12

As the sun slowly lowered behind the apartment building, the house turned into a party as the ladies began to get ready. Freddie constantly cursed Crystal out, as she sang along to a Keyshia Cole song in her room, which prohibited Freddie from hearing her jazz clearly. Not trying to be out the loop, Remy and Angel also partied to a Rick Ross rap song that blasted on the radio as they both applied good smelling lotion and perfume in all the right places.

Sandi returned to the house with her nails done up in a red polish with metallic palm trees on each nail. She walked in switching hard, trying her best to show off her new outfit. She even got her eyebrows arched to perfection.

She strolled in Remy and Angel's room. "Let's get this show started ladies. I'm feeling hot tonight. I need to make my money back and then some." She was obviously in a better mood.

"Girl, how many dicks did you have to suck in order to look that good?" Remy asked.

"Just one. Then, I had to blow in his ass to get the eyebrows." Both Remy and Sandi started laughing.

That's a nasty girl, Angel thought. "We never did decide what I was gonna wear tonight, Remy," Angel remarked.

Freddie yelled from her room, "Starr, come in here. I got the perfect outfit for you."

Remy looked at Angel and shrugged her shoulders like she didn't know what was going on. Freddie had never bought any of the girls' clothes, so this was new to everybody.

"Go on in there and get that Catholic school uniform she wants you to wear," Sandi said laughing. She then turned around and walked to her room.

Angel's nervous demeanor could be seen a mile away as she walked up to Freddie's door and knocked, even though it was open. "You only have to knock when my shit is closed," Freddie instructed.

When Angel walked in, she was surprised at what she saw. Unlike the rest of the house, Angel was shocked to see how clean and well kept Freddie's room was. However, even more surprising were the black satin Dolce and Gabanna pants with the matching crop jacket lying across Freddie's king sized bed. Her eyes became big as fifty cent pieces.

"Well from the look on yo' face, I can tell 'dat you know the outfit is for you." Angel shook her head, but didn't say a word. "Well try it on, and see if it fits." Freddie picked up the jacket and held it up to Angel.

"I can't believe you did this for me."

"You worth it," Freddie replied. After handing Angel the jacket, she turned around and picked up a diamond studded belly chain with the necklace to match. "Here you go, add this."

"Oh my God, this is beautiful," Angel replied, taking the jewelry out of Freddie's hands. She looked like a kid at Disney World the way she admired the sparkling diamonds.

"Don't get too damn excited cause 'dat shit ain't real. It's costume jewelry," Freddie said, with a smile. "Now go try everything on."

"Okay, I'll be right back."

"No, try it on right here. I wanna be the first one to see it on you."

"Sure," Angel replied hesitantly. She slipped off the terry cloth robe that Remy gave her, exposing her bare breasts and sexy green g-string. Freddie began to lick her lips, which made Angel uncomfortable, but with the excitement of the new outfit, she quickly ignored her stares. "How does it look?" Angel turned around showing her plump ass and flat washboard stomach.

"Like a fuckin' dream," Freddie replied. "I knew you was gonna look good in 'dat shit." She then went under her bed and pulled out a box that contained a pair of Jimmy Choo shoes. "This should set off the outfit." Again, Angel was speechless, and couldn't believe that Freddie was being so nice to her. Moments later, Crystal arrived to do her makeup.

"Wow, you look great, Starr," Crystal said. "You picked out that dress, Freddie?"

"Listen, do your job. I need her to look legal, but don't go over board. Keep the colors light," Freddie ordered.

Fifteen minutes later, Angel couldn't believe the transformation. When she looked in the mirror, someone else stared back at her. The colors Crystal had chosen really brought out her beautiful light brown eyes. "I can't believe this is me."

"Well believe it because yo' ass is stunnin'. Good job Chris," Freddie said. "Now let's get this show on the fuckin' road."

ન૦ ન૦ ન૦

When the Hummer pulled up to the front of the club in Liberty City, thirty minutes later, all the women seemed ready to party expect Sandi. Ever since she'd seen Angel in her new dress, her attitude had changed completely. It also didn't help that Remy and Crystal kept complimenting Angel during the entire drive. A smile came over the ladies faces when they saw the long line stretching around the corner, which meant lots of money for everyone.

Angel watched as two large bouncers walked over to the truck, and opened the passenger door. Sandi exited the truck first, and when she did several men and even a few ladies yelled and whistled. Sandi waved and blew kisses to the crowd as she strutted inside. Each girl got the same reception when they got out.

"Welcome to Freddie's Penthouse, Starr," Freddie said. "Go ahead, they won't bite you unless they pay me first."

Angel took a deep breath and finally stepped out the truck. All the men went crazy. *This is how Beyoncé must feel walking the red carpet,* Angel thought as she waited for Freddie. Once Freddie was beside her, they both smiled, winked and slowly walked toward the front door.

Angel was completely overwhelmed when she entered the smoky club to find ladies dancing on small stages, with little to nothing on, girls in lingerie serving drinks behind the bar, and several other girls giving lap dances. Angel then looked up to see Sandi, Remy and Crystal heading up the steps to a second level.

Angel tapped Freddie on the shoulder. "What's up those steps?"

"'Dats where my girls work. They all started down here dancin', but when they were ready, I gave them they own private room upstairs. Can you dance?"

"A little bit, I guess," Angel replied nervously.

"Well if you can't, you better learn fast because if you want to stay wit' me and the girls, you have to earn yo' keep."

Angel looked at Freddie, who had a smirk on her face, and finally realized what this was all about. Freddie wasn't nice, she was a businesswoman. The dress and the shoes were all bait to lure Angel in.

"Yo' ass is next on stage, so don't fuck up," Freddie said, before walking away. She hadn't even given Angel a chance to process anything.

I thought she said I could see how I liked things before making up my mind. This is such bullshit. Angel watched several of the other dancers as they did their set before she heard the worst words of her life.

"Freddie's Penthouse, let's show some love to our beautiful new girl, Starr," the DJ announced. It wasn't long before the song, *I'm N' Love Wit' A Stripper*, by T-Pain and Mike Jones blasted through the club's speakers.

Angel couldn't believe it was her turn already. When she looked around the club, she and Freddie locked eyes, but Freddie wasn't cracking a smile or clapping like everybody else, which immediately made Angel nervous. She quickly lowered her head as her body began to shake uncontrollably. A part of her wanted to turn around and run out the front door, but her feet felt glued to the floor. She stood there for a couple of seconds, until she looked up at Freddie, who now appeared to be extremely irritated. At that moment, Angel began to think about Lexus, and tried to get herself together.

"Hey, Starr where you at, baby?" the DJ called out. "The song is almost over."

Come on Angel you can do this. You don't want Freddie to beat you down like she did Lexus. Just act like you're dancing in front of Wink or Poppy. Trying to keep those thoughts, Angel finally stepped up on the stage like a pro. The crowd went wild as Angel slowly moved her body to the beat of the music. She made several moves she'd seen off the late night videos and constantly swayed her hips from side to side. When the song went off, the crowd cheered, even though Angel hadn't taken off one piece of clothing. The adrenaline rush of dancing on stage, made Angel feel good. She smiled from ear to ear as she walked up to Freddie, who was now finally clapping.

"Good job, Starr. Now go upstairs because these thirsty-ass dudes are gonna try and attack you, and I don't think you ready yet."

Wow, why couldn't my father ever protect me like this. "Good idea."

Angel was in the middle of the hallway on the second floor when she heard some commotion coming from inside one of the rooms. Not sure if she should run and get Freddie, Angel decided to crack the door to see what was happening, and when she did, her eyes grew two times the normal size.

She burst into the room, as a guy attacked Remy, and began hitting the man with anything she could find in the room. It didn't take long for the man to get upset. He turned around and pushed Angel, causing her to fly into the nightstand. However, Remy retaliated by kicking the guy in the groin area. He let out a loud moan before falling to the floor. As Remy tried to walk over and kick him again, he grabbed her legs and snatched her down to the floor with him. She began kicking and punching with all her might.

Holding on to her side, Angel ran and jumped on the man's back when she saw him trying to mount Remy. She dug her nails into his face, then peeled his skin back like an orange.

"Coke!" the man screamed.

"That's enough Starr, he gives up," Remy said. When Angel didn't stop, she got even louder. "Coke is the magic word that means stop, Starr. Get off of him!"

Angel released her fingers one at a time from the man's face as blood slowly began to drip, and hopped off his back. "What's going on here? I thought he was attacking you," she replied, breathing heavily.

"I'm sorry Starr, but this is my baby, Marlin. Marlin likes to get rough during our time together. He's a sweet man with a soft wife at home that can't whip that ass like me. I fuck him up a little; let him wrestle me to the ground, then fuck him until he explodes."

Angel was speechless.

"Look at my face. My wife is going to be pissed," Marlin cried looking into a mirror.

Remy walked over to him. "Give me your wallet."

"Why?" he asked.

"I'm going to keep all your cash, then mail your wallet back to you in the mail, so you don't have to change your information. You can tell your wife you got robbed on the way home," Remy answered.

"But I didn't even get to finish our session. Little Bruce Lee over here messed up my damn nut."

Remy held up her arms. "It goes like that sometimes, baby. Think about all the times I went the extra mile to get you off. I'll make it up to you next time." Remy covered herself with a fishnet baby doll dress, then escorted Marlin out.

"Shit, I had no idea that's what y'all were involved in up here. Shit, you're a prostitute, Remy. You fuck for money," Angel said.

"Let me ask you a question. When you sucked that lil' boy's dick in school, what did you get for your work? Oh, that's right, you got expelled from school, in trouble with your father and ran away from home. Whereas, I just sucked Marlin's dick, got five hundred, and got my frustration out by beating that nigga's ass."

Angel laughed. "Well when you put it like that, I feel stupid."

"Let me school you, Starr. The dancers downstairs make about two to three hundred dollars a day. Now up here in the Sex Kingdom, we make two to three thousand a day. All of us get paid to do what we love…fuck. I can still go downstairs and dance if I want some bullshit-ass lunch money or something. But the Sex Kingdom is why I got all that shit in my closet."

"So all the girls in the house work up here?" Angel asked.

"Yeah, except Freddie and now Lexus of course. Freddie owns the club and lets all of us stay in her house for free. She also roughs niggas up when they get out of line around here. That reminds me, I can't believe the bouncer let you barge in here like that."

Angel shook her head. "I didn't see anybody at the door. As a matter of fact, I didn't see anybody when I came upstairs."

"Wow, Freddie would be pissed if she knew that shit."

"I like Freddie. She's so damn cool."

Remy looked at her like she was crazy. "I don't know about that, but I do know that you'll probably be asked to join the team tonight. I can tell by the way Freddie looks at you that she thinks you're special. If you want to stay, she's gonna call you to her room, then fuck you into the group."

"What?" Angel yelled.

"I'm serious. Freddie likes you, and it's what she does to welcome the new girls. So, do you still think she's cool now?" Remy asked, followed by a huge laugh.

Angel appeared to be in a daze. "What if I don't want to have sex?"

"Well in that case Freddie will probably have Sandi beat your ass for taking her money, and then put you out in the street again."

Angel was at a loss for words.

Despite Freddie's instructions, Angel sat downstairs at the bar, watching the other girls dance, set after set. She decided to stay away from Freddie after what Remy told her, and turned down guy after guy until the night came to an end.

124

The girls waited in the truck as Freddie closed the books and locked up for the night. The ride home was just as loud as the ride over because the girls never seemed to stop partying. However, there was one voice that was never heard. Angel replayed Remy's conversation and the vision of Lexus being stomped on the ground over and over in her head as she rode in the back seat in complete silence. *What the fuck am I going to do now?* she thought.

CHAPTER 13

Angel sat on the couch in the living room and watched as Crystal, Remy and Sandi counted their earnings from the club. She had to admit, seeing all that money made the Sex Kingdom job very tempting, but was still nervous about being with strange men and having sex with them for money.

"That's what the fuck I'm talking about!" Sandi yelled, as she counted her last twenty dollar bill. "I almost pulled in four grand tonight!" She gave a slight smile, then looked at Crystal and Remy. "And y'all bitches didn't think I was the baddest one in the crew."

"You're not," Remy countered.

Four thousand? Maybe I should give this job a try, Angel thought. She was waiting on the microwave to finish popping a bag of butter flavored popcorn, when Freddie called her name.

"Starr, come in here. I need to talk to you."

Crystal and Remy giggled because they automatically knew what Freddie wanted. Both of them had gone through it. Sometimes, more than once. Sandi however, didn't find anything amusing. She was the only girl in the house, who thought she was Freddie's favorite, so it pissed her off that Freddie was giving so much of her attention to someone else. Sandi stared at Angel like a bald eagle as she headed toward Freddie's bedroom.

"Good luck, girl," Remy said, through her laughter.

Angel didn't bother to knock, when she saw the bedroom door open this time. However, she just stood in the doorway with her arms folded, and didn't bother to walk all the way in. The candles, which took over the two nightstands, had the room smelling like vanilla ice cream. When Freddie looked up from her Jet magazine and saw Angel standing there, she pushed several of the decorative pillows on her bed onto the floor, then patted the mattress, instructing Angel where to sit.

As Angel began to take baby steps over to the bed, Freddie stopped her. "Now you can close my shit."

As crazy as the idea was, Angel decided to act as if she was closing the door, but left it open slightly. Luckily, Freddie's attention had gone back to the magazine, so she wasn't paying much attention. To Angel, leaving the door open, meant someone could possibly rescue her if assistance was needed. She slowly walked over to the very edge of the bed, and then sat down.

"You seem so nervous. Are you afraid of me? Do I scare you or somethin'?" Freddie asked finally putting the magazine down. She adjusted her black silk robe then moved closer to her prey.

"I've never had sex with a woman before," Angel admitted.

"So, what makes you think 'dat's the reason why I called you in here?"

Angel didn't want to snitch on Remy, so she shrugged her shoulders. "I don't know. I guess because of the way you looked at me when I tried on the outfit you gave me."

Goose bumps rose on Freddie's arms as she thought about Angel's body. "Well you right. I do wanna fuck the shit outta you, but I also want to see if the Sex Kingdom interests you at all?" She slowly began stroking Angel's hair.

Angel still hadn't made up her mind about the job yet, but from the expression on Freddie's face, it didn't look like she was going to take no for an answer. Angel felt obligated to join the team. "Yeah, I'm interested."

Freddie displayed a huge smile. "Good 'cause I can make a lot of money off you…I mean we can make a lot of money. You gon' be my shinin' star!" Freddie moved her index finger down to one of Angel's nipples and began to rub it gently. After feeling its stiffness, Freddie smiled and gave it a playful little tug. She knew once Angel didn't resist, it was show time. "If I'm gonna be yo' first, I have to make sure I do everythin' just right," she said, leaning closer to Angel's ear.

Freddie kissed Angel's neck, then twirled her tongue like a number eight. As her hand began to caress Angel's back, Freddie could tell that she was no longer the only one with goose bumps. "Don't worry, I'll take it slow," she assured.

Enjoying how Freddie made her clit throb, Angel's fears of the unknown slowly began to disappear as she allowed Freddie to remove her clothes along with her thongs. She felt sexy standing in her birthday suit. A feeling she'd never experienced before. The cool air began to make both of her nipples stiff and started the juices flowing between her legs.

Freddie slowly guided Angel down on the bed, and was surprised when Angel laid back and spread both her legs to expose her drenched pussy. Accepting the open invitation, Freddie kissed Angel's ankles with little pecks, then quickly made her way to Angel's thighs. At that point, she glided her hand up to Angel's treasure, and gently rubbed around the perimeter, causing Angel to arch her back.

"You like 'dat?" Freddie asked, as she massaged Angel's clit in a circular pattern with her index finger. As Angel shook her head up and down, that was Freddie's cue to take off her robe, exposing her naked body.

Angel's soft moans began to amplify when Freddie's tongue dove deep inside her wanting pussy. The warmth and movement of Freddie's tongue made her body tingle in a way that no other man was able to do. Freddie began to suck and lick faster as Angel moved her hips to fuck Freddie's tongue. The taste of Angel's sweet cookie, immediately caused Freddie to start generating juices of her own, and without a seconds notice, she got up, climbed over Angel and placed her body in the 69 position.

Surprised by the erupt feeling of ecstasy, Angel opened her eyes to see Freddie's perfectly manicured pussy luring overhead. Not to be outdone, Angel didn't waste anytime lifting her head and began to devour Freddie's treasure. Although she was a rookie, her tongue worked like a pro.

"Damn, baby," Freddie blurted out. "Lick this pussy like you mean it." It wasn't long before Freddie inserted two of her fingers inside Angel and began moving them in and out at a rapid pace. "Cum for me baby." Freddie's finger fucking session caused Angel to start moaning again. Seeing that Angel was completely turned on, Freddie kept her fingers inside with one hand and used her other one to pull open the drawer on the nightstand. "I got somethin' special for you baby."

Angel became lost in the moment when Freddie pulled out a cordless bullet, and placed the cold silver egg shaped vibrator against her clit. Freddie's fingers continued to push deeper and deeper as a strong surge of cum came bursting out Angel's overflowing pussy.

"Oh shit," Angel moaned.

"Wait...I ain't done," Freddie responded. She left the bullet against her clit as she went back in the drawer, pulled out a strap-on, then secured it through her legs, and around her waist. The black, nine inch dildo teased Angel just before venturing inside her pussy.

129

Angel felt the bullet tapping against new erogenous spots as Freddie rotated her movement to wiggle the dildo further inside. As she started to speed up, Angel rocked her head back and forth frantically. At that point, she was past the moaning stage and the screams of delight could be heard all over the apartment.

The girls laughed as they heard the sounds that many of them made when Freddie had inducted them into the house. However, Sandi was the only one not laughing. She just stared in the direction of Freddie's room and bit her bottom lip.

Angel loved how Freddie worked her body, and soon forgot all about being with a woman. She even allowed Freddie to use several of the toys to bring her to orgasm after orgasm. Angel was in complete heaven.

ॐ   ॐ   ॐ

Two hours later, when Freddie went inside the bathroom to take a piss break, Angel felt alive. Her body still shook from the multiple orgasms as she felt a cool breeze blow across her naked body. She lifted her head to find the bedroom door open, and Sandi standing in the door frame. Neither said a word, but Sandi's look of hatred spoke volumes.

Freddie walked out the bathroom to find Sandi staring at Angel. "Explain why you believe it's okay to open my fuckin' door when I know I closed it."

Sandi looked over at Freddie and immediately noticed the dried candle wax over her naked breasts and hips. She then rolled her eyes and turned her attention back to Angel. "I'll let you continue to house train your new bitch."

Rage quickly built up in Freddie's body as she slapped Sandi across her face. "Muthafucka, you done forgot yo' place!" Freddie shouted. She wrapped Sandi's weave tightly around her

130

left hand then yanked her down to the floor. "Crawl, dog. Crawl over to the bed and beg Starr for her forgiveness."

Not knowing what to make of the whole ordeal, Angel quickly sat up in the bed. "That's not…" she started to say.

Freddie cut her off. "'Dat's not what? Did I tell yo' ass to say anythin'? Now hold out your hand so this hoe can beg for yo' forgiveness. She ain't got no right to be callin' you no bitch. She's the bitch!"

Sandi crawled on all fours as Angel's eyes watered. When Sandi got to the bed, she sat on her knees and bent her arms in front of her, then panted like a dog. Scared that Freddie would treat her like Lassie next, Angel held out hand as Sandi kissed it repeatedly.

"Please forgive me, Starr…please," Sandi said.

"You mad 'cause I ain't fuck you, huh?" Freddie asked. "Well since you wanna be fucked so bad, I'ma let yo' ass have it." She reached into the nightstand and pulled out a twelve inch strap-on this time, then quickly stepped into the straps. Freddie pushed Sandi's face down onto the floor, and forcefully spread her legs apart.

"Please don't do this," Sandi pleaded.

"Why not, you wanted to be fucked so bad, so now here's yo' chance," Freddie replied, as she yanked Sandi's hot pink boy shorts down. She didn't even bother to use lubricant before ramming the huge dildo into Sandi's dry asshole.

Sandi yelled out in pain. "Oh my God no, please stop!"

"Fuck no, take this fake-ass dick like a solider!" Freddie yelled.

"Starr, please help me…please," Sandi begged.

Angel immediately covered her ears, to try and drown out Sandi's constant pleas for help. She knew there was nothing that she could do, especially if she didn't want the same thing to happen to her.

"Starr, help me," Sandi repeated.

Freddie turned her attention to Angel. "I wish you would bring yo' ass over here." She gave Angel another evil look before directing her attention back to the crazy sexual encounter.

Freddie snatched Sandi by her fake hair, and pounded her ass with rapid speed, until the dildo was covered in blood. At that moment, Angel tried to hold back, but the tears ran down her face as if it were her being raped by the rubber dick.

Once Sandi's body became limp and she stopped screaming, Freddie finally stopped. "Don't forget your fuckin' place again, bitch," she ordered, pulling the dildo out.

Angel continued to stare at Freddie in complete and utter disbelief as she threw the bloody dildo on the bed, then walked out the room. A few seconds later, the bathroom door was slammed and almost came off the hinges. Apparently Remy and Crystal knew better than to eavesdrop at the door because they were nowhere to be found.

Trying desperately to get out the room before Freddie came back, Sandi tried to get up, but was in too much pain. As soon as Angel heard the shower water start, she slid out the other side of the bed, wrapped a sheet around her body, then ran over to help Sandi. She pushed Angel's hands away at first, but the pain was so severe she had no other choice, but to accept the assistance.

Angel put one of Sandi's arm around her neck, then slowly helped her to the living room. With every small step she took, Sandi moaned in pain. So what normally would've taken five seconds, took almost ten minutes.

When Angel finally helped Sandi onto the couch, Remy and Crystal were staring at her with tears in their eyes. In their minds, Freddie had gone too far, but no one was dumb enough to approach her.

"She needs to get to a hospital," Angel suggested. Sandi cried like a baby as the blood rushed out her ass, but Remy and Crystal didn't budge. "Why are y'all just standing there? Can't you see she's hurt?"

"Because they might be scared 'dat I'ma fuck them up if they help her stupid-ass that's why," Freddie replied, with a towel wrapped around her body. "Look, you ain't been around here long enough to be suggestin' shit around here, Starr."

"I'm sorry," Angel responded, in a weak tone.

"Umm…I'm not trying to step out of line here, Freddie, but I think Starr might be right. Sandi's hurt pretty bad, and just might sit here and bleed to death or some shit if we don't take her," Remy added.

Freddie was about to go off, but quickly stopped herself when she thought about the possibility of a charge on her hands. That type of drama wasn't needed. "Get her ass outta here."

"Can we take the truck?" Remy asked.

Freddie laughed. "Look, now you goin' too fuckin' far. That bitch ain't gon' bleed on my seats. Go ask one of them nigga's across the street that Sandi fucks on a regular to take y'all."

Freddie could barely finish her sentence before Remy was out the door. She returned a few minutes later, with exactly what Freddie suggested, two guys from across the street who Sandi fucked on a regular. By this time, both Freddie and Angel had slipped on something more appropriate.

"Hurry up guys," Remy said, as she covered Sandi's half naked body with a sheet. The men didn't waste any time picking Sandi up and carrying her outside. "We're gonna go to the hospital and make sure she's okay," Remy said to Freddie.

"So when you say we, who are you talkin' 'bout?" Freddie asked.

Remy looked around the room at the other girls, who were both ready to go. "Me, Crystal and Starr."

"You and Crystal can go, but Starr stays here," Freddie responded. Angel looked like she was about to cry. "Don't look at me like 'dat. Shit, we need to spend some more time together since Sandi decided to interrupt us. We ain't done."

Before Remy and Crystal left, they both looked back at Angel, who followed Freddie like a trained dog toward her bedroom. She never bothered to look back.

Four hours later and completely worn out, Remy and Crystal made their way back to hell on earth. As they entered the apartment, both women tried their best to walk softly so Freddie wouldn't be disturbed. However, that was only wishful thinking because it didn't take long for Freddie to call Remy's name.

"Shit," Remy whispered under her breath as she walked toward Freddie's room. When she stood at the door, Freddie was sitting on the bed smoking a Black and Mild. She looked over at Angel, who was sleeping like a baby.

"Yeah, you should know how I roll. Five orgasms will do 'dat to you," Freddie said. "Now where's that bitch, Sandi? She needs to come clean up this fuckin' blood off my carpet."

"She's still at the hospital. The doctor said she's gonna need some reconstruction to her anal canal," Remy replied.

"Well that's good enough for her. I bet she'll stay her *ass* out my business from now on," Freddie said laughing. She thought her joke was funny, Remy however didn't. Freddie looked at Angel and lightly rubbed her face. "Oh well Starr, I guess you up to the bat next."

ॡ   ॡ   ॡ

The next night, the girls abandoned their normal ritual of listening to loud music as they got dressed, and settled for complete silence. There also wasn't any blasting of music when they jumped in the Hummer, and drove to the club. Everyone was silent and seemed to be in their own world, except Freddie. She sat in the driver's seat with a small smirk the entire time. She was also the first to speak up, when they arrived at the Penthouse.

"Look, I've dealt wit' the silent treatment shit since we left home, but now it's time to get those game faces on. It wouldn't be wise to fuck wit' my money ladies," Freddie blasted as one of the bouncers opened the passenger side door. Remy was about to step out, when Freddie grabbed her arm. "Make sure you help the new fish. I would hate to repeat last night's drama if you know what I mean?"

Remy shook her head up and down, before stepping out the truck and blew kisses at her men. It didn't take long for Crystal to follow suit. However, as Angel was about to get out, Freddie instructed her to wait. After walking around the Hummer, Freddie grabbed Angel by the arm before they proceeded to move past the crowd. On their way into the club, Freddie made sure to greet a few VIP's who spent tons of money, and made Angel flash her sexy smile as well. Freddie instructed the bouncers to let the VIP's in before everyone else, then made her way inside. It didn't take long for Freddie to escort Angel to Sandi's room in the Sex Kingdom, and gave her the ultimate pep talk.

"You ain't scared are you?"

"A little bit," Angel replied.

"Well, you need to get out 'dat shit quick because you got customers to serve," Freddie said, in a harsh tone. "I would really hate for our relationship to change, so I need for you to make just as much money as Sandi did. Besides, these men ain't nothin' but sex toys, so just use 'em to satisfy yo' needs 'cause I know you like to fuck. Close your eyes if you have to, but never let 'em see yo' weakness. All dogs can smell fear."

"I'll do whatever it takes."

"Good, now take yo' clothes off," Freddie replied, before finally leaving Angel alone.

When the club doors opened, it only took a few minutes for the clients to start rolling in. Visions of Sandi screaming in pain consumed Angel's mind as her first client entered the room. Taking Freddie's advice, she closed her eyes when the gruesome three hundred pound man got on top of her. Angel wanted to cry but remembered what Freddie said.

All Angel's clients that night didn't want to have sex with her. Some just wanted head, while others wanted to watch her play with herself using different objects, but nevertheless her pussy was still sore when the night finally ended.

"You handled yourself like a real pro tonight," Freddie said to Angel as all the girls walked down the steps from the Kingdom. "All the clients had good things to say 'bout you."

"Well, good because I'm sore as hell."

"Don't worry, Starr. That happens on your first time. You just need to get home and submerge your kitty in a hot bath," Crystal said.

As they all walked out the club, Angel began to think about Antoine, and how she remembered seeing him take woman after woman in his room as a child. *So this is what it feels like to have sex without a care in the world*, she thought. *But shit...at least I'm getting paid for it.*

CHAPTER 14

Antoine walked around the house like a complete zombie. It had been over a week since Angel ran away, and he still hadn't heard anything. Calling Detective Gilliam to see if there were any new leads had become a part of his daily routine, but everyday Antoine received the same disappointing news. He even found himself spending countless hours on the internet doing research on runaway teens, which eventually caused him to stress even more. That had to stop. Antoine did however, manage to post Angel's picture, along with her information, on a few missing person's websites, to see if anyone recognized her.

Antoine constantly blamed himself for Angel running away. It had taken him twelve years to finally realize how much of a terrible father he was, and how the relationship with his daughter was ruined by emotional neglect. Even though he'd provided for Angel financially over the last few years, he still considered himself a deadbeat dad because of his lack of support in Angel's life over the years. It was bad enough that her mother decided to abandon her, so Antoine could only imagine the pain Angel had been through. Because of this, he was more determined than ever to find his daughter, so they could start over.

Before going downstairs to fix something to eat, Antoine decided to go into Angel's room for the second time that day. Every morning after he woke up, he always checked her room to see if she'd decided to come back home, and so far she hadn't turned up yet. This time, he wasn't checking to see if Angel was there, but to see if something in her room could possibly tell him where she was. Although Detective Gilliam had already conducted this same type of search, Antoine felt the need to do it again.

"Who knows, maybe we missed something that last time," Antoine said to himself, as he opened Angel's bedroom door.

Surprisingly, Antoine could still smell a hint of her body spray when he entered the room and started looking around. The first place on the agenda was her walk-in closet. A place she loved and spent a lot of time. He went through several of her jacket pockets, and raided countless pairs of jeans, but didn't come up with anything. He then went through several of her shoe boxes, but again, there was nothing unusual. He stayed in the closet for a few more minutes before finally coming out.

"It's no way in hell a teenager is gonna be this careful," Antoine said, to himself as he went over to her dresser. He quickly scanned the top of the furniture before opening each drawer. Again, after opening five of the six drawers, he still hadn't found anything. Once Antoine opened the last drawer and realized that was where Angel kept her panties, he quickly closed it back.

Hell no. I can't go through my daughter's panty drawer, that's disgusting, he thought. *That seems like some incest type shit.* Antoine walked over to the bed, and was about to look under it, when suddenly he stopped. *But what if something is in there, and I don't look? Wait a minute, so that means Detective Gilliam went through her panty drawer?*

Antoine walked back to the dresser, pushed his concerns aside, and slowly opened the drawer. He found himself pulling out one colored thong after the next, and became extremely upset. "How in hell did she even get the money to buy all this shit?" Antoine asked himself, as he pulled out a sequined pair that looked like it belonged to a stripper. "And where the fuck did she plan on wearing these?"

Antoine pulled out several more thongs until he reached the bottom of the drawer and saw something wrapped in red tissue paper. *This must be real special, since it's wrapped all up and shit.* He didn't waste time pulling off the thin piece of paper. Inside, were a pair of diamond studded red thongs, a DVD and a note. Antoine immediately began to open and close his fist as he read the very first line on the piece of paper.

Angel,

Thanks for the banging head job yesterday. I hope you enjoy the gift because I can't wait to see you in them. Oh, I hope you enjoy the movie as well (smile).

Your Lover 4 Life

Antoine quickly grabbed the DVD and almost broke his neck trying to get downstairs to the family room to see what was on it. Whatever it was, he wanted to see it on his big screen, to make sure he wouldn't miss anything. He inserted the DVD in the player and pushed several buttons on the remote before the picture finally appeared on the T. V. Antoine was astonished at what he saw.

He stood in complete disbelief as he watched Angel giving oral sex to a man, who appeared to be older than he was. Within a matter of minutes, Antoine's anger had instantly turned into sadness as a single tear rushed down his face. It was one thing to know Angel was having sex, but to see it was a different story. He couldn't believe his daughter was so out of control, but only had himself to blame. Antoine immediately turned off the T. V. then retrieved the DVD from the player before breaking it into tiny pieces.

At that moment, Antoine knew the best thing for him to do was to get out the house, so he wouldn't keep thinking about Angel or visualizing her mouth wrapped around someone's dick. The entire situation was starting to become too much to handle. He looked at the clock on top of the cable box and thought for a second. *Even though my vacation isn't over yet, I can just go back to work early. Plus it's only eleven-thirty, so I can still see some of my regular afternoon clients when I get there.*

Antoine ran back his room, and jumped in the shower. Thirty minutes later, he walked downstairs, grabbed his backpack along with his keys and headed out the door in his workout gear. It was a cloudless beautiful spring day in Miami, and for once Antoine started to feel a little bit better as he climbed in his truck, started the engine and opened the sun roof. The warm breeze felt good against his five o'clock shadow, and it wasn't long before he started bobbing his head to a Robin Thicke song on the radio.

Antoine's problems had been pushed to the back of his mind, until his cell phone began vibrating. Every since Angel had run away, he always thought it could be her whenever his house or cell phone rung, so Antoine turned the music all the way down, and quickly answered without looking at the caller ID. "Yes, this is Antoine Moore."

"Oh shut the hell up. Your ass ain't that damn professional."

Antoine frowned at the sound of Mariah's voice. "What do you want? I'm not in the mood for your games."

"Why aren't you at your work? You know the job where you rub on people's elbows for a living and shit," Mariah joked.

"Why aren't you somewhere minding your fucking business?" Antoine snapped back. "What do you want?"

"Well, I just called to see if you finally decided to end this dumb-ass child support case. I mean…I'm trying to get you out this shit before you go to court and lose."

"Honestly Mariah, I haven't even thought about the case because I've been so worried about our daughter over the past week or so. She's also the reason why I haven't been to work."

"Oh yeah, so what did her ass do now?" Mariah asked.

Antoine got quiet for a moment, then continued. "She ran away from home a week ago, so if you happen to see her, please call me. I'm worried to death."

"Wow you really got something on your hands. So anyway, what about that court case?"

Antoine was furious. "Did you just hear what I fucking said? Our daughter has been missing for over a week, and I don't know where she is!"

"Look, don't raise your voice at me. Now, I thought I made it clear the last time we talked that Angel's your problem, not mine."

Antoine couldn't believe how insensitive Mariah was to her first born. "Call me when you become a little more concerned about *my* daughter," Antoine said before hanging up.

ॐ   ॐ   ॐ

When Antoine arrived at the center, he decided to make a quick run to the Starbucks across the street before starting his day. Besides, it had been a while since he indulged in his favorite Iced Caffe Mocha, and it was calling his name. As soon as Antoine walked into the popular coffee store, he looked at the woman in front of the line very carefully. She had a familiar face, but Antoine didn't want to say anything until he knew exactly who she was. After what he was going through, the last thing he needed was one of his scorned women causing a scene. When the woman turned to the side to point out the muffin she wanted, Antoine's face lit up. It was his sorority sister, Loren Brent, who's nickname was Lady B.

Antoine waited for her to walk past him, then quietly snuck up behind her. Before she reached the door, he tapped her on the shoulder softly.

When Lady B turned around, she seemed just as shocked to see him. "Is that Antoine Moore of the Ho Phi Ho fraternity?" she asked, with a huge smile.

Antoine returned the smile. "Girl, don't play with me. I left my hoe days in college," he lied. "Now give me a hug because you know I'm a Phi Beta Sigma for life."

Lady B continued to smile as she and Antoine gave each other a long embrace. "You still look the same, boy."

"You're still a bad ass motherfucka yourself," Antoine said, as he stared at Lady B's fair complexion and light green eyes. It didn't take long for his eyes to travel to her shapely figure that filled out the fly business suit she wore. *Damn, why didn't I ever hit that in school?*

"Yeah, I haven't changed much," he finally answered. "You sure did, though. I can't believe you cut all that long hair. But I like that nice spiky cut you rocking."

"Thanks. I was a little self conscience when I first got it done," Lady B replied, rubbing the back of her head. "So, what's been going on? How's Terrell? Oh, and let's not forget that bitch of a baby mother, Mariah?"

"I almost forgot how much you despised Mariah back in school. Shit, it took her hair a long time to grow back after that big fight y'all had too." Antoine laughed.

"Yeah, if I saw her right now I would probably beat that ass again."

"Terrell's cool, but I'm like you…who gives a fuck about Mariah. If you really wanna know though, maybe you should go ask that football nigga she's married to."

"Oh no, so let me guess, you must be dealing with that baby mama drama stuff, huh?"

Antoine shook his head. "Well it's a little more complicated than that. We'll be here all night, if I got into that shit," he replied. "But enough about me, what are you doing back in Miami? I thought you were in New York, Ms. Big Time Fashion Buyer? I hear you doing big things up there."

"I was, but Saks transferred me here, and I'm not complaining. I missed the weather in Miami so much."

I'm glad they did too, now I might have a chance to hit that, this time. "What about me? Didn't you miss me?"

Lady B began to blush. "Actually I did. I used to think about you from time to time. . ."

As Lady B continued to talk, Antoine's eyes drifted when he noticed Natasha coming into the store. It wasn't even a question in his mind if she was going to cause a scene once they made eye contact, so he had no other choice but to brace himself for the storm. Natasha didn't waste any time walking up to Antoine, with a serious attitude as usual.

"It's bad enough that your ass ain't been to work in almost two weeks, and now you over here socializing when you should be workin'," Natasha commented.

Antoine was completely embarrassed. "Don't come over here acting like a ghetto-ass hood rat. If you came to get coffee, then go stand your ass in line."

"I didn't come over here for no damn coffee. I saw when you got out your car about ten minutes ago, and I've been waiting for you to come to the center ever since. Dr. Wolenski wants to see you, so I suggest you wrap this little shit up." She looked at Lady B, who never said a word. "Trust me, don't waste your time with this asshole."

"Can you fucking leave now? I'll be at the center in a second," Antoine responded. Natasha stared at Lady B for a few more seconds before turning around and walking out the door. "I'm sorry about that. Natasha's definitely not playing with a full deck," Antoine said.

"It's okay, but it doesn't look like your hoe days are over with to me."

Antoine was surprised. "You got tons of jokes, huh? I haven't done anything with that girl."

Lady B looked at Antoine like he was full of shit. "You don't have to explain yourself to me. What you do in the privacy of your bedroom is your business. Even though I'm sure you have sex in more places than that," Lady B joked. "Well, it was nice seeing you, but I need to get going. I'm on my way to Bal Harbour, and I just stopped for some of this liquid crack," she joked.

"Do you think we can keep in touch since you're back in Miami?"

Lady B seemed hesitant at first, but finally gave in. "Sure, do you have a pen?"

"No, I'll just put it in my phone," Antoine replied. He pulled out his blackberry and started turning the track wheel on the side.

After exchanging numbers, he and Lady B walked outside, and then gave each other another huge hug. Antoine loved the way her hips moved as she walked away, and it wasn't long before his dick started to throb.

Not right now, player. I know we haven't had any pussy in a while, but I'll get you some, just hold fast, Antoine thought as he turned around and headed for the center.

However, when he walked into the door a few seconds later, and looked toward the receptionist's desk, he was more than surprised to see Dr. Wolenski caressing Natasha's shoulders from behind. Antoine was floored. From where he stood, the massage didn't appear to be for Natasha's rehabilitation. He quickly looked around the waiting area to see if there were any patients waiting for service, but it was completely empty. Not wanting to see anymore, Antoine began to clear his throat to get their attention.

"Oh, hello Antoine. I had no idea you were standing there," Dr. Wolenski admitted. He quickly took his hands off Natasha, and placed them in his pockets.

Damn, I would've never known that you like a little chocolate in your milk, Wolenski. "I just actually got here," Antoine stated.

"Well, follow me to my office. There's something I need to talk to you about."

Natasha started snickering as Antoine walked by. *As the head therapist around here, I'm definitely gonna suggest that we get rid of her crazy-ass.* He wasn't exactly sure what Dr. Wolenski wanted, but the look on his boss' face didn't seem too happy.

"Listen Antoine, I'm gonna get straight to the point because as you should know, I don't like to beat around the bush," he said, taking a seat behind his desk.

"Yes I do, and I certainly respect that."

"Good because respect can take you a long way, especially when you start working for someone else."

Antoine's eyebrows scrunched up. "Excuse me."

"I'm sorry Antoine, but I've lost a lot of business over this past week all because of you not being here, and I can't have that."

"So, I can't take a fucking vacation!" Antoine shouted. He walked closer to the desk. "Besides if that's the case, you're gonna lose even more business if you fire me."

"Mr. Moore, I'm not going to ask you but one time to calm down, and reframe from using that type of language in this office. You're not in the hood with one of your homies."

"I can't believe you just said that racist shit." Antoine was extremely pissed. "So, this is how you repay me after busting my ass around here?"

"Don't play games Mr. Moore. Just because I'm not in the center most of the time doesn't mean I don't know what's going on. Everybody around here knows that you spend more time trying to get in everybody's panties rather than working. So, that's another reason I'm letting you go."

"That's not true."

"Oh yeah, well what do you think the results would be if I tested some of the semen samples on my gym equipment around here?"

Antoine wanted to walked over and punch the frail Jewish man in his face, but knew that would only make matters worse. It also didn't help that he was right. "I've already hired a replacement for you, so I would appreciate it, if you would gather up your things and leave now. Your last check will be mailed."

Antoine couldn't believe what was happening. "Fine…if you wanna carry the situation like this, I'm down for whatever." Antoine turned around to leave, then stopped dead in his tracks. "If it's the last thing I do, I'm gonna make sure I take all your fucking clients." He never gave Dr. Wolenski a chance to respond before slamming the door.

Antoine didn't bother going to clean out his desk, because he knew it didn't contain anything important. All his contacts were kept inside his backpack, so making a pit stop wasn't needed. He quickly stormed through the center, and was headed for the door, when Natasha stepped in his path.

"I told your ass not to fuck with me, didn't I?" she asked. "Now your ass is out of a job."

"So did you have something to do with this shit?"

Natasha smiled. "Of course. I've been sucking the doctor's little pink dick all week to make this happen. However, if it makes you feel any better he didn't want to do it. I had to end up blackmailing him in order to get rid of your ass."

Antoine was furious, but tried to remain calm. "Can you get out my damn way?"

"No, I'll move when I get ready."

He went to grab Natasha by her arm, but quickly stopped himself when another therapist walked by. "Listen, you crazy bitch, move before shit gets worse than it already is."

"Fine, I think I've done enough damage anyway," Natasha stated as she moved to the side. "Oh, but then again, I guess spray painting your house was a good one too."

Antoine was only a few steps away when he heard Natasha admit to damaging his property, and it took everything within him not to turn around and slap the shit out of her.

CHAPTER 15

Angel became a hit at the club instantly. Within the two weeks that passed, she'd become the most requested girl, and Freddie's top money maker. From males to females, her tight young pussy had the minds of everyone spinning. Angel herself also started to become turned out from all the sex, and began to live out all her wildest fantasies. From fucking three men at the same time to role playing as a crazy dominatrix, she never seemed to be satisfied. Angel craved the attention and the money, so regardless of what her clients wanted, she was up for the challenge.

Monday nights were usually slow at the Penthouse, so Angel and Crystal went to Remy's room for a short break while Freddie ran to the store to get more pretzels. She made sure to keep tons of salty things at the bar, so people would constantly order drinks. When the girls walked in, Remy held up two glasses of Moet.

"It's time to celebrate, bitches," Remy yelled. Both Angel and Crystal laughed as they walked over and grabbed their glasses. "Welcome to the team, Starr," Remy added.

"Yeah, welcome," Crystal chimed in.

"Thanks…I'm glad to be here," Angel replied.

The girls held up their glasses into the air as Remy made the toast. "Pussy is power, so let's get this paper!"

Both Crystal and Angel said they would drink to that as all three ladies clanked their glasses together. It didn't take long for the glasses to be turned upside down and filled back up again.

"So how does it feel to be making all the damn money around here?" Crystal asked, looking at Angel. "I mean you done came in here and took all Sandi's clients and then some."

Angel shook her head. "I'm not gonna lie, it feels damn good to be making this type of money for doing something I like to do."

"Yeah, that's how the fuck I feel. This shit is like taking candy from a baby," Remy said.

The girls laughed again and continued to toss back the champagne, until Crystal pulled out a large zip lock bag filled with weed called, Bin Laden. "I'll roll the first one and then it's the rookie's turn," she said. "Since she's so good at giving head and shit, let's see if she can roll a blunt."

Angel took the plastic bag out of her hand, and held it up in the air. "Hold on...so...so...let me get...this straight," she said, as her words began to slur. "We.... getting ready to smoke something with the name of a terrorist on the shit? I know I'm a little drunk, but does anyone else besides me think that's a bad idea?"

Crystal started cracking up laughing. "Give me this shit, rookie and just sit back."

Minutes later, Remy's room was so cloudy from the smoke you would've thought something was on fire. The girls continued to talk shit and inhale the potent drug while lying on Remy's bed, when the door flew open. They all jumped up thinking it was Freddie, but was surprised when Sandi limped into the room.

"What up you hoe's?" Sandi asked.

Remy and Crystal ran up their friend, and almost knocked her over. "Oh, my goodness, why didn't you call somebody and tell us you was getting out the hospital? We could've picked you up," Remy said.

"It's cool," Sandi responded. "One of my niggas came and got me. He also took me to the mall, so I wouldn't come up in here looking broke down, and I know y'all bitches wasn't gonna do that."

"You're a hundred percent correct, but we're so glad to see you, boo," Crystal added.

No one ever realized that Angel hadn't bothered to welcome Sandi back yet. Even though Angel was happy that she was okay, a part of her wanted Sandi out the Penthouse for good. She felt threatened that Sandi was going to come back and steal her fame, so at that point, Angel was willing to do whatever it took to remain the top girl.

"Man, I'm not feeling this soft side of y'all. Don't treat me any differently than you did before," Sandi said with a laugh.

"Well in that case, sit your broke tight asshole down," Remy shouted.

"Now that's better," Sandi replied. "So what's been going on while I've been gone? Who's making all the money around here now?" Remy and Crystal finally looked at Angel, who displayed a cheesy smile. "You mean to tell me, her ass is making all the loot now?" When Remy and Crystal shook their heads, Sandi shot Angel an evil look. "So...how does it feel to be me?"

Angel sucked her teeth. "Shit, I'm better than you."

Sandi looked as if she was about to go off, when Remy stopped her. "Look don't start no shit Sandi. Besides, your ass just got out the hospital from Freddie fucking you up. Do you want to go back?"

Sandi thought about what Remy said, and calmed down. "Yeah, you right. I'm not gonna let this lil' snotty nose bitch get me all out of whack. As soon as I heal good, we'll see who the top bitch around here is."

"My point exactly," Remy replied. Both her and Crystal helped Sandi to the bed, and didn't waste any time offering her some weed. After Sandi took the blunt, the three girls started another puff, puff pass session. "When was the last time you had that pussy ate?" Remy asked Sandi.

Sandi looked at Angel who had decided not to join their party, and was posted up against the wall. "Well, my women clients have done their thing, but Freddie hasn't given me an orgasm since her ass came."

Remy hopped up and grabbed a pair of scissors from the bag she brought with her everyday, then crawled back on the bed. "Well I'm horny as shit, so you're gonna get an orgasm today." Remy looked at Crystal and said, "Help me out." They gently pushed Sandi on her back as Remy took position between her legs and began to cut Sandi's clothes off.

"You bitches are gonna pay. Do you know how expensive this Prada shirt is? Why didn't you just take my shit off? I'm going to…"

Sandi immediately was at a loss for words when she felt Remy's tongue enter her vagina. Her eyes closed instantly as her nipples hardened.

"I bet you didn't think Remy's tongue could be just as good as Freddie's," Crystal said, as she joined in on the fun by rubbing Sandi's double D's.

"Don't stop!" Sandi shouted.

I can't believe this shit. I didn't know they were all bisexual, Angel thought.

Remy and Crystal took turns taking off their clothes, and offered Angel to join them, but she declined. However, she did enjoy watching from the sideline as the sex acts increased. Within minutes, a full blown orgy had started. Becoming hornier by the minute, Angel was about to join the party, when Freddie opened the door. She froze immediately. The other girls were so wrapped up into each other they never noticed Freddie standing there.

"So, who the fuck idea was this?" Freddie asked. Hearing Freddie's voice almost made Sandi turn a different shade, and her body started to tremble. Crystal began biting her nails, which meant she was nervous as well. "Somebody better fuckin' answer me!"

"Umm...I guess we just got a little carried away Freddie since it's slow around here tonight," Remy finally said.

"So, instead of goin' downstairs to get new business, y'all decided to stay up here and fuck each other?" Before Remy could reply, Freddie walked over to Sandi in her normal manly strut. "And you...nobody said you could bring yo' closed up ass in here. What good are you to me like 'dat?"

"Do you think I can come back once I heal?" Sandi asked, in a childlike voice.

"Well yo' room in the Kingdom has been taken over by a real profitable young lady," she replied, glancing over at Angel. "So I'm not sure yet, but since you already naked, you can definitely stay tonight. I gotta client downstairs who wants three girls anyway, so y'all bitches freshen up. I'm sendin' him up in five minutes." Freddie motioned for Angel to follow her out the room. Once they stepped out, Freddie grabbed Angel's hand. "Now, I got a real treat for you. There's a regular VIP client waitin' downstairs, so I need you to freshen up too. Oh, and make sure you treat him well 'cuz his money is long up in here."

Angel smiled. "Thanks. I'm sure you could've given him to one of the other girls if you wanted."

"Are you crazy? It ain't nothin' like fresh new pussy."

☙ ☙ ☙

Ten minutes later, Angel began her session by riding the VIP's dick like a trained jockey. When she couldn't get into it, she demanded that they switch into her favorite position. "Fuck me doggy style."

The VIP instantly got turned on. Normally he was the one who called the shots at the Penthouse, so this was new for him. He got up as Angel turned around and placed her ass in the air. For a moment he tried to deep stroke Angel's pussy in order to impress her, but failed to do any damage. Little did he know, the size of his dick had already disappointed her, so he could've done the entire zodiac sex chart and it wouldn't have made a difference.

As the VIP continued to pound Angel from behind, she felt that something had changed right away. His dick felt different, causing her to tell him to stop.

However, with his orgasm rushing up to the top of his dick and the tingling in his body ready to go haywire, he couldn't just stop. Angel tried her best to pull away, but with him holding her hips, it wasn't easy. After several attempts, she finally succeeded.

"Why'd you do that? I was about to cum," he said.

Angel looked at his shrinking dick. "Oh shit. I knew something wasn't right. The fucking rubber broke."

He looked down to see the rubber around the base of his dick. "You clean right? You better not give me nothin', hoe!" The VIP started freaking out.

"Fuck you, asshole. Your nasty ass better not give me nothing. Get out!" Angle yelled.

"Hold up. I paid six-hundred dollars to be with you, and I ain't cum yet. I want my fuckin' money back!"

A bouncer walking pass Angel's room heard the commotion, and burst into the room. "We got a problem, Starr ?" he asked.

"No, he was just about to leave, Big Slim."

"I ain't going nowhere until I get my money back from this bitch," the VIP shouted.

"Get the fuck out of here little dick before Big Slim fucks you up!" The bouncer laughed at Angel's comment, which really pissed the VIP off.

"Little dick?" he pointed at himself. "Fuck you trick. All I know is I better get my money back," he kept saying, as he put back on his clothes.

"You heard her main man, let's go," Big Slim said, stepping closer.

"I ain't going nowhere!"

"Look, we can do this the easy way or the hard way. You decide," Big Slim said, as he got closer to the VIP.

The situation was about to get ugly when Freddie rushed into the room. "What the fuck is goin' on in here?" She looked at Big Slim and then at Angel, but they didn't say a word. "Well, answer me!"

"Well I told my client to leave, but he refused, so that's when Big Slim got involved," Angel finally replied.

Freddie walked over to Angel and slapped her twice before she could even blink. "So, you makin' the rules now?"

Angel sobbed. "No."

"So, if you ain't makin' the rules why the fuck did you tell one of my best customers to leave? Do you know how much money he spends in here?"

Angel shook her head left to right as the tears ran down her red cheeks. "No, but the rubber broke, and when it did, he had the nerve to call me a hoe. Like I got a disease or something."

Freddie slapped Angel again. "You young lil' bitch, you are a hoe. Don't think 'cuz you got the best pussy 'dat you callin' shots 'round here. This is my fuckin' establishment. If a rubber breaks, you keep on fuckin' unless I tell your ass not to. You got 'dat!" All Angel could do was nod her head. "Did you get yo' nut?" she asked the VIP.

It seemed like he didn't want to get Angel in trouble, but finally answered. "No, I didn't."

"Well take yo' clothes back off because Ms. Starr here is gonna finish the job." Freddie turned toward Big Slim, "Come on fat man. Let's give these people some privacy."

As they walked out the door, Angel felt numb. She knew at that point, she really wasn't going to enjoy having sex with the VIP. However, she didn't have any other choice. She couldn't believe Freddie was willing to risk her life over a dollar.

Angel hesitantly made her way back over to the bed. "Are you ready?" she asked the VIP through her constant sniffs.

"Don't worry about tonight," he responded.

"What do you mean?"

"I mean, there's no need for us to have sex at this point."

Angel looked at him like he was a fool. "Are you kidding me? What are you trying to do, get me in more trouble? You heard what she said."

"Yeah I did, but she's not in this room is she, so what Freddie doesn't know won't hurt her."

The expression on Angel's face said that she was still skeptical. "Trust me, I won't say a word. You can make it up to me next time. Shit, I'm here damn near twice a week."

"Are you sure?" Angel asked.

"Positive." He walked over and kissed Angel on the cheek, then turned toward the door.

"Wait, you can't go this soon. It hasn't even been five minutes."

The VIP smiled. "Don't worry, if I see Freddie, I'll just tell her, I'm a one minute brother when the pussy is good."

At the end of the night, Angel walked down the steps from the Sex Kingdom holding her swollen cheek. When Remy saw her coming, she walked around the bar, and filled a hand towel with ice from the chest underneath the counter. "Put this on your face," she said, walking up to Angel.

"Well, well, well, how the tables do turn," Sandi said, with a smirk.

"Shut up Sandi," Remy replied. "I don't know why you keep blaming Starr for your ass getting raped by a damn dildo."

Sandi rolled her eyes before turning around. Seconds later, Big Slim walked up to Angel. "Hey Starr, the VIP from earlier told me to give you this," he said, handing her a white envelope.

"Thanks," Angel said.

"Which VIP did you have tonight?" Remy asked.

"I'm not sure, but our session turned out well."

As bad as Angel wanted to share what happened between the two of them, she decided to keep it to herself. Besides, Sandi was a hater and would've told Freddie in a heartbeat. When Angel opened the envelope, she smiled. Inside were two one hundred dollar bills, and a small note.

Here's a tip. Thanks for the wonderful time even though it started off rough. Can't wait to see you again.
VIP

"It looks like you got your first admirer," Remy said.
Angel's smile widened. "I guess so."

CHAPTER 16

While Angel smoked weed and downed several glasses of Moet every night, Antoine sat alone in his pitch black bedroom with a bottle of Hennessy and sulked. He couldn't believe it had been almost three weeks, and there was still no word from Angel or the detectives. Antoine knew the last resort was to contact a private investigator because as bad as he blocked it out, in his mind Angel could've been dead. The thought made him feel so helpless. As the days rolled by, he decided to take things a step further, by making a heartfelt appearance on one of the local news channels, and hoped that someone would contact him. However, the only people who called were his countless number of women, who he ignored. In fact, Antoine ignored everybody except Lady B, who'd become very supportive.

Lady B was someone to talk to when he felt lonely or depressed, so after days of talking until the wee hours of the morning, she eventually started coming over. It wasn't long before Antoine and Lady B began spending all their free time together, which was therapeutic to a man who believed he'd lost everything. Antoine's parents had died in a car accident during his second year of college, so to him, Angel was the only family he had left.

Lady B tried to encourage Antoine, but when the days turned into weeks, it became difficult to motivate him, especially since he was unemployed. He'd gone on several interviews with a few other rehabilitation centers, but after requesting an overly paid salary, no one ever offered him a position, which only added salt to his open wound.

Antoine pulled up to his house after a long day of interviewing, and immediately noticed that the lights were out, which was strange because since giving Lady B a key, she normally got there before he did. After getting out his truck and walking to the door, Antoine turned the key and entered his house. Nevertheless, when he clicked the light switch, he almost jumped out his skin when he saw a huge group of people jump from behind different pieces of furniture.

"Surprise!" everyone yelled in unison.

Antoine's eyes became two times their normal size as he scanned the room, and saw several of his old college buddies, a few old co-workers, Terrell and Lady B all clapping like they were at a concert. Antoine was completely shocked.

"Happy Birthday," they screamed again. The guys laughed when they saw how Antoine looked like a deer caught in headlights.

"Boy, look at you. You look like you're about to cry," Terrell said, tapping Antoine's back.

Antoine looked around and saw everyone looking at him with huge smiles, and even though he really didn't feel like dealing with anyone, he didn't have the heart to ask them to leave. Besides, he'd forgotten about his birthday on purpose. The last thing he wanted to do was celebrate. After looking at the excitement on everyone's face for the second time, Antoine decided to put his feeling aside, and walked around, greeting people he hadn't seen in ages.

NAUGHTY Little Angel

Minutes later, Lady B brought out food from the kitchen, and before long the dining room table was quickly hidden by several bowls, platters and three chafing dishes that she'd arranged to perfection. As Lady B made her way back into the kitchen, Antoine wasn't far behind.

"Whose idea was all of this?" he asked.

Lady B smiled. "I just thought you needed some cheering up, so I went through your cell phone, and got all your friends numbers. I hate seeing you like this. Not to mention, it's your birthday."

Antoine walked over and grabbed his new woman by the waist, then planted a small kiss on her lips. Despite the way he was feeling, Antoine knew she was only trying to help. "Thanks, baby. I appreciate this."

"I figured you could use some male bonding with your boys, so I just hope it helps."

"Me too," Antoine replied, before stepping back. He turned around to leave, when Lady B spoke up.

"Are you sure your hoe days are over?" she asked.

Antoine looked at her with a weird expression. "Why do you say that?"

"Well, considering you have over a hundred phone numbers for all the women you deal with, I just need to know what I'm getting myself into."

Antoine walked back over to Lady B and grabbed her by the waist again. "I'll delete all of those numbers, if it means I can spend all my time with you."

"Shut up," Lady B said, smacking her teeth.

"No, I'm serious. I love being with you. I don't care about those other women. They were just...how do I put this...kind of like one night stands."

"And how do I know I'm not a one night stand?"

159

"You've been here for more than one night, haven't you?" Antoine joked. When he saw that Lady B didn't find his joke too amusing, he continued. "Seriously, you're very special to me, so I would never treat you like that, baby."

Antoine was glad Lady B didn't pull away as he pulled her close and gave her a passionate kiss. As their tongues continued to dance with one another, Antoine could feel his manhood slowly rising. It had been a while since he had sex, so he knew his dick was starving for attention.

Antoine was about to pick Lady B up and place her on the granite counter top when Terrell walked in. "Man, come on. Why did y'all call all the guys over here if y'all was gonna go off in a quiet corner and make out."

Embarrassed that they'd completely forgotten about their guests, Antoine and Lady B quickly got themselves together. "Shut up, Tightness," Antoine replied. "You're just jealous because Lady B's fine-ass ain't all over you."

"Yeah whatever, just come out of this kitchen and entertain the people who came over here to celebrate with your old ass," Terrell replied.

Antoine hit the back of Terrell's head as they both walked back to the family room. When they arrived, the rest of Antoine's guest were sitting in front of his Plasma T.V. watching the Mayweather vs. De La Hoya fight that he'd recorded on his TiVo. Antoine fixed his famous Hennessy and coke and walked over to join the gang.

"What round is it?" Antoine asked, as he took a sip.

"2nd," someone hollered.

Although Antoine never stopped thinking about Angel, having his friends and old co-workers over did give him a little bit of relaxation, even if it was just for a moment. They watched all twelve rounds of the boxing match, giving each other high fives, imaginary punches and throwing back shots of Hennessy and Patron.

"See, we need to do this shit more often. We need a guys night out, and I know just the place. It's called Freddie's Penthouse," Terrell said.

"I heard about Freddie's. It's supposed to be off the chain," another one of Antoine's buddies answered.

"Man, I'm telling you, it's supposed to be these rooms upstairs called the Sex Kingdom, where you go to have all your wildest dreams come true. I say we move this party over there," Terrell continued.

"Yeah, I could use some phat ass in front of my face right now!" someone yelled.

"I also heard they got a new chick over there in the Sex Kingdom named Starr, who's supposed to be off the hook. They say she can do some amazing things with her mouth, if you know what I mean," Terrell said, pointing to his crotch.

"You're still a damn hoe," Lady B said, as she walked in the room and sat on Antoine's lap. "No wonder you couldn't hold on to Nina back in college."

The sound of Nina's name made Terrell even more hype. "Man, fuck Nina. It's her fault we ain't together now anyway!" He gave Antoine a funny look. "Now back to what I was saying. I heard the girl, Starr can pick up a forty ounce bottle with her pussy."

Antoine seemed to be contemplating about the idea of going to the strip club, but when Lady B moved her ass to the perfect position, it instantly caused his dick to jump. Lady B smiled when she felt his slight hard on, and decided to have a little fun as Terrell continued to sell the guys on Freddie's Penthouse. She slowly began to move her ass back and forth until Antoine's dick was fully erect, and at that point, she knew he was excited.

"So, what do you say, Ant? You down?" Terrell asked.

"The only place Antoine's going is upstairs," Lady B interrupted. "He can get a lap dance right here. Besides you're not taking my man to some disease infested titty bar."

"Ain't nobody talking about taking Antoine out to sleep with other women and bringing you a disease. I was thinking of some harmless fun," Terrell's eyes begged for the chance for his boy to tag along.

"We can do it some other time," Antoine finally said. "I really just wanna spend some time with Lady B tonight." Antoine couldn't wait to take her upstairs and release his monster on her.

She turned around and smiled. "I couldn't agree with you more. I'll show every one out," Lady B replied, as she rubbed Antoine's shoulders.

"Well, I think the party's over," Terrell said, before taking one last shot. "It's cool, Ant. We'll wait for you before we go to the Penthouse."

Lady B stood up. "Well you might have a long wait, Tightness," she said sarcastically. "Let's go, guys."

The boys let out a few moans. They weren't ready to go just yet, but could tell Antoine and Lady B had other plans. As she followed everybody out to the foyer, Terrell stayed behind.

"I'm outta here man," Terrell said, giving Antoine a pound. "What time are you putting Lady B out, so I can call you for all the details?"

Antoine shook his head. "I'm afraid you won't be getting the details this time, and believe me she's not leaving anytime soon."

"Wow, what in the hell did she do to yo' ass? I ain't never heard you talk about a broad like this."

"I don't know…shit is just a lot different for me now, I guess."

As Terrell was about to respond, Lady B yelled from the foyer. "That goes for your ass too, Terrell. Let's go!"

Terrell smiled. "She's a bossy thing too, huh?" He gave Antoine another pound, before heading toward the front of the house. When he reached the foyer, he gave Lady B a kiss on the cheek before heading out the door. "Don't put it on him too bad tonight."

"I'll try," Lady B responded, as she stood at the door and thanked everyone for coming.

Once the house was clear, she and Antoine cleaned up a little before he told her to stop. "I'll take care of everything else. You go ahead upstairs. I'll be up there in a minute."

"Are you sure? This place is a mess."

"Of course, you've done more than enough tonight."

Lady B didn't waste any time running upstairs to fix herself up before Antoine came up. Since it was their first time being intimate, her body was overwhelmed with anticipation, and she couldn't seem to stop smiling. When Lady B reached the master bedroom, she quickly removed her tight fitting Seven jeans, baby doll tee, and her sexy underwear before spreading baby oil all over her body. She wanted her skin to feel extra soft. Lady B then turned off the lights, before lighting a cherry scented candle and turning on the CD player. She swayed her head from side to side as Tank's hypnotic voice came through the speakers. His newest baby making CD was bound to put anybody in the mood.

When Antoine opened the bedroom door, a few minutes later, the light from the hallway shined inside, showing Lady B, who was naked and stretched out on the bed on her hands and knees. Antoine licked his lips as his eyes scanned her body, which looked like a beautiful cheetah. When he opened the door wider to shine in more light, Lady B sat up on the bed displaying a bright red rose tattoo on her shaved goodies.

"Wow! Your body is amazing," Antoine said, walking into the room.

"Meow," was the only response she made.

"Oh, is that the sound a cat makes?"

"Meow," Lady B said again.

When Antoine reached the bed, she crawled over to him slowly, and looked up. Antoine smiled. "What are you doing? Are you stalking your prey or something?" As Antoine stroked Lady B on the middle of her back, his dick began to stretch further with every stroke. Lady B rubbed her head against his right leg. "Here kitty-kitty," Antoine whispered.

Lady B used her nose to tickle his erect shaft then sat up to unbutton Antoine's pants. It didn't take long for Antoine's dick to poke its stiff head out the slot of his underwear. Lady B grabbed his dick firmly.

"I want you to holler my name," she moaned.

"Hey, what happened to my kitty cat?"

"Oh, play time is over. You need to get ready. I'm going to fuck you like never before."

"Bring it on baby. Let's see if your bite is as bad as your bark," Antoine responded, in a stern voice.

"Go get your condom," Lady B said.

Antoine let out a slight laugh. "A what…are you kidding? Come on baby, I wanna be able to feel that pussy."

"And you'll still be able to feel it. Look, since this is our first time, I need you to strap up. Besides, don't forget about all your one night stands."

Not trying to spoil the moment, Antoine quickly obliged by walking over to his nightstand and pulling out three magnums that had been in the drawer forever. "I hope these things didn't dry up and shit," he joked, as he tore open one of the packs. His smile couldn't be erased when he glided the condom on with ease, then walked back over to the bed.

Lady B didn't hesitate pulling Antoine onto the bed, then threw her leg over his body. He looked up to see her move the tip of his dick around the perimeter of her vagina. His body quickly became at ease.

"Get ready to scream out my name, baby," Lady B replied, with a laugh.

Lady B inserted his rock hard manhood inside her moist pussy. She began to rotate her hips in a slow circle, then used her legs to move up and down Antoine's dick. Lady B's pussy felt like a warm jacuzzi as she rode Antoine like a famous polo player. Her breathing began to increase as his dick tapped the spots between her voluptuous thighs. Lady B quickly picked up her pace, which intensified the feeling on Antoine's manhood.

Not wanting to cum, he lifted his body up and switched positions with Lady B. He loved the smell of her pussy, as he spread her legs apart. He used his hands to gently massage around her throbbing moist erotic zone, then softly licked her pussy until she screamed out in ecstasy. The orgasm that quickly rushed through her body was so overwhelming that her body began to jerk.

"Oh, daddy," she moaned.

Each tingle of Lady B's pussy seemed to mesh with the pounding of her heartbeat. Her moans were very seductive, which made Antoine's dick seem harder than any of his other sexual encounters. She held him tight, and scratched the back on his neck as the jerks never seemed to stop.

However, little did Lady B know, the night was just beginning for them. As their bodies glistened from the sweat, Antoine got up and went to his closet. Having no idea what was going on, she looked at him like he was insane as he went through his closet like a maniac. After throwing several items out, he finally found what he was looking for, and returned to the bed with a small black bag. Ignoring Lady B's strange looks, Antoine pulled out what looked like a bunch of parachute cables. She continued to watch as he walked over to the corner of the room, stood on a step stool and fastened a large silver clamp to the ceiling. When the black straps fell, Lady B finally knew what he had. It was a swing. A huge smile over came her face.

"Get that pussy over her," Antoine demanded.

Lady B didn't hesitate to rush over to him. He held her legs as she climbed inside and locked her hips in place. After getting her in place, he took off the old condom, and placed a new one on, so it could be nice and wet before he positioned his body between her legs and instantly began to dive deep into her pussy. Lady B held onto the straps as Antoine grabbed her ass cheeks with both hands. He squeezed them firmly as his huge dick grinded through her pool of cum. The faster he moved the more cum dripped from her pussy. Lady B let out another seductive moan when she felt another orgasm rushing through her body. She then began to pull on her nipples as her firm breasts bounced from side to side. Antoine loved the sight of Lady B pleasing herself.

Suddenly, her moans quickly turned into screams as his dick stirred her pussy like no man had ever done. The more Antoine pounded her treasure, the more she seemed to be feeling light headed. Lady B felt drunk as the room started to spin, and it felt like she was about to vomit. However, none of this caused Antoine to hold back. He used the thick straps to get deeper inside her walls, which caused even louder screams. She couldn't hold back.

"Work this pussy, Antoine!" she yelled.

Antoine flipped her leg over his body and began hitting her

from a horizontal doggy style position. The flexibility of the swing was amazing. She began to push her body back to pound against him, and made her pussy walls tighten to massage his dick as he went in and out.

It wasn't long before Antoine felt the urge to explode. "I'm about to cum!" he yelled.

"That's right, cum for me, daddy," Lady B responded, as Antoine continued to beat her pussy like a piece of meat.

Seconds later, Antoine lifted his head in the air and let out a huge moan. He never stopped pounding as a large amount of cum shot into the condom, making his dick feel like it was drowning. However, when his strokes finally slowed down, his body began to jerk.

"Damn, that felt good, baby," Antoine said, completely out of breath.

"Yeah, I guess," she responded in a nonchalant tone.

Antoine's dick immediately went limp, and fell out of her pussy. He looked at Lady B. "Hold up, so what you saying, it wasn't good or something? I mean, I could've sworn you got yours."

She shook her head. "I did, but here I was talking all that shit about you screaming out my name, and you never did. Shit, I did most of the damn yelling."

Antoine laughed, then gave Lady B a huge hug. "Are you serious?"

"Yes, I'm very serious."

"Well I tell you what, I'll make it up to you in the second round because we're just getting started." He could feel his dick getting hard again, as he played with one of her nipples. "Your ass might need some ear plugs after I'm done this time."

They both laughed. *Good because I want you to crave this pussy until the day you die*, Lady B thought.

CHAPTER 17

Over the next week, Angel began receiving gifts every night from the special VIP, who quickly became her and Freddie's favorite customer. It all started with the two hundred dollar tip, he'd given her after their first encounter, but soon turned to sexy lingerie, expensive jewelry and even bigger tips. Even though Angel was skeptical about accepting his tokens of affection at first, it didn't take long to reel her in. She loved all the attention, especially all the jealously from the girls. They were dying to know and frequently asked Angel who the mystery VIP client was, but she never told them anything. Her only response was a huge smile whenever she modeled her newest gift. Under Freddie's strict rules, Angel was to keep her mouth shut about the VIP, which she didn't understand, but wouldn't dare question Freddie's reasons. Whenever the VIP came to the Penthouse, he always treated Angel with love and respect, which she quickly got attached to, so the condom incident was quickly deleted from her memory. He made her feel special, especially when they had sex, so despite Freddie's rules about keeping all the clients at a distance, Angel decided to take a chance.

She began going out with the VIP after everyone in the house went to sleep at night, and found herself clinging to him every time they were together. They often found themselves going to get something to eat or just sitting in his old custom white '74 Buick

Apollo around the corner from Freddie's apartment, and talking until the sun was almost up. Whatever they did always made Angel happy, and as long as she was in his presence, everything was fine.

Angel was having a good night in the Sex Kingdom one evening, and even though her regular clients were spending money, she still couldn't get off with any of them. Normally the money they spent, or the different freaky positions they put her in determined how motivated and excited she would get, but this time things were different. She found herself taking countless numbers of breaks to use KY jelly just to stay moist, which was definitely out of the norm because her pussy stayed wet. Angel just wasn't into anyone, but knew she had to do something quick before one of her clients complained to Freddie.

As Angel sat on top of her last client's dick, she closed her eyes and began to think about her VIP, which instantly started the juices flowing between her legs. She thought about how he sucked on her clit softly then licked the outside of her pussy like a lizard before sticking it all the way inside. Angel could feel herself getting hornier as she put one foot on the floor, and fucked her client a little bit harder. The more she thought about the VIP swallowing every once of cum after each of her orgasms, the harder she pounded her pussy against her client's dick. When Angel finally opened her eyes, she saw her client pulling on the sheets for dear life.

"Are you ready to cum?" she asked.

"Yes, baby. This is the best pussy I've ever had in my entire life. Keep riding this dick, until I cum!" he shouted.

Angel closed her eyes again and tried to fantasize about her VIP again, but this time nothing happened. She squeezed her eyes tighter, and blocked out her client's constant grunts,

169

but again there was nothing. Disappointed that the moment was over, Angel slowly opened her eyes, but to her surprise, as soon as she did her client's body began to jerk. A smile crept on her face because at that point, she knew everything was over. Angel didn't waste anytime climbing off her client, and covering up with her black French lace teddy, compliments of Mr. VIP.

"Wow that was amazing. Do you think I could see you again?" the client asked.

"Sure baby, just make sure you hook up with Freddie, and she'll take care of everything," Angel replied.

Not wanting to carry on a long conversation, Angel quickly put on her four inch heels, then walked to the door so the client would get the point. After getting dressed, he walked over to her, and held out a fifty dollar bill.

"Here's your tip. Thanks again for the wonderful time."

Fifty dollars? Man, this is bullshit compared to what my boo gives me. "Thanks."

"Anytime, sweetness," he said, before planting a wet kiss on the side of her face.

Angel almost wiped her skin off as she went downstairs to get a bottle of water. After talking to a few of the intoxicated men at the bar, she watched one of the dancers perform on the pole when she saw her VIP over in the corner. Her pussy instantly began to throb as they both smiled at each other.

"What are you doing here?" Angel mouthed. To her knowledge, he was skipping a night at the Penthouse to take care of some business. *Maybe he couldn't stand to be away from me, so he changed his mind*, Angel thought as a waitress walked up to her carrying a cocktail napkin.

"This is from him," the waitress said, pointing to the VIP.

Once Angel opened the napkin and read what it said, she shook her head up and down. Seconds later, she ran back upstairs to the Kingdom and quickly washed up in the bathroom. Even though, he probably wouldn't mind, Angel didn't want to be around her VIP without a fresh cookie. She'd served several men that night, and didn't want to take a chance smelling like a bag of dicks.

After freshening up, Angel got dressed, hurried down the steps and ran out the door while Freddie was in her office. Again, Angel knew she was taking a huge risk, by disregarding Freddie's rules but didn't care. Besides, in her mind, the VIP could end up taking her away from Freddie's Penthouse for good. Once she got outside, the VIP was waiting at the corner in his car just like the note stated, when Angel ran up and got in. They gave each other a big kiss before driving off.

Fifteen minutes later, the car came to a stop at the Midtown Inn Motel Biscayne Boulevard. Angel sat in the car while the VIP went inside to get a room. A few moments later, he came outside with the key in hand, and a smile that could be seen for miles. Convincing Angel that he wanted total privacy, they decided to leave his car in the front of the motel while they walked around to the back where the room was located. As crazy as the idea sounded, Angel never questioned his reasoning. She was just excited to finally be alone with him.

Angel smiled from ear to ear as she walked into Room 128, and didn't hesitate to plant a huge kiss on his lips as soon as the VIP closed the door.

"I want this evening to be so romantic."

"I see you're happy to be here, huh?"

"Are you serious? Now we can take our time, and I don't have to worry about serving another client when you leave. I want my body to be all yours tonight," Angel replied.

The VIP looked at her up and down. "So, can you say that pussy belongs to me?"

"Of course daddy," Angel said, walking up to him.

"Good, then you won't mind what's about to happen." Within seconds, the VIP forcefully pushed Angel on the bed, and grabbed several inches of her long hair. She shrieked in pain when he yanked her head back. "You better not make a fuckin' sound either!"

Angel wondered where all the anger was coming from. He was using so much force while he pulled her hair that the roots were starting to pulsate.

"You're hurting me," Angel cried, despite his demand.

"Whore, didn't I tell you to shut the fuck up!"

The VIP ripped her shirt off with one tug. Angel's heartbeat raced as she began to feel that she'd made a major mistake by coming with him without anyone knowing her whereabouts. As a violent smack whipped across her face, Angel tried to ball up into a knot, but nothing seemed to work. He then began yanking at her pants.

"Please stop. I don't like it like this," Angel pleaded.

"Bitch, I don't give a fuck what you like, and now you gonna get it because I told your ass to be quiet." He punched her in the stomach with a hard body shot to get her to release the hold she had on the waist of her jeans, and continued to pull them down until they finally came off.

Angel hurried to crawl toward the top of the bed trying her best to get away. Her mind was running out of control from fear.

"Get your ass back down here!" he yelled.

Angel tried to kick him as he stepped onto the bed but missed, causing the VIP to kneel down and unleash a flurry of blows to her side and back. Angel cried out in pain. He gave her another slap before ripping her panties off, and held her arms down while he pulled out his penis and rammed it inside.

The pain of his dick scraping the inside of her pussy made tears well up in her eyes. Angel swung her hands frantically to get him off, but all she did was to upset him more.

"Oh now you wanna act like you don't want this dick," he said, blocking her hands. He reached his left hand around her throat and began to squeeze while smacking her several times with his right hand. Angel could barely breathe, and tried her best to fight him off, until she had nothing left.

        ॐ   ॐ   ॐ

Two hours later, Angel opened her eyes. She tried to get up, but her hands and feet were tied to each post of the bed frame. Angel called out for the VIP, but there was no answer. She looked around the room, then began to tug on the ropes, but couldn't get them to loosen, then stopped when she heard a key being put into the door.

Oh God, please let this be a maid. A sense of relief came over her body, until she saw it was the VIP, and her mood instantly changed to fear.

"Why am I tied up to this bed?"

He let out a wicked laugh and placed a brown grocery bag onto the table, then picked up her blue thong off the floor.

"I have to use the bathroom. Take these ropes off me!" Angel yelled.

"You're very fuckin' hardheaded," he replied, before walking over to the bed and sticking her thong into her mouth. He then tied it in place with a black strap. "This will teach your ass to shut up."

Angel began pulling on the ropes with all her might, but they didn't give. She twisted her hips and tried to kick her legs to get the ropes to unfasten, but to no avail. She watched as he pulled out several different size candles from the bag, and a few razors, then placed them on the table. You could almost smell the fear leaking out of her pours.

Angel began to cry. *What the fuck have I gotten myself into now?* She had no idea what he was getting ready to do to her.

"Do you understand that you're a no good whore?" he asked.

Angel made eye contact with him, but didn't answer. Her heart rate increased as he stood in front of her and laughed before taking his clothes off. "A dirty girl like you must be cleansed to become pure again. I must release the wicked demons living inside you," he uttered, grabbing one of the razors.

Angel's eyes widened when he took the razor and made a large cut over his own nipple. He didn't make a sound as blood began to slowly run down his chest. He seemed emotionless except for the rising of his dick.

This sick motherfucka is getting off on the pain, she thought.

He reached inside his bag again, and pulled out some white powder and placed it all over her body. He then dove his face into her thighs and began sniffing. It was cocaine.

"Somebody please help me," she tried to mumble.

The VIP sniffed from her thighs all the way to her kneecaps, then finally lifted his head. His entire face was covered with the white substance. A crazy laugh came out his mouth as he stood up from the bed and walked over to retrieve the razor again. "I must begin to release the demons from your evil body."

Angel tried to scream at the top of her lungs for help, but couldn't be heard. When he walked back over to her with the tiny silver object and sat down, tears began to stroll down her face.

"Don't worry, you'll feel better once the demons are free," he said, making several cuts on Angel's cheeks. The pain was horrific as she screamed at the top of her lungs even though no one could hear a sound.

The VIP made several more cuts along the sides of her mouth then moved to her neck, shoulders, and chest before finally putting the razor back down. By that time, Angel was almost numb from the pain. He quickly jumped back between her legs and began sniffing the cocaine until his nose felt like it was on fire.

Angel continued to pull and twist the ropes as he slowly made his way down to her treasure. She wanted to throw up when she felt his tongue twirling inside her pussy. She tried to twist her hips to get him to stop, which only pissed him off. He jammed his fingernails into her thighs and held them still while his head continued to move at a rapid pace.

He then climbed up on top of Angel and rammed his dick into her pussy with tremendous force. She muffled out another scream just before he locked his hands around her neck. With his bare hands, he choked Angel, banging his dick further inside her at the same time.

"You nasty whore. You have no respect for yourself. I must purify your wicked ways," the VIP chanted. He sat up and punched Angel again. His hand felt like a concrete boulder slamming into her face causing the tears to run down her face like a waterfall.

"I'm so sorry. I love you. I must do this so we can truly be together. I know this hurts so believe me when I say, this hurts me more than it hurts you."

Angel tried to use the pity in her eyes to beg him to stop, but it didn't work. His dick continued to bang inside her causing her pussy to ache tremendously. All she could do was sit and endure the pain until somebody came to rescue her, or until she was dead. Whichever came first.

CHAPTER 18

"Has anybody seen Starr?" Remy asked, as she walked up to the bar. She hadn't seen Angel in at least two hours which was odd. Normally when Angel was done with her clients, she always went to Remy's room so they could exchange crazy stories or compare tips. Now that the club was closed, it was really usual that she wasn't around.

I ain't seen her," Crystal said. "What about you Sandi?"

"Why would I wanna keep up wit' her? Shit, hopefully she took her ass back home."

Remy frowned. "When are you gonna get over the fact that Starr took your room? It's not her fault."

"When I get back up in the Kingdom is when I'll get over it. Do you think I like being downstairs, dancing for this lil' ass piece of change?" Sandi asked, showing her one dollar bills. "I been down here all night, and all the fuck I made was three-hundred dollars. You know I ain't used to that shit!"

"Well take your concerns to Freddie then. It's not Starr's fault that you didn't mind your damn business that night," Remy added with a smirk.

Remy watched as Big Slim and another bouncer walked downstairs. Usually when they came down, all the rooms upstairs were completely clear. "Hey Big Slim, was Starr in her room when you checked it?" Remy asked.

He nodded. "No, why?"

"Where the hell could she be?" Remy asked out loud.

"The last time I saw Starr, she ran into her room like she was rushing, then a few minutes later, she came out with all her clothes on. Maybe she went to do something for Freddie," Big Slim said.

"Shit, the only thing we can do for Freddie is make money," Crystal added.

"Like I said, hopefully her ass ran the fuck back home," Sandi said, with a huge grin.

Remy gave Sandi and Crystal the look of death as they started laughing. "That's why your dumb-ass only made three hundred tonight, and that's probably before Freddie gets her cut," Remy said, looking at Sandi. "Is your body sore from swinging on that damn pole all night?"

Remy's question made Crystal bang the bar with her fist, as her laughter continued to pour out.

"Fuck you, Remy!" Sandi shouted. "And who side are you on, bitch?" she said, directing her question toward Crystal, who had tears in her eyes by this point.

However, Crystal didn't have a chance to respond before Freddie walked out of her office, and over to the bar like she meant business. From the look on her face, everyone could tell that she was pissed, which wasn't good. An immediate silence fell over the room like God himself had just appeared.

"Why the fuck are y'all so damn loud? Don't y'all muthafuckas know all 'dat fuckin' laughin' and loud talkin' is keepin' me from countin' my money right," Freddie yelled. "And Crystal yo' ass is the main one I hear. You better shut the fuck up before I make yo' red ass turn blue!" Crystal looked as if she wanted to make a comment, but quickly decided against it. "What? You got somethin' to fuckin' say?" Freddie asked her. "Speak the fuck up!"

177

Crystal cleared her throat and looked like she said a quick silent prayer. "I'm sorry Freddie, but it's Remy's fault. She the one down here, asking all those damn questions about Starr and shit."

"You bitch!" Remy yelled to Crystal. She could tell Sandi was laughing under her breath.

Freddie looked at Remy. "So what's yo' concern about Starr? If you wanna know about any of my bitches, you need to ask me."

Remy contemplated for a few seconds about whether she should have the conversation with Freddie, but she couldn't seem to ignore her concerns about Angel. "I'm sorry Freddie, but I haven't seen Starr in a while, and I was just worried about her."

"Well don't be. She in good hands right now."

At that moment, the cocktail waitress who'd given Angel the note from the VIP earlier came from behind the bar. "Are you sure she's in good hands because that nigga Cutty is deranged."

Remy, Sandi and even the bouncers let out gasps one by one. Not only because Cutty was a crazy customer who was known to torture girls in the past, but also for the waitress, who obviously had no idea what she was getting herself into by questioning Freddie. Everyone knew not to do that type of shit if you didn't want a beef.

Freddie was furious. Big Slim and two other bouncers immediately ran over to Freddie to hold her back. "Who the fuck told you to add yo' two fuckin' cents, bitch! If I say she in good muthafuckin' hands, 'dat's what it is. As a matter of fact, get out! Get yo' ass out my club right now, since you wanna stick yo' nose where the shit don't belong!"

"Who the hell is Cutty?" Crystal softly whispered to Remy.

"The VIP, who always does crazy shit, but buys you gifts at the same time. You know…the one who gave Lexus all those damn roses."

"Oh, him," Crystal replied.

The waitress looked around the room like she expected someone to come to her defense, but everyone looked the other way. "Fine," she said, throwing down the hand towel.

"And gimmie that money you made tonight too," Freddie said, as the waitress started to walk away.

The waitress turned around. "Are you serious? I already gave you a portion of my tips."

"Somebody better tell this bitch I'm dead serious."

"Please, do what she says before shit gets out of hand," Big Slim added, as he continued to hold onto one of Freddie's arms for dear life.

Seeing that Freddie was just as crazy as Cutty was, the waitress went in the back pocket of her tight fitting pants, and pulled out a small stack of money. Tears welled up in her eyes when she looked back at Freddie.

"Bitch, you better be glad these niggas holdin' me back. Now, get the fuck out my spot and don't bring yo' meddlin'-ass back." The whole room watched as the shapely waitress turned around and walked out the front door. "Take y'all fuckin' hands off me!" Freddie ordered to the bouncers.

As they followed Freddie's demands, Remy was still in awe about Angel being with the client from hell. She also remembered when he got crazy with Lexus a few months back, Freddie promised them, that she wouldn't allow him in the Kingdom anymore.

Despite the outcome, and even though she didn't want to be in the waitress' shoes, Remy knew she had to say something. "No disrespect Freddie, but are you sure Starr is safe with Cutty because he tried to set Lexus on fire the last time."

"Yeah, he kept trying to burn me with a cigarette the last time I was with him," Sandi said boldly.

"Shut up whinin' bitches. Cutty's been paying me a grand to be wit' Starr up in the Kingdom, and fifteen hundred to take her ass to the Midtown Motel tonight, and 'dat's more money than any of y'all dried up pussy bitches have made, so I don't give a fuck what he does. As long as he don't kill y'all, my business can go on as usual."

Remy couldn't believe what she'd just heard. She knew Freddie was a coldhearted person, but this took the cake. *I gotta find a way to go get her*, she thought as Freddie continued to fuss.

"Yeah, Cutty and Starr have been fuckin' wit' each other for a while now. She didn't think I knew about all the sneakin' around she been doin' wit' him, but I know everythin' y'all bitches do. Shit, I was the one who told him he could be wit' her ass at the motel. Her dumb-ass is just too stupid to know 'dat. Don't nothin' get pass me, so think 'bout that shit, before y'all hoes try and pull somethin' over on me," Freddie preached.

The whole room was quiet as Freddie started up again. "Now, like I said, be the fuck quiet, so I can finish countin' my damn money," Freddie added, before walking back into her office. As soon as she closed the door Remy jumped into action.

"Sandi, I know you might hate me right now, but I need your help. We gotta get Starr away from Cutty's crazy-ass before he does something to really hurt her."

"Yeah I know. I don't even like Starr, but I don't wish Cutty on nobody. Do you think he's the one who been giving her all those gifts?"

"Of course. He and Freddie set this whole shit up. I mean, Freddie even let Starr go with him before the club closed, so I wouldn't be surprised if he gave her more than fifteen hundred," Remy responded.

180

"So, what do you need me to do?"

"Well, since you the only one who can eat Freddie's pussy and have her going insane, I need you to make a pass at her before we leave. That way she'll probably tell us to stay out the house, so y'all can have some privacy, and that'll give us time to go find Starr."

Sandi sucked her teeth. "Come on, Remy. I ain't really feeling Freddie like that since she raped me. Can't I do something else to help?"

"I feel you," Crystal added. "I couldn't lick her pussy either if she had done some shit like that to me."

"Come on, Sandi. You know that's the only thing that'll work," Remy pleaded. "I'll even give you a hundred dollars."

The sound of someone talking about money was music to Sandi's ears. "Make it two hundred, and you got a deal," she replied.

Remy finally smiled. "Deal." She then looked over at Big Slim and the other two bouncers, who thought the girls were always entertaining. "I need your help too."

"You ain't even gotta ask us Remy. We been dying to stomp that crazy motherfucka, so it would be a pleasure. Just as long as Freddie don't find out we went behind her back, everything's cool," Big Slim responded, as the other bouncers nodded in agreement.

With everything in order, everyone waited on pins and needles until Freddie came out of her office. When she finally appeared twenty minutes later, Remy looked over at Sandi, who'd started pushing up her breasts like she was preparing for a date. It didn't take long for Freddie to walk over toward them, and bark a few more demands.

"Big Slim get ready to lock up. Girls, get yo' shit and let's go," Freddie said, as she adjusted the bag on her shoulder.

However, before anyone could move, Sandi hopped up, and immediately whispered something in Freddie's ear. When Remy saw Sandi pull out the charm, by licking Freddie's ear lobe, she knew the plan would work. Everybody joked about how Sandi's name should've been lizard.

Freddie's smile almost lit up the room. "On second thought, fuck 'dat. Big Slim, me and Sandi are gonna head home. You take Remy and Crystal's ass somewhere for a couple hours, so they don't fuck up my time wit' Sandi. Then bring 'dem bitches home later." Freddie didn't even wait for a response before she grabbed Sandi's hand, and made a quick exit.

"Thanks Sandi," Remy said softly, as she could only imagine what Freddie was gonna have her doing.

ô   ô   ô

Two of the bouncers along with Remy and Crystal arrived at the Midtown Inn Motel a few minutes later. As soon as they pulled up, Big Slim immediately noticed the old Buick parked in front one of the rooms

"That's his old piece of shit car right there. I remember seeing the nigga pull up in front of the club a few times." Big Slim quickly pulled his Navigator into a parking space, and put the truck in park. "Remy, go work your magic with the desk clerk while we sit here because they might get a little suspicious if we all go in there. You need to find out exactly what room they in."

"And hurry up," Crystal said. By the sound of her voice everybody could tell she was nervous.

"Calm your ass down Crystal. I got this," Remy replied. She pulled out her compact mirror from her purse, and played with a few strands of hair before getting out.

They all watched as Remy switched to the front office, which was located a few feet away from where they were parked. When Remy opened the door, she was relieved to see a young black guy working behind the counter. Even though it didn't matter, she knew it would've taken a little extra work if it had been a woman.

"Umm…excuse me, I'm looking for my brother who drives that Buick over there and I was wondering if you could tell me, what room he's in," Remy said, in her best Marilyn Monroe type voice. She bent over the counter so the clerk could see her breasts from the low cut shirt she wore.

When the guy looked up from his King Magazine, his eyes almost popped out of his head. "Damn, hello gorgeous. What did you say you needed?"

Remy batted her eyes. "I'm looking for my brother and his girl. He drives that car right there," she said, pointing her finger. "Can you tell me what room they in?"

"Now you know I'm not supposed to do that."

"Come on, baby. My brother ain't answering his cell phone, and I need to talk to him."

"What can you do for me if I give up that information?" the clerk asked with a huge smile.

"Well let me just say this, I have a girlfriend in the car, and we willing to give you the best fucking blow job you ever had," Remy replied, licking her lips. "Shit, I can taste that big thing in my mouth right now."

The clerk, who looked like he hadn't had sex in months, was already drooling by the time he finally managed to speak. "Damn, I can't wait."

"So what's the room number, daddy?"

"Oh, your brother's in Room 128."

"It's a girl in there with him, right?" Remy asked.

"Yeah, I believe so."

"You're wonderful. I'll see you in a little bit," Remy said. She blew the clerk a kiss before turning around and switching out the door. She couldn't believe how easy it was to get the information. "I didn't even have to show no skin," Remy bragged to herself as she got back into the truck. "Okay, he's in 128, which looks like it's on the other side of the building. He obviously just parked his car on this side. Are y'all ready?"

"Yeah, we ready. But once we drive around, I think Crystal should stay in the truck and hop in the driver's seat, just in case we need to roll out," Big Slim suggested.

"That's fine with me, let's just hurry up," Crystal stated again.

A few minutes later, Remy and the two bouncers jumped out the truck and ran up to the door. They could hear Cutty screaming all sorts of profanities from inside the room, but didn't hear Angel's voice at all.

"Oh, my God, kick the door in," Remy said, as thoughts of Angel being terribly hurt danced around her head.

It didn't take much for Big Slim to use his size fourteen shoe to kick the door in with rapid force. When he did, they all quickly rushed inside the room to find Angel tied to the bed, naked and covered in white powder. Her face was swollen with tiny cut marks all over her cheeks and her mouth was covered in blood.

"I'ma kill this sick motherfucka," the other bouncer said, as he and Big Slim jumped across the bed, grabbed Cutty by his throat, then began to punch and stomp him repeatedly.

Remy rushed over to Angel, and started to remove the ropes from her legs and arms. "Oh, Starr, I'm so sorry this happened

184

to you," she said, removing the pair of thongs from her mouth. Remy grabbed the blanket from off the bed and used it to cover Angel before helping her to her feet.

"We should cut your dick off since you like cutting people," Big Slim said, as he grabbed one of the razors off the nightstand. "Is that where you got the name Cutty from?" When Big Slim put the razor under his throat, Cutty began to yell out in fear. "What the fuck you yelling for bitch?" Big Slim asked.

"Don't do it," Angel finally said. They all looked at her like she was crazy, and couldn't believe after all he'd put her through, she still didn't want him to get hurt.

"Man, take her to the truck, Remy, so we can handle this," the other bouncer said.

"I don't wanna get in trouble for doing something to him," Angel pleaded.

"Take her ass to the truck 'cause she must be delirious or some shit," Big Slim replied.

"Come on, Starr," Remy said, as she helped Angel outside. "The last thing we need is to sit here and watch them beat Cutty like he stole something."

Once Crystal and Remy helped Angel get in the truck, her body continued to shake in fear. She put her head on Remy's shoulder and cried like a baby. Emotionally and physically, she was beyond hurt.

"It's all over now," Remy said, rubbing her back. "I won't let nobody else hurt you. I swear."

CHAPTER 19

Mariah was on the couch watching her favorite TV show, CSI when her husband walked into the room. She gave him a small smile and winked her eye, but he didn't respond. Normally when she winked, he always winked back, so Mariah knew something was getting ready to kick off. She decided to focus back on her program as he started to pace around the room.

However, right before the character Warrick Brown was about to say something, her husband snatched the remote off the coffee table and turned the television off. Mariah sat up wondering what was going on. He then threw the remote against the wall breaking it into tiny pieces.

"When the hell were you going to tell me?" he yelled.

A blank look consumed Mariah's face. "What are you talking about, sweetie? Did you have a bad day or something?"

"Oh, so you don't know what I'm talking about? You trying to play me?"

Mariah fell back against the cushions. "I'm not in the mood for the games you playing. If you have something to say, just say it all ready, so we can go upstairs and have some fun."

He reached into one of his back pockets and pulled out a white envelope. "Why the fuck have you been keeping secrets?" He flung the envelope at Mariah, hitting her in the face.

Mariah jumped off the couch. "Have you lost your damn mind?"

"No, but I do need for you to get your shit and get out. I don't want to see your face. I can't trust you anymore."

Still not knowing what her husband was talking about, Mariah picked up the envelope off the floor and pulled out the papers inside. When she saw the child support and restraining order documents, she almost fainted. She didn't know what to say. "I didn't think you needed to know about this. You have so much on your mind already with the league and all. I'm taking care of this," Mariah replied.

"So, you didn't think that I should know about a fucking kid you had seventeen years ago? And on top of that shit, your kid's father got a restraining order against you. So you been going over that nigga's house and harassing him and shit?"

"It's not what you think. I'm not harassing him," Mariah tried to explain.

"So why the fuck would the nigga have a restraining order against you? I can't believe this shit. My own damn wife has been lying to me."

"Dwayne, I didn't lie. I just failed to tell you about my past, that's all."

He looked at her like she was stupid. "So, that excuse is supposed to fucking make me feel better? You got another kid, Mariah!"

She walked over and tried to touch him, but he pushed her away. "I'm sorry that I didn't tell you, but I was young when it all happened. I made a mistake by having her."

"So, why didn't you keep her?"

She lowered her head. "Her father wanted her more than I did." Mariah tried to touch him, but he pushed her away again. "Come on Dwayne, I told you I was taking care of everything. Trust me, this is not gonna affect our marriage."

"But you're using my fucking hard earned money to take care of this. I married you and vowed to take care of you and our family. I'm not getting my body knocked around like a car crash every Sunday to pay for a child that's not even mine. I pay for everything around here, so you're not taking care of shit."

"Am I hearing you correctly? Are you saying that because you're the only one who works, that the money is all yours and not ours?" Mariah asked.

"You damn right. I don't see your ass contributing to the bank account."

Mariah looked for something to throw. "I take care of this house and our children. If you believe that it's your account, that's a problem. It's our account."

"First of all, you don't take care of shit. You don't even fucking work and we still got a maid and a damn nanny. Employees that I pay for. All this is because of me," Dwayne ranted, sweeping his hand around the room.

Mariah followed his hand. She felt her temperature rising to her blowing point as she walked over to the mantle and grabbed the glass case with his autographed basketball from the Chicago Bulls team after winning the '96 NBA championship.

"Don't even think about it!" he yelled.

Mariah squinted her eyes. "Fuck you." She lifted the case high into the air, and threw it on the floor. The glass holding the prized possession shattered all over the marble tile. She laughed without concern as the ball bounced across the floor and knocked over his fraternity shield display that sat on one of the end tables.

Mariah didn't even flinch when Dwayne ran over and grabbed her by the collar of her shirt. She used both of her hands to snatch his hand away. "What's wrong, you told me to get my shit." Mariah then turned around and began pushing over his NFL trophies and plaques as she walked toward the front door. "Remember your vows, Dwayne. For better or for fucking worse. I'm not letting you put me out my own house. I'm only leaving so neither one of us catches a charge," she uttered with defiance in her voice.

Mariah grabbed her purse that was sitting on the table in the foyer, and slammed the front door. She cursed all the way to her truck, then jumped inside and pulled off. Mariah wasn't sure where she was going, but knew it had to be far away from her house.

She drove around town for almost an hour before finally stopping at a sports bar near South Beach. "Fuck this, I need a drink," she said, getting out of her truck. Normally Mariah would've check her appearance in the mirror several times before getting out, but this time she could've cared less how she looked.

When Mariah walked into the rowdy establishment, she ignored the men who were desperately trying to get her attention and headed straight for the end of the bar. As soon as she sat down on the hard stool, she ordered two shots of Grey Goose.

"Coming right up," the bartender replied. A few minutes later, he walked back over to Mariah with two shot glasses, which she downed before they could touch the bar. "Wow, either you were thirsty, or really needed a drink," the bartender joked.

"Give me another one, and make it a double this time," she ordered.

"Cool, but after this, you need to take it easy pretty lady, especially if you're driving."

Mariah looked at him, and almost jumped across the bar. "Don't fucking tell me what to do. Do your fucking job, and just get me my drink. I can handle myself!"

The bartender looked at her for a few minutes, before turning around.

Mariah was downing her third drink when the doors opened and Antoine and Terrell walked inside. She couldn't believe her luck. Antoine was the root of all her problems and all of the bars in Miami, he had to end up at the same one she was in. It was like God was teasing her.

When Antoine and Terrell walked over to the bar, neither one of them saw her at first, but after placing their order, Antoine was the first to see Mariah's face in the mirror behind the bar. He smiled, tapped Terrell on the shoulder, then pointed in her direction. When they both turned their heads, Mariah was staring at them with an evil smirk.

"Do you wanna go over there?" Antoine asked.

"Hell no, it looks like she's about to kill somebody," Terrell commented.

"That's exactly why I think we should. It looks like she's having a bad day."

"Man, we don't even hook up like we used to since Lady B came into your life, so I was hoping that it could just be a boys night out tonight. I don't wanna get involved with Mariah and her damn drama," Terrell said.

"Damn, Terrell you would think it was your baby momma instead of mine. If anything she's gonna have a lot of shit to say to me, not you. Come on, it looks like she could really use a friend right now," Antoine replied.

After their drinks came and several more minutes of convincing, Antoine and Terrell finally took their shots of Hennessy and slowly walked over to Mariah. Terrell and

Mariah locked eyes, which Antoine didn't pay any attention to until neither one of them would take their eyes off one another. When Terrell finally glanced over at Antoine and realized that he was watching them, he changed his mind about going.

"Naw man, you go by yourself. Y'all probably need to talk anyway," Terrell said, tossing back his shot. He didn't give Antoine a chance to reply before walking back over to the other end of the bar.

Deciding not to challenge Terrell's decision, Antoine continued toward Mariah, and could sense something different about her as soon as he sat beside her. She sat on the stool with a distant type of aura. "You look like you're about to slit your wrists or something," he said.

"Look, don't come over here with any fucking jokes because I'm not in the mood right now."

Antoine held up his hands. "Damn, don't shoot me. It's just that I've never seen you like this."

"That's because I've never had these problems before," Mariah responded.

"Oh yeah, well join the club baby because we all got problems. Shit, I know your ass could care less, but I still have no idea where Angel is, and it's killing me."

Mariah seemed unfazed about Antoine's concerns about their daughter. "How did we end up here? I mean we both had so much going for us in college. Who would've thought our lives would turn up like this?" She turned her third shot glass upside down.

Antoine shook his head. "I know exactly what you mean. My plan was to never have children, make a lot of money and travel around the world meeting all sort of exotic women until I died fucking some twenty year old."

Mariah ordered two more double shots, and had a few nasty words with the bartender, before turning her attention back to Antoine. "Fucking women forever was your master plan? I'm starting to rethink that shit about you having potential."

All Antoine could do was laugh. He ordered two more shots to go along with Mariah's and downed them as soon as they arrived. After Antoine gave the bartender an extra fifty dollar bill to keep serving them, he and Mariah continued to slam down shot after shot. The drinks really began to disappear once they began talking about Angel.

"I couldn't believe when I missed my period and took that pregnancy test and the little plus appeared in the indicator. I didn't know what to do. I was scared to tell anyone. I felt so alone," Mariah admitted.

"Well, I'm not gonna lie, when you told me you were pregnant, I was pissed because I knew I didn't want any kids, even though I always wanted to be a better father than my dad," Antoine replied. "I have to piss like a race horse," he blurted out of the clear blue, then slightly stumbled to his feet.

"Why do all guys say that shit?" she asked with a laugh.

"I don't know why other guys say it, but I say it because my dick is just as big as a horse," Antoine replied, walking toward the bathroom.

"You need some help holding that horse dick?" Mariah shouted, with a burst of laughs.

Antoine looked around for Terrell on his way to the bathroom, but didn't see him. He figured that his friend was probably upset about their boy's night out, and decided to leave. He knew he would have to call Terrell and get back on his good side at some point.

When Antoine got back to the bar a few minutes later, several guys were standing around talking with Mariah. A beautiful drunk woman at the bar alone always brought out the perverts. Antoine knew he had to save her. He quickly stepped between the guys and grabbed Mariah before planting a long wet kiss on her lips. The other guys stood around and watched in awe. Mariah never backed away.

"Mariah, you're wasted. I better get you out of here before one of these no good niggas try and rape you or something." Antoine helped her to her feet. "What's that jock going to say with you coming home like this?"

"He won't...be...saying...shit. I'm so...so mad...at his ass. He gone...tell me...that...that...I gotta leave...he...putting me out," Mariah responded, slurring ever other word. "I...I should...go...back and...burn...the motherfucking...house down."

"I'm sure he's just joking," Antoine said. He put her arm around his shoulder, and walked her outside to her truck. Mariah couldn't even deactivate the alarm with the key. Instead she kept setting the alarm off.

"You're in no shape to drive, so where do I need to take you?" Antoine asked.

"Shit...take me...me...home. I need...to kick...my husband's...ass...anyway."

"No, we can't have that. Where else?"

"I...don't know...fool. Take me... to...to... your house," Mariah slurred.

Antoine was feeling a little twisted, but he wasn't that fucked up. He knew Lady B was at his house, so that idea was out. "How about I take you to a nice hotel, and you can come get your truck in the morning?"

"My...head is...spinning." Mariah leaned on his shoulder. "I...I...don't care...where you...take me."

Antoine helped Mariah into the back seat of his truck, then drove to the Loews Miami Beach Hotel. With Mariah's new status, he knew she would only want to stay in the best. Antoine left her in the car until he went to check in, and when he came out she was asleep. He carried her into the hotel over his shoulder, and struggled to get her to the room. When they finally reached the ninth floor, he stood Mariah up against the wall while he used the card key to open the door.

After getting her inside, Antoine immediately placed her on the king size bed. He then went into the bathroom and soaked a washcloth in cold water to place on her forehead. For some reason, the crazy remedy always helped him when he was hung over. Antoine returned to the bedroom to find Mariah pulling off her shirt.

Mariah fumbled with her bra until she was able to unlatch the back, and Antoine watched as her huge 36D breast bounced out to greet him, then sprung back into position. He stood with his mouth open. *Damn, I don't remember those things being that big back in school, so she had to pay for those babies, but they look good though*, he thought.

When Mariah moved to take off her jeans, she fell on the floor, and Antoine let out a laugh. Mariah looked up and threw her shoe at him, which landed right on his forehead. Soon, Mariah was the one laughing.

"Did I hurt the poor baby?" she said, walking over to him with one leg still in her jeans.

"I'm probably gonna have one hell of a headache," Antoine replied rubbing his head.

Mariah reached down and began to massage his dick. Even though he was surprised, Antoine stopped rubbing his head, and allowed her full access. He closed his eyes as his penis continued to harden.

"I missed this big dick," Mariah groaned, tussling with his belt. It didn't take long before Antoine's pants were down by his ankles, and Mariah was stroking the tip of his dick with her thumb.

"We shouldn't be doing this. You're only doing it because you're upset with your husband," Antoine said, pushing her hands off him.

Mariah's only response was kneeling down, and putting several inches of Antoine's cock into her mouth. The softness of her lips and warmth of her moist mouth broke his fight. Mariah twirled her tongue up and down his shaft, then dug her nails into his thighs.

Antoine couldn't wait to feel his dick between her legs, so after feeling her soft lips a few more seconds, he pushed her off him. He snatched the rest of his clothes off, and quickly removed hers before picking her up and carrying her to the bed. Their naked bodies felt good up against one another. It had been seventeen years since they felt the warmth of each other's touch.

As Mariah laid on her back, she opened her legs and allowed Antoine to play with her pussy. He slid in and out using two fingers until she was soaking wet, and couldn't hold back from pushing his massive dick into her wanting pussy. Mariah let out a loud moan.

Her husband was a good lover, but his dick never filled her entire pussy the way Antoine's dick could. He always seemed to tap the spots that made her whimper and moan. Mariah began to feel his dick pressing against spots that hadn't been touched since the last time he fucked her. The warmth of his tight body holding her around her waist and squeezing her breast rushed though her body. Mariah's soft moans quickly became screams of ecstasy.

However, things suddenly changed. When Antoine looked at Mariah, the only thing he could think about was Lady B. He thought about her waiting for him at home, while he was out having sex with another woman. A woman Antoine knew he didn't have feelings for. Deep down, Antoine knew he hated Mariah for what she'd done to him and their daughter. It was time for him to stop thinking with the one eyed man between his legs. He quickly pulled out of her pussy and jumped up. "I can't do this."

Mariah's eyes became big. She could feel her vagina returning to its normal size, and the reforming of her inner walls shot tingles up her back. "You can't do what? Put that dick back inside me now!"

"I'm sorry Mariah, but this is wrong. I shouldn't have allowed this to happen."

"What are you talking about? The only thing that needs to happen, is you putting that dick back inside of me, so I can cum. I need this orgasm."

Antoine ignored her demands. He got up and started to put his clothes back on. "Look, I've found someone who I really care about, so this shit doesn't feel right. This is not me anymore. I need to change my life. I'm not fucking up with this woman."

Mariah sat up with her back against the headboard. "You can't be serious? You...found someone special. You let me suck and slob all over your dick, then we have sex and now you want to stop. Fuck you and your special bitch!"

"I'm sorry. I should've never been misleading like that, but as you can see I'm trying to change."

Mariah laughed. "Don't even play yourself. People like you don't change."

"So, what about you? Are you telling me that you changed into a better person? I hope not because if that was the case, you would've called and asked about our daughter."

Mariah figured if she could convince Antoine that she cared about Angel, maybe they could finish their steamy sex session. "Well I'm asking now. Did you find her yet?"

Antoine was furious. "Her? You can't even say *her* name can you? Mariah, do you even realize the reason why our daughter's gone is because both of us are fucked up parents. If we'd showed Angel how much we love her, she would be home right now instead of out in the street somewhere. Doesn't that even bother you?" When Mariah didn't respond, Antoine shook his head. "You're fucking pathetic."

"Fuck you mister perfect. You turned her away from me since the day I dropped her off. Don't think you can talk to me like I'm some fucking child."

Antoine finished putting on his clothes, then turned to look back at Mariah. "I'm going to remove the restraining order and stop the child support case immediately, and after that I don't want anything else to do with you, so stay the fuck away from me." He turned around to walk out the door.

"Yeah right. You'll do anything for a piece of ass, so I'll get you to change your mind," Mariah screamed back.

"No wonder your husband put your ass out," Antoine said, opening the door.

Mariah had heard enough. She jumped out of the bed and ran after Antoine like a raging bull. When he saw her coming, he ran down the hall, and managed to make it onto the elevator before it closed. Mariah got halfway down the hall, then realized she wasn't wearing any clothes.

An old white man coming out his room had to take a double look. His wife went to cover his eyes, but he pulled her hands down. He stared at Mariah's perky breasts and neatly manicured vagina, and almost drooled. His wife just looked at Mariah with disgust.

Mariah glanced over at the elderly couple. "What the fuck are you staring at? Shit old man, for five hundred you can touch and for a thousand the wife can join us," she joked.

The husband reached into his pocket searching for his wallet, but his wife hit him in the arm and pulled him down the hallway.

Mariah walked back to the room, to find the door locked. "Shit!" she said, out loud.

She didn't have any other choice but to walk naked to the front desk downstairs. Mariah stood at the elevator, waiting as if nothing was wrong. On the way down to the lobby, it seemed like someone was waiting for the elevator on every floor. The faces amused her when the doors opened and they saw her naked frame standing there.

Mariah strutted out of the elevator and to the front desk with confidence. It was almost if she had on a St. John suit the way she carried herself. The clerk was shocked as Mariah stood in line instead of walking straight up to the counter. A female clerk ran to the back to get her a robe to cover up, and offered to assist her immediately. After explaining the situation and despite the fact that the room was in Antoine's name, Mariah managed to get a key.

On her way back, Mariah couldn't figure out if she was upset that Antoine had said all the things that were true about her, or the fact that he'd met a special woman that was making him change his ways, and that woman wasn't her.

CHAPTER 20

Angel closed her eyes tightly as the hot water ran down her back. The pain from the water hitting the numerous cuts on her body was excruciating, but Angel knew she had to endure the pain. Over the past two days, she'd taken at least three showers a day, to wash off the scent of the man, who she was beginning to fall in love with. A man who'd turned out to be a lunatic, and not the lover she so desperately hoped for. Tears began to run down Angel's cheeks, as she began to think about all the disappointments in her life. She was tired of all the let-downs and more importantly tired of trusting people. Every time someone came into her life, they always managed to hurt her, which was why she was starting to become immune to love.

As Angel continued to let out all her emotional distress, Remy walked into the hotel room. "Starr you in there?" she asked, walking up to the bathroom door. Remy could hear the water from the shower running. However, when there was no reply, she immediately became concerned. *Oh shit, I knew I shouldn't have left her up in this hotel room by herself*, she thought. *What if Freddie found out where she was?* At that point Remy didn't waste anytime barging into the bathroom, and snatching back the shower curtain like she was looking for a cheating husband. "Starr are you okay? Why didn't you answer me?"

Remy could tell she'd been crying. Angel covered her face with her arms. "Get out. I don't want you to see me like this."

"Girl, do you know how many naked women I've seen in my life."

Angel continued to cover her face. "I'm not talking about my body; I'm talking about my face. Look what that bastard did to me," Angel whined, finally dropping her arms.

Remy looked at Angel, who did remind her of the character, Edward Scissorhands, but she didn't want to make her feel bad. Luckily the swelling had gone done. "Are you serious? You're still beautiful as ever. It's nothing that a little makeup can't cover. Don't worry, I'm sure Crystal can hook you up."

"If I hadn't looked in the mirror myself, I would probably believe you."

"Well you need to believe me. Shoot, all we need is some cocoa butter to get a head start on those scars, and everything's good. Shit, and if you wanna go old school, we can put some regular butter up there like my grandmother used to do when I was growing up," Remy replied, with a huge grin.

Angel finally smiled. "Yeah, I guess."

"Well hurry up in here, I need to talk to you," Remy said, as she turned around and closed the bathroom door.

A few minutes later, Angel finally came out the bathroom wearing one of the white hotel supplied bathrobes, and looking like a lost little girl. It was at that moment, when the thought of Angel's age finally crossed Remy's mind. "Do you want me to call someone in your family, so they can come get you?" Remy asked, lighting up a cigarette.

Angel contemplated about calling Antoine for a brief moment, then changed her mind. "Hell no. I don't see a need to go home. Besides, my father doesn't give a shit about me anyway."

"Now why would you say that? I'm sure he's worried sick about you."

Angel sucked her teeth. "Please Remy. You have no idea what kind of childhood I had with a father like mine. He's always been more concerned with the bitches he fucks than me, so I doubt if he's worried at all."

Remy inhaled the smoke from her cigarette then let it out. "Starr, I know it may seem like your father doesn't love you, but I bet you all the money in my pocket that he does, and I don't intend on losing my shit like Sandi did at the restaurant that day." Both Remy and Angel started laughing. "I just think you might be better off back at home then at Freddie's."

Angel's smile instantly turned into a frown. With all the drama and chaos that had happened over the past couple of days she'd completely forgotten about Freddie, and how pissed she was going to be. "Freddie is probably pissed, huh?"

"Shit, that's putting it mildly. She's been asking everybody who comes through the doors of the club if they've seen you or Cutty. All I gotta say is, if you don't go home, you need to get your ass back to the Penthouse because Freddie is going crazy. She's threatening to do some terrible things to you if you don't."

Angel took a while to respond. "Why can't I just stay here?"

Remy put her cigarette out. "Are you serious? Starr, you've already been gone for two days. You must don't understand. If Freddie finds you, it's not gonna be pretty. Don't you get it? She's talking about really hurting you. Shit, soon she's gonna find out that I've been lying about knowing where you are, and I'm not trying to get my ass ripped apart by no dildo."

Angel went over to the bed and sat down as the tears flowed. She was so confused about what she should do.

"Starr, please go home. This is not a place for a smart girl like you," Remy said, trying to console her young friend.

"No, I'm going back," Angel replied, as she wiped her tears. "I wanna go back to the Penthouse."

Disappointed with her decision, Remy knew they didn't have much time to go back and forth. After watching Angel put the clothes on that she'd brought her, Remy started applying a little bit of makeup to Angel's face. "If you go back to the club looking like shit, and not the top money maker, Freddie will definitely kill you then."

Angel never thought things would go that far and hoped Remy was only kidding. "Kill…me?"

At that moment, there was a knock on the door, which immediately put Angel in panic mode. "Oh shit, who is that?"

"Chill out, it's probably just Big Slim. He drove me over here, but I told him to wait a while before he came up to the room so you could get dressed."

Remy walked over to the door and looked out the peephole before opening it. When Big Slim entered the room, he smiled at Angel, who had always been his favorite girl. "How you feeling, beautiful?" he asked.

Angel lowered her head to shield her face. She was slightly embarrassed to let him see her like that. "I'm fine."

"Don't try and hide that pretty face from me. I don't care what that crazy motherfucka did," Big Slim responded. "You still beautiful."

Angel forced a smile. "Thanks."

"How you been holding up over the past few days? Have you been eating?"

Big Slim was starting to remind Angel of a father figure. "Shoot, the only thing I've been doing for two days is eating," Angel replied. "I hope I didn't gain any weight."

"We need to go," Remy said, looking at Big Slim. "You know how Freddie is. If we don't get Starr back, who knows what that crazy bitch will do."

As Angel slid her feet into a pair of Remy's expensive shoes, she contemplated about her decision again, and began to think that the streets were not for her. She thought about how easy her life was back at home, and wondered if her father really was worried about her. Angel looked over at the hotel phone, and thought about calling Antoine to tell him that she'd made a big mistake and wanted to come home, but her thoughts were interrupted.

"Starr hurry up. We need to get out of here. The club is already open, and I need to get back. Shit, Freddie only sent me to the store to get some more of her damn pretzels. I should've been back," Remy informed.

Big Slim and Remy helped Angel as she slowly walked out the hotel room, and downstairs to his truck. Once helping both ladies in the back, Big Slim jumped in the driver's seat and pulled out the parking lot on damn near two wheels. Angel stared out the tinted window watching the downtown scenery change as Remy slid closer and began to rub her back lightly. Remy knew there was nothing she could say that would comfort Angel at the moment, but she wanted to express her support in any way she could.

When the truck pulled up in front of the club fifteen minutes later, Angel braced herself. She knew that whatever Freddie had in store for her wasn't going to be good, so she had no other choice, but to take it like a woman. Big Slim opened the back door, and helped both Remy and Angel out. It didn't take long for several men, who were standing outside to begin yelling out pathetic pickup lines, but the girls ignored them. They had more important things to direct their attention to.

Freddie was standing at the downstairs bar talking with some customers when Remy and Angel walked through the doors. When a few men started calling out their names, Freddie quickly turned her head toward their direction. Remy could feel Angel's entire body shaking as Freddie didn't waste anytime walking up to them. She also didn't waste anytime slapping Angel as soon as she was within arms reach. The impact was so hard spit flew from Angel's mouth.

"Where the fuck you been? I should kill yo' ass for thinkin' you could just up and leave for two fuckin' days. Bitch, who do you think you are?" Freddie grabbed Angel's throat and applied deep pressure.

"Please, let her go Freddie," Remy pleaded.

Freddie removed her forceful grip and looked over at Remy with anger in her eyes. Angel began to cough hysterically. It was obvious she could care less that the entire club was looking at them. "And where the fuck did you find her? How did you know where she was at?"

Remy cleared her throat. "Starr called me and told me to come get her from the Courtyard downtown."

"How the fuck did she get there? Her ass was supposed to be at the motel with Cutty!"

"I don't know," Remy lied.

"If I find out you lying, I'm fuck yo' ass up too," Freddie threatened. She then turned her direction back to Angel. "I been callin' Cutty for two fuckin' days, and he won't answer his phone nor has he been up in here spendin' money. What happened over there at that motel?"

"Nothing." Angel's voice was barely a whisper.

"I see he must have roughed yo' ass up a lil' bit," Freddie said, holding up Angel's face. "Well, I really don't give a fuck what happened. Yo' ass just better hope he comes back up in here. You should know by now it's not wise to fuck wit' my money."

At that moment, a customer at the bar called Freddie over. When she went to see what he wanted, they whispered in each other's ear for a moment before Freddie yelled for Angel to come over. Despite Freddie's angry looks, Remy helped Angel to the bar.

"Remy, don't you got somethin' to fuckin' do?" Freddie asked. "Now...Sam this is my shinin' Starr. Starr, Sam would love to go upstairs with you for an incredible evenin'," Freddie smiled exposing her famous gold tooth.

"I'll take care of him," Remy jumped in.

Freddie's dark skin almost turned blue. "Who fuckin' club is this? I think all y'all muthafuckas around here are forgettin' who's in charge around this bitch. I said 'dat he wants Starr, not you Remy." Freddie reached for an empty Heineken bottle and broke the glass on the bar. "Starr get your ass over here, now!"

Angel slowly walked over and stood next to Freddie like a little child. Remy backed up not knowing what to expect as several other customers and dancers continued to watch the drama.

Freddie grabbed Angel by the hair and yanked her down to the floor. "Open your fuckin' pants and take out your dick!" Freddie shouted at Sam.

A confused look over came everyone's face, especially Sam who kept looking at Freddie, then down at Angel. "Umm... Freddie don't you think we should go upstairs?" he asked.

"Fuck 'dat...you heard me. I want you to take out yo' dick right here, right now. This lil' unfaithful bitch is gonna suck your dick in front of everybody in this fuckin' club. What's wrong? You can't get your dick hard in front of people."

"Oh my dick is already hard. I love to be watched," Sam said, unzipping his pants and whipping out his penis.

"You better suck his dick good and swallow every ounce of cum or I'm gonna use my bob wire dildo to rip your pussy apart!" Freddie yelled at Angel, pulling her hair tighter.

Tears rolled down Angel's swollen cheeks as she closed her eyes to try and hold them back. Quickly, trying to get herself together, she opened her eyes, sat up on her knees and opened her mouth. After tasting the salty flavor of Sam's dick, Angel soon realized that she no longer had control over her life or the things that were happening in it.

Daddy, I wanna come home, Angel thought, wishing for the first time since she'd left that her father could hear her thoughts.

CHAPTER 21

Mariah felt great as she pulled away from the Bal Harbour Shops, having put a major dent in the Hermes and Marc Jacobs stores. Being married to a pro football player with a seven figure salary definitely had its perks, and weekly shopping sprees were at the top of her list. When Mariah heard the popular *Solider Boy* song come on the radio, she turned up the radio and tried to imitate the dance moves she'd seen on BET a few times. Despite how crazy she probably looked, doing the silly dance instantly reminded her of how she and Antoine used to have dance contests back in college.

As Mariah pulled up to a light, she begin to think about Antoine and how much fun they used to have. A week had gone by since the night she ran into him at the bar, and even though he'd pissed her off by cutting their sex short, it was hard not thinking about Antoine when she went to bed at night. Her panties became moist as she thought about his naked body. Mariah hated to admit it, but her former lover was the only man who could hit her pussy in all the right places, and cause her to have multiple orgasms. Not to mention, his dick was two times bigger than her husband's. Deep down, Mariah knew she still had feelings for Antoine, and blamed Angel everyday for tarnishing their relationship.

Several cars started honking their horns, breaking Mariah from her short trip down memory lane. She placed her foot on the accelerator and put the air conditioner on full blast before giving herself some advice.

"Let me stop thinking about Antoine's ass, before I fuck around and lose my husband. What we had was over." She quickly turned the volume back down and changed the station to jazz. "But shit, who am I kidding. It's gonna be hard trying not to masturbate with the thought of that nigga's big dick banging this pussy."

When Mariah arrived in her exclusive Miami Beach neighborhood a few minutes later, there were several people walking in the streets causing her to slowly creep to her house. She wondered where all the people were coming from or going, but the closer she got to her Mediterranean waterfront estate; the more she realized something was going on at her residence. Mariah pulled over when she saw her circular driveway blocked by several cars.

"Shit, I hope Dwayne don't have his team over because I'm not in the mood for entertaining," she said, jumping out her truck. However, the large sign hanging above their black iron gate that read: EVERYTHING MUST GO- .75 OR LESS in bold print confirmed there was no gathering going on. "What the hell is going on around here? Dwayne didn't say shit to me about a yard sale, and I can't think of anything in that house to sell for . 75 fucking cents!" Mariah talked louder as she walked closer to her house.

She stopped dead in her tracks when she realized that everything on the tables, hanging on racks, and on the ground only belonged to her. *Oh my God, this nigga has lost his mind*, she thought. Mariah immediately started pushing people out her way looking for her husband.

"Get the fuck out my yard before I call the police!" she shouted walking through the crowd. "This shit is not for sale!" Even though some people looked at her, they continued to shop.

Her husband was taking two dollars from a woman with a pair of Mariah's favorite Giuseppe Zanotti sandals and Chanel handbag when Mariah ran up on him. Mariah went ballistic when she saw her expensive shoes and purse in the woman's hand.

"What the fuck are you doing, Dwayne? Why is all my shit outside?" Mariah asked in a crazed voice.

"I'll be here all day, so tell all your friends," Dwayne said, handing the woman fifty cents back. "Enjoy your things."

Oh, I gonna make you buy me three more bags for selling my shit. "Don't ignore me!" Mariah ordered, grabbing her husband by his arm.

He looked at her like she was crazy. "Get your damn hands off me. You got some nerve showing your face around here!"

"What the hell is wrong with you? The last time I checked, I live here too. Shit, I just left a few hours ago. Do you need to be on some type of medication?"

"Correction, you used to live here, but not anymore."

"Why are you doing this? What did I do? Why are you selling all my things?" Mariah asked snatching the price tags off her shoes.

Dwayne smirked. "*Your* things. Your broke-ass didn't pay for one single item up in that fucking house. Not even these," he replied grabbing her fake breasts.

"But I don't understand. What did I do? We just talked about all our problems yesterday?"

"Okay, since you're gonna sit up in my face and play the dumb blonde role, check this…our team just had a mandatory physical a few days ago."

Mariah looked confused. "Okay, so…"

"Bitch, do you know how stupid I looked when the trainer came back and told me that I had fucking Chlamydia?" He waited for a reply, but there wasn't one. "I didn't believe him at first because we always joke around the locker room, but when I knew he was serious, it almost killed me. The only person I've been with is you, Mariah. I had to pretend that I was cheating on my wife to save the embarrassment of the guys riding me because my wife is a fucking whore."

Tears began to well up in her eyes. "I don't know what you're talking about. I don't have an STD. The test must've been wrong." Mariah tried to plead her case but then it hit her.

The night she and Antoine had sex, she couldn't recall them using any protection. *Oh my God, that no good motherfucka. How could this shit happen to me?* As Mariah continued to think back, she also remembered making up with her husband the very next morning when she came back home. They always participated in make-up sex, so the thought of her begging Dwayne to 'fuck her harder' started to become crystal clear.

"I knew your ass was going to deny it. First I find out that you got a seventeen year old daughter that you never told me about, now this shit. You know what, all those times I had fucking groupies in my face wanting to fuck me after the away games, I never cheated on you, and this is how you repay me?"

Mariah wanted to answer, but when she saw the nanny with her two small children looking out the window, the tears wouldn't stop. She quickly started walking toward the house, when Dwayne ran from around the table, and blocked her entrance. Mariah went to walk around him, but he kept getting in her way.

"Where the fuck do you think you're going?" he shouted. At that point, he could care less how many people were looking at them, or the fact that he would probably be on the six o'clock news once the news got out.

"If you're putting me out, I'm going to get my children."

"You're joking right? There is no way in hell you're taking my children with your trifling-ass."

"Excuse me, are all these dresses really . 75 cents?" a woman asked, holding several garments.

"Bitch, put my stuff down. None of this shit is for sale. You need to get your ass off my property before I have you arrested!" Mariah shouted.

"Don't listen to her ma'am. Everything in your hand is free. Whatever you can carry is yours," Dwayne responded.

Mariah pushed his chest. "Get away from me. I need to go get my children!" She looked toward the window again to see if the nanny was still there, but she wasn't.

"Why, so you can leave them on somebody's doorstep too? I know your history now."

"You don't understand. I was young back then."

"I don't care how young you were. What kind of mother would do that to her child? And you know what. . . I did a little research and found out your first born is working down at Freddie's Penthouse selling her body for money. From what I hear she's pretty good too. If you were a real mother, you would be rushing down to save her."

Mariah stood glassy eyed from the tears strolling from both eyes. She stared at the window even though her two children weren't there, then grabbed a huge purse off the ground and began stuffing it with anything she could get her hands on. Several women grabbing some of Mariah's designer belts and sunglasses stopped and watched as she continued to stuff the items.

"Don't take everything honey. Save some for us," one of the women said. Mariah looked at the woman and rolled her eyes before walking down the driveway.

"I'll let you keep the truck for now, but I want all my shit back!" Dwayne yelled, as Mariah hopped in the driver's seat.

"Yeah well you're gonna have to hunt me down before I give it up," Mariah said to herself. She quickly drove off, but stopped when she got a few feet away. As tears started to flood her eyes again, she took out her cell phone, and dialed a number. "It's me. I need to talk to you right now."

CHAPTER 22

When *Jesus Will Work it Out,* by the Pace Sisters came blasting through the alarm clock on Antoine's nightstand, he quickly rolled over to turn it off. Surprisingly, the usual aches and pains he woke up with every morning from all the stress of worrying about Angel were not evident. He looked over and smiled when he saw Lady B on her side of the bed. Despite her light snores, she looked beautiful when she slept, and even her elbow that was usually in his face every morning, was under control.

This might be a good day, Antoine thought as he slid his feet into his chocolate colored slippers and headed for the bathroom. After twisting the knob for the shower to start, he used his nose hair clippers while waiting for the water to get hot. Once the temperature was just right and he stepped inside, Antoine placed his head under the water to massage his scalp, but suddenly the once relaxing water began to burn his body.

"Ouch! What the hell?" he screamed out.

"Oh baby, I'm sorry. I forgot how hot the water gets when you flush the toilet," Lady B explained.

Antoine stuck his head through the curtain, and looked Lady B up and down. "So, I guess we're really moving our relationship to another level."

She smiled. "Why? What makes you say that?"

"Because you're starting to pee now while I'm in the shower, when before you would use another bathroom. I even think I heard you let one rip," Antoine replied, with a little laugh.

"Boy, stop playing. You will never catch me releasing any body odors in front of you now or fifty years from now."

"No need to be embarrassed. Everyone does it. Besides, piss shouldn't smell like that, and if it does your ass needs to drink more water."

"Oh, you got jokes, huh?" When Lady B flushed the toilet again, she let out another loud laugh after Antoine yelled from the change in the water temperature again.

"Get out of here, now woman!"

"That'll teach you," Lady B said, closing the bathroom door.

Twenty minutes later, Antoine emerged from the bathroom wearing a towel around his waist. Looking at Lady B sitting on the bed, he began to dance around the room, making his dick move up and down. Little did he know, his seductive moves were starting to turn Lady B on.

I love to watch that big dick move. I wonder if he knows how much I wanna fuck him right now, she thought. She watched as Antoine made his way toward his closet. *But no...he has an important day ahead of him, and I wouldn't want him to lose focus.*

He slipped into his walk-in closet and came back out with a black, pin-striped Armani suit. Antoine wanted to look sharp for his meeting with a leasing agent regarding renting a space for his own rehab center. After going on countless dead-end interviews, he knew it was time to start something of his own. His clientele was already there, all he needed now was gym equipment, and a place to put it. The dream of Five Star Therapy was beginning to show itself.

Antoine gave Lady B a quick New York runway modeling show as he finalized his outfit with his gold Presidential Rolex watch. "How do I look, baby?"

"Absolutely stunning. I could see you on the cover of GQ magazine." Lady B crossed her legs, causing the baby blue robe she wore to open a little bit.

Antoine paused and stared at her smooth thick thighs before making his way up to her beautiful green eyes. *Damn I'm really feeling this girl.* Antoine slid his way over to the bed, then leaned over and kissed her forehead.

"Is that all I get? Wow, the look in your eyes lied to me. I thought you were gonna give me something to think about all day," Lady B said, in a flirtatious tone.

Antoine held a huge grin. "Did you brush your teeth this morning?"

"Get your ass over here!" Antoine leaned back down to Lady B, and their mouths moved slowly toward one another. He could care less if she'd brushed or not. The feeling of her soft plush lips made it worth while. "Thank you. That should hold me over until you get home," she said.

"My pleasure."

Antoine stopped at the door and watched as Lady B got back in the bed and curled up under the comforter. *I've finally found the one,* he thought leaving the room. As Antoine made his way downstairs, he thought about the night he came home late from being with Mariah. Being that Lady B thought it was a boy's night out, she never said a word when he came home. She allowed Antoine to have his space, and didn't crowd him, which was another thing he loved about her. She was damn near perfect, and he knew he had to hold on to a good thing.

Lady B popped from under the covers when she heard the front door close. Antoine starting his car confirmed that the coast was clear. She reached for the cordless phone, and dialed across the keypad, "You need to hurry up. Antoine just left," she said, into the receiver.

಄   ಄   ಄

Two hours later, Lady B had taken a shower, put on a sweat suit and was getting ready to fix herself a cup of tea when the doorbell rang. She hurried over to the door, and looked through the peephole before opening it. "Where have you been? You took your own sweet time, didn't you? Antoine is not gonna be gone much longer," Lady B said, walking back toward the kitchen.

Mariah walked into the house and slammed the door. "Don't fucking question me. I needed to talk to your ass yesterday!"

"Sorry, but I couldn't get away. Antoine and I were together all day."

Mariah was heated. "Yeah, I can see y'all getting real damn cozy around here."

"Damn, who got your panties stuck up your ass?"

Mariah paced around the kitchen. "Are you having fun playing house with this motherfucka? I didn't pay you to fall in love with Antoine. You only had one goal, to keep fucking tabs on the nigga, and get some dirt, so I could use it against his ass in court. But you took getting close to him to a whole other level."

"I had to get him to open up and trust me. Do you know how hard it was to get Antoine to trust a woman? Hell, I should get extra money for completing that task alone."

Mariah walked around the marble island. "Do I owe you extra for spreading your legs and fucking him? Do you get a big bonus for your nasty pussy giving him an STD?"

Lady B looked at Mariah and laughed. "Whatever. My pussy is disease free. What would make you think I gave him something?"

"Because…I had to get it from some damn where."

"What the hell are you talking about?" Lady B looked at Mariah closely.

"Look, Antoine and I slept together the other night."

Lady B looked crushed. "Are you serious?"

"Hell yeah, I'm serious. When my husband told me yesterday that I gave him Chlamydia, I did the math. Antoine probably fucked you without protection then turned around and gave it to me. He was so busy trying to get at this pussy, he forgot to use a condom."

"Listen, whether you fucked him or not, like I said I don't have a damn STD."

Mariah smirked. "Well maybe Antoine got it from another woman he's fucking."

The thought of Antoine having sex with someone other than her, was devastating. "Maybe so," Lady B replied. She paused for a second, and then continued. "So, what happened with your husband?" *Even though I could care less.*

"He kicked me out the house, that's what happened."

Lady B watched Mariah pick up the kettle filled with boiling hot water then put it back down. *This bitch better not do something stupid with that pot,* Lady B thought to herself. "Maybe you need to check your man instead of blaming Antoine. I bet he was the one out fucking and brought that shit to you. And in true pimp form, he picked a fight with your ass before you had time to know what the hell was going on." Lady B laughed.

"And you need to mind your fucking business. Like I said, I didn't pay you to sleep with Antoine, and possibly fall in love with him, so that's all you need to worry about," Mariah repeated.

"Well, you fucking him wasn't the smartest idea either. We used a condom, so maybe you should've done the same since this has obviously turned into some kind of competition."

Mariah laughed. "Trust me when I say, this is not a competition. Besides, if it was, you wouldn't even be in my league."

"What, the minor league? Honey, in case you didn't know Antoine has allowed me to move in. He leans on me for support and I got his nose wide open, so my pussy must be in the major league, bitch."

Mariah laughed again. "Don't let that nigga fool your dumb-ass. As you can see by him fucking me while y'all supposed to be a couple and shit, he's not loyal to anybody."

Lady B knew Mariah was right, but wouldn't dare agree with her out loud. "Look, what difference does it make now anyway? He told me the other day that he talked to someone at the court about stopping the restraining order and the child support case, so you should be happy. Now all this shit can be over."

Mariah put her hands on her hips. "Are you serious? My husband just put me out, and you want me to walk away like everything's okay? Antoine is the reason for all this shit in the first place. Now my money is about to be short," she said. "Fuck that, pay back is a bitch."

"Do you ever get tired of playing games? I mean, you've been doing this shit since college."

"And when the fuck are you gonna get tired of being so naïve? Your stupid-ass the one sitting up here thinking, Antoine was gonna be faithful to you."

Lady B tried her best to act as if Antoine sleeping with Mariah wasn't a big deal, but in fact it was. In reality, she really did have feelings for him, so the news came as a complete surprise.

"I still can't believe you fucked Antoine. What happened to you hating him so damn bad? You know what…your husband should've put your ass out 'cause that was some foul shit."

Mariah became furious. "Fuck you, bitch. Don't get mad at me. If you would've stayed focused, and did what your ass was paid to do, I doubt if you would even care!"

"Yeah, well I do care. By you doing that, it's allowing him to stay in that comfort zone of being a player. Now he's probably never gonna settle down," Lady B replied.

"How could you defend a no-good, selfish ass nigga like him? I don't know about you, but he's messed up with me for the last time," Mariah stated.

"No, I actually think you've messed up for the last time," a deep voice said.

Mariah and Lady B turned around to find Antoine standing in the doorway. As they stood in silence, both of them looked at each other then back at Antoine.

"I would expect some conniving shit like this from Mariah because that's the type of woman she's always been. But Lady B, I've never thought you would do something like this." Antoine walked further into the kitchen. "So here I am thinking y'all hate each other, but actually that's not the case."

The look on both their faces told the entire story. They wondered just how long he'd been standing there and how much he'd heard. Lady B walked around the island to get closer to Antoine, but he backed away.

"I want both of you to get the fuck out my house!"

"Antoine, it's not what it looks like. Mariah just came over to give us some new information about Angel. That's the only reason she got through the door," Lady B tried to explain.

"Don't use my fucking daughter as an excuse to get out of this shit. I heard a lot more than you think. Now, you and your boss need to get out my house." Antoine walked closer to both of them.

Mariah reached for the kettle again. "I wish you would bring your ass any closer. I'll burn your ass like Al Green."

Antoine instantly stopped in his tracks. "Look, just get the hell out! Both of you are trespassing right now."

All three of them continued to look at each other until Lady B finally made the first move, and walked out the kitchen. A few seconds later, Mariah followed. However, she never put the kettle back down just in case Antoine tried something as he walked behind her. Lady B stopped when she got to the front door.

"Antoine can we just talk without her being around?" she asked, looking over at Mariah.

"*Her?* Bitch I got a name," Mariah responded.

"Lady B just go. There's really nothing else to talk about. I just hope the money was worth it," Antoine said.

"Oh, don't worry…she won't be getting paid now, since my husband probably drained my damn bank account by now," Mariah interjected. Lady B looked like she was about to cry.

"Oh well…maybe you'll get lucky on the next assignment," Antoine said to Lady B, as both women made their way outside. "And Mariah since you're homeless now, you can go ahead and keep the kettle because you might need it."

The look on Mariah's face wished death on Antoine as he slammed the door in their faces.

CHAPTER 23

Antoine paced the floor back and forth like a mad man until he heard two cars start up outside. He jetted to the window and looked out to make sure Mariah didn't do anything to his car again, then let out a sigh of relief once both women pulled off. Hurt instantly began to set in as the thought of Lady B deceiving him invaded his mind. For the first time in his life, Antoine felt as though he'd finally found the right one and was beginning to fall in love, so the thought of being played crushed him.

Antoine felt terrible. He lowered his head as he walked into the family room and sat on the couch. After looking at the bottle of Hennessy that sat on the bar across the room, he contemplated about taking a shot, but his thoughts were interrupted when the phone rang. He checked the caller ID before taking the phone off its base, and the word private blinked on the screen.

"Who the fuck is this?" he asked himself, pushing the talk button. "Yeah."

"Antoine, don't hang up," Lady B pleaded.

"What the fuck do you want?"

"I need to talk to you. Trust me, it's important."

Antoine clenched his jaw. "Talk about what? I don't have shit to say to you. Go play games with somebody else!" he yelled, before slamming the phone down. He jumped up to unplug the power cord to the main cordless base, so all the phones wouldn't ring. Just in case Lady B decided to call back, he didn't want to be annoyed, but the phone rung again.

"I thought I told you I didn't have shit to say!" he yelled into the phone. This time he didn't bother to look at the caller ID.

"Damn, who in the hell pissed you off?" Terrell asked laughing.

"Oh, what's up man. I'm sorry I thought you were Lady B."

Terrell laughed again. "Trouble in paradise, huh? What happened?"

"That bitch played me…that's what happened." Even though Antoine was extremely pissed off, he was happy that Terrell called. He needed someone to talk to.

"Man don't worry, these bitches been playing me for years."

Antoine got quiet for a moment. "Yeah, well I don't get played. I'm the one who's supposed to do that shit."

"Tell me what happened."

"You're not gonna believe this shit."

Terrell got hyped. "Oh shit, Lady B had a dude up in your place." He was always guessing before he knew the full story.

"Hell no!"

"Well shit…did she have a woman up in your place?" Terrell said laughing.

"Man, no. If that shit happened, do you think I would be on the phone with you?"

"I give up then. What is it?"

Antoine sighed. "I caught Lady B and that bitch-ass Mariah up in here talking about how they had an agreement to fuck me over."

Terrell didn't respond. Antoine listened closely to see if the line went dead. "Did you hear me? I said Mariah fucking paid Lady B to spy on me. She was playing me the whole damn time."

"Wow! Now that's really fucked up," Terrell finally said.

Antoine began to go into several outbursts as he told Terrell the rest of the story. When he started repeating the same thing over and over again, Terrell knew he needed to help.

"I'll be right over Ant. We need to do something to get your mind off those bitches." Terrell closed his cell phone before Antoine could turn down the offer, then turned his car around and headed for his best friend's house.

It took Terrell thirty minutes to get over to Antoine's house, and another twenty minutes to talk him into going down to Freddie's Penthouse. Despite Antoine's anger, he was still hesitant about being around any women at the moment, but Terrell wouldn't stop begging until he finally gave in.

On the drive to Liberty City, Terrell kept boasting about the new girl at the club who he couldn't wait to bang. He also told Antoine about all the incredible stories he heard about how good her pussy was and the things she could make her mouth do.

"I'm so glad you finally decided to come with me Ant. I've been holding off on going to the club because I wanted my Ho Phi Ho frat brother to be with me," Terrell said with a huge smile. "I'm telling you man. Once you fuck this girl, your ass ain't even gonna be think about Lady B. You're gonna be like Lady who?"

Antoine however, just sat in the passenger seat staring out the window, and constantly asked himself questions about why Lady B would do something like that to him. He was so upset that he didn't even notice when they arrived at the club. Terrell had even managed to park the car and everything.

"You ready to get this pussy?" Terrell asked, as he looked at himself in the rearview mirror.

Antoine shook his head. "I guess so."

"Man, snap out of that shit. I ain't never seen you like this."

"I'm cool," Antoine replied in a low tone.

Terrell stared at him. "So, you ain't gonna look at yourself in the mirror or anything? You never go into a spot with bitches without doing that."

"Can we just get this over with?" Antoine asked, opening the car door. He stepped out and looked around before looking back in the car. "Are you coming?"

"Whatever you say, bro," Terrell answered.

Antoine followed Terrell into the club doors. When he looked around at several of the men who appeared to be enjoying themselves, a smile finally managed to spread across his face. However the smile quickly faded, when he looked at the beautiful girl on stage dancing to R. Kelly's *Sex Me* song. She immediately reminded him of Lady B.

Shit, this is gonna be a long night, Antoine thought as he watched the girl grind her body to the beat of the music.

Seconds later, Freddie came around the bar to greet her new customers. "Welcome to Freddie's Penthouse gentlemen, I'm Freddie. Whose pussy can I get for you tonight?"

Terrell took six hundred dollars out his pocket and waved it in Freddie's face. "Well Freddie, we want a threesome with your new girl."

Freddie laughed. "Honey, yo' ass only gave me six hundred. My new girl Starr, don't come out for nothin' less than a thousand, and that's just for the basics. The price goes up for any of her freaky shit."

Terrell looked disappointed. "Shit…well what do we get for six hundred?"

Freddie pushed her blond weave from her face then took the money out of Terrell's hand before sticking it in her bra. "Crystal, Remy, come down downstairs right now!" Freddie shouted into her portable walkie-talkie radio. Minutes later, the two girls strolled down the steps wearing lace teddies.

"This will work I guess. I'll take the red bone," Terrell said, referring to Crystal. "But I'm coming back for the new chick… believe that."

"Well when you get yo' money right, come see me," Freddie replied walking away.

Remy looked at Antoine and instantly liked what she saw. She grabbed his hand and led him upstairs as Terrell and Crystal followed close behind. On her way up, she glanced over at Sandi, who was giving a guy a lap dance with a serious frown. She seemed pissed that it was Remy going upstairs with a client and not her.

Antoine was halfway up the steps when he looked back to see Terrell already slapping Crystal's ass. Antoine wanted to turn around and go back downstairs, but he knew Terrell was going to be pissed.

When they got upstairs, Remy walked ahead of Antoine and opened the door to her room, and went inside, but Antoine didn't follow. He just stood in the doorway looking like a scared child at the doctor's office.

"What are you waiting for?" Terrell asked, pushing Antoine into the room. Once he was inside, Terrell closed the door then hurried to catch up with Crystal.

"Wow, I've never had to force a guy into my room before. Usually it's the other way around," Remy said, walking over to the bed.

"I'm sorry. Were you talking to me?" Antoine asked.

"You're not even listening to a word I'm saying."

This was new for Remy. At first she was upset, but then found it kind of arousing that he wasn't all over her. Remy instructed Antoine to take a seat on the bed. When he slowly walked over, she asked him his name. However, Antoine didn't respond. He just sat looking around the room at all the items hanging from bed posts and hooks on the wall.

Man I hope this dude is not crazy. We don't need another Cutty episode around here. "Are you okay?" Remy asked.

"Yeah, I'm fine."

"So, what's your name, then?"

"Antoine."

"Well, Mr. Antoine. Are you ready for a night that you'll never forget?" Remy asked in a seductive tone.

"I finally thought I found Ms. Right. I've been doing everything I can to change my ways and just focus on her. Then I find out she was just playing me," Antoine revealed.

"Umm…that was a lot of information," Remy responded. She moved closer to Antoine and began to rub his shoulders. "I hope you don't mind me asking, but who are you? Are you some kind of athlete because your body is amazing?"

"No, I'm just a regular guy out here looking to survive just like everybody else. But instead of my life being simple, my daughter Angel is missing, her bitch-ass mother is out to get me, and my girlfriend is a hired snitch."

At that point, Remy decided that Antoine really needed to get his mind off all the negative shit that was going on in his life. She used the remote on her nightstand to dim the lights and turn on the custom made slow jams CD. Once the music started playing, Remy stood up and started dancing, taking off her teddy and placing it around his neck. She then leaned over and began to suck on his ear lobe like a newborn baby. Antoine just sat there like he was a piece of furniture.

Remy grinded her body up and down his legs before separating them with her knees. As she danced seductively between Antoine's thighs, she slid her tongue from his ear to his neck. Her hands then slowly went down south and stopped at his pelvic area. Remy's eyes lit up when she used her hand to find the imprint of his dick.

Oh shit, his dick is huge, and it's not even fully hard. Remy went to unfasten his belt and zipper to get a view of what he was working with, but was denied. Antoine removed her hands.

"Let me ask you a question. Why did she have to do that to me?"

"Who are you talking about?"

"My girlfriend…you know the Ms. Right I was talking about."

"I don't have the answer to that," Remy answered, going back for his pants.

Antoine stood up. "I can't believe this. I really wish my daughter would come back home 'cause I really need someone right now. I never thought I'd miss having my child around, and for all I know she's probably dead. The police still don't have any leads. What the fuck is God doing to my life? As soon as I start to care about someone, he yanks them out from under me." He made his way to the door.

"Antoine, I really would like to get your mind off your problems," Remy said standing up. Besides, you know you can't get your money back."

"You know what? Here's my business card. If you ever need a trainer, give me a call. I wouldn't be any good to you like this, so just keep the money." Antoine extended his hand. "Oh, and don't tell my friend I left."

Remy took the card and stared at Antoine for a few seconds. "I hope you find your daughter," she said, as he walked out the room.

"Now 'dat was fast," Freddie said, as Antoine walked past her on the steps. "You one of 'dem two minute niggas huh?"

"Yeah, it's amazing what the right woman can do for you," Antoine said, never looking back.

CHAPTER 24

The next night Angel sat in her room up in the Kingdom, and put the finishing touches on her makeup. She still had no idea that her father had only been a few feet away from her the night before, and probably never would. Ever since the Cutty incident, Freddie wouldn't allow Angel to leave her room anymore during business hours, so she had no idea what was going on outside of her room's four walls. Freddie wouldn't even allow the other girls to interact with her. Angel missed going downstairs to flirt with clients or to get a drink from the bar. Everything was sent to her room by a bouncer or even Freddie herself. She was constantly monitored. Even outside of the Penthouse, Freddie watched her like a hawk when they got home. Angel felt like a prisoner. She'd even overheard Freddie telling one of the bouncers to install a camera in her room to make sure Angel didn't try anything. Being at the Penthouse had turned into a living hell.

I don't care if it kills me, I have to find a way to get outta here, Angel thought to herself as she put on her mascara. At the moment, she could hear Freddie walking in the hallway yelling for everyone to get ready, because the doors were about to be open. Trying not to get in trouble, Angel quickly sprayed a few squirts of her Dolce & Gabbana Light Blue perfume between her breasts and made sure her hair was in place. Suddenly, her door opened and Freddie stood in the doorway.

"Get your shit together, Starr. We expecting a few playas from the Miami Heat up in here tonight, so I'll let you go downstairs," Freddie said.

Angel was ecstatic. "Oh, okay." She rushed around the room to grab her things before Freddie changed her mind. She smiled from ear to ear as she walked to the door in a sexy little strut.

"Now let me warn yo' ass before you get any ideas. I'ma be watchin' you at all times, so don't get cute. I wouldn't wanna embarrass you again," Freddie said, with a stern look.

"I understand. I promise to be on my best behavior."

"'Dat's my girl," Freddie replied. She licked her lips and grabbed Angel's ass before letting her pass.

Angel did everything she could not to throw up on her way downstairs. Another one of Angel's VIP clients, Richard led the rush of men once the club doors were opened. Angel took position at the end of the bar as men scurried around the club to get their favorite chairs. The party that took place every night in the Penthouse was about to be on.

Richard stopped to hug a few of the waitresses before noticing Angel sipping on her usual Romance Caribeno mixed drink. He slowly tipped a waitress and directed her to bring his Long Island Iced Tea over to the end of the bar. Richard had a sinister smile on his face as he walked toward Angel, reached into his pocket and positioned himself behind her. She glanced up at his reflection in the large mirror at the back of the bar and wondered what he was up to. Richard then pulled out a lovely white gold necklace with a heart diamond pendant from his pocket and slid it around her neck.

Angel reached up with her right hand and smiled. "What's this?" she asked, looking at the jewelry. "Is it for me, or are you seeing what it might look like on your wife?"

"It's for you. I just wanted to get you a little something for all the special things you do to me. I love our times together, and this is something I thought would look good on you," Richard said, softly. He licked around her ear as he fastened the clip. When Angel spun around on the stool, the smile she had before was gone. "What's wrong? I thought this would make you happy?"

Richard's gift instantly made Angel think back to when Cutty showered her with nice things. "I can't accept this," Angel said, trying to take off the necklace.

Richard grabbed her hand. "Why not. It's perfect and beautiful just like you."

"Look, another one of my VIP's used to give me all sorts of gifts before his bipolar-ass flipped out on me." Angel began to rub the cuts on her cheeks that had almost healed. "I'm not trying to go through that crazy shit again, so you can keep your tokens of affection if that's what comes after this."

Richard took a step back. "Starr, I would never do anything to hurt you. Trust me…I love you more than my damn wife. Why do you think I'm here every night?"

Angel laughed. "To get your dick sucked. You already told me your wife stopped providing that service two years ago."

"No, it's more than that. Nobody makes me feel the way you do."

When Angel was about to respond, she glanced over at Freddie, who watched her every move. She knew Freddie didn't like her girls to talk too long before making a deal to go upstairs, so Angel decided to step it up a notch. Especially if she didn't want the drama Freddie was known for. Angel pulled Richard by his tie between her legs, then smiled before giving him a deep kiss. As she wrapped both arms around his neck, she made her tongue wiggle inside his mouth then bit his lower lip.

"I love the necklace. Thank you."

Richard's dick began to expand and poke Angel's inner thigh. He moved in closer to press his body against her as the smell from her perfume intoxicated him. He lowered his head into the center of her breasts and took a deep breath. Angel moved her right hand down to his waist, then reached inside his pants and repositioned his erect dick to get a good hold before massaging his shaft. Richard looked like he was in heaven.

"I love you so much. I can't wait to get you upstairs," he whispered.

Angel couldn't lie she was just as horny, but was still weary about Richard's sincerity. *Even if he is lying, maybe he can help me get out of here or even let me use his phone to call my father. I need to play my cards right.* "I don't know if Freddie's gonna let you go with me tonight, since there's supposed to be so many pro athletes coming through."

"Don't worry…I'll pay double. Triple if I have to, but you're gonna be with me."

Angel smiled. She loved the attention. "Go give Freddie your money. Then we can get started, daddy. I have some new toys I wanna try out."

Richard didn't want to approach Freddie with a pitched tent, so he decided to wait a few minutes before walking over. As he and Angel waited for is dick to soften, the front door to the club opened. Mariah stepped inside like she owned the place.

Wearing a tight cream colored halter dress, she stood a few feet inside the door and began searching the club. A waitress walking immediately took Mariah as a high class lesbian and offered to show her to a good seat.

"I'm looking for someone in particular," Mariah shouted over the music.

The waitress raised her eyebrows. *Another upset housewife looking for her man who's probably up in here spending the mortgage money*, she thought walking away.

A few guys whistling and making loud passes at Mariah, caught Angel's attention, and when she glanced toward the front door, she had to do a double take. *Damn, that woman looks like my mother*, she thought. *But no, it couldn't be...that lady barely looks a day over twenty-one, and she's wearing the hell out that dress.* Angel looked back over at Freddie, who was being bombarded with basketball players by that time.

Mariah continued to search the club until she finally spotted Angel at the end of the bar. They immediately made eye contact. When Angel realized it was her mother, she slid her hands from around Richard's waist as Mariah began to walk over.

"What's wrong princess?" Richard asked.

"Now that's funny. Those are the same words I used to say to her when she got upset as a little girl," Mariah said, walking up on them. She stood directly beside Richard.

"Oh, that must've been before you fucking dropped me off on my father's door step," Angel shot back.

When Richard turned around, his head went back and forth between Angel and Mariah several times. It was like looking at a shadow. "Starr, I didn't know you had a twin," he said, with a little laugh.

"I'm not her sister asshole, I'm her mother. Now get from between my daughter's legs before I mace your nasty ass," Mariah threatened.

Richard stepped back and held his hands in the air like he was under arrest. Angel instantly jumped off the bar stool. The five inch stilettos made her tower over Mariah. As Angel stepped in front of her, the two stood looking at each other like pit-bulls in a dog fight.

"You're not running shit in here. It's way too late to try a play the damn mommy role."

Mariah's head jerked. "Who the fuck do you think you're talking too? I'll smack the taste out your nasty mouth."

Angel mimicked the head move. "I'm talking to you. Don't come in here disrespecting my clients like that. I'm the big dog up in this spot. All the men want me."

"Do you know how dumb that shit sounds? You're a fucking prostitute at seventeen years old," Mariah fired back. "Look at this place. You're in a dirty club with old, broke dick men who probably need blue pills just to get their shit hard."

"I know you're not passing judgment on me. You're the same woman who dropped her first born on a doorstep, and now you think you're the shit because you're married to a football player. Oh wait, my bad…you're headed to divorce court. Dwayne Wright is your husband's name right? Well he told me all about how he kicked you out after I fucked him last night. Shit, the way he spends money, he could be one of my best clients."

Mariah balled up her fist and went to raise her hand when Freddie walked up to see what all the commotion was about. Freddie grabbed Mariah's wrist as she reared back to take a swing at Angel.

"Hold up, bitch. Are you fuckin' crazy? Nobody hits my girls, especially Starr," Freddie said, holding Mariah's arm tight.

"Freddie, I want you to throw her ass out!" Angel shouted.

"If you upset because yo' man is comin' down here messin' wit' my Starr 'dat's somethin' you need to be discussin' wit' him. It's her job to please my customers."

Mariah was slightly intimidated by Freddie's massive size, but she didn't let that stop her from responding. "Her job! Her fucking job! This little girl is my child. Her name is Angel Moore not Starr as you call her. She's only seventeen years old!" Mariah shouted at Freddie.

So her parents finally came to get her, Freddie thought. *Well that shit still don't matter. I'm not giving up my Starr that easy.* Freddie looked at Angel, then motioned for Big Slim to come over. "Starr, take yo' client upstairs to yo' room, now," Freddie ordered. "Big Slim, keep shit in order up there."

Even though Angel knew leaving with Mariah was a chance to get out, she wouldn't give her the satisfaction. She grabbed Richard's hand, and pulled him upstairs to her room, and never looked back.

Mariah stood in amazement. In that moment, she knew just how much control and influence Freddie had over Angel. Mariah reached in her purse and pulled out a wad of cash. *If I can get this woman to help, I'll have the leverage I need to get Antoine back.*

"Why you pullin' money out?" Freddie asked.

"Money is the one thing that I know talks in a place like this. I'll pay just to discuss something with you," Mariah replied.

"Now you speakin' my language."

As Freddie and Mariah negotiated, Remy quickly made her way downstairs. She hoped like hell Freddie didn't notice that she was late, due to her difficulty finding the perfect outfit. When pro athletes were in the building, everybody wanted to step their game up. Once Remy saw the look on Angel's face as she passed her on the steps, she wanted to stop and ask what was wrong, but Angel kept moving like a speeding car. Remy was surprised to see Angel out of her room anyway, being that she'd been locked down for so long. When she reached the last step, Remy strolled over to the bar and ordered a frozen Margarita.

Freddie sat down on the barstool nearby. "So let's talk. I ain't got all night."

Mariah sat next to her. "I really don't want to cause any trouble around here for you."

"Are you threatenin' me?" Freddie shouted. She jumped off the barstool like she was ready for battle.

Trying not to look in their direction, Remy knew something was about to kick off from Freddie's reaction. She waited on her drink and pretended not to be in Freddie and Mariah's conversation.

"Angel or Starr is my child, but she was living with her father, Antoine when she ran away from home. I've been looking for her for a long time," Mariah lied.

"Okay, so I still don't understand what 'dat has to do wit' me, "Freddie said, sitting back down on the stool.

Remy moved even closer to Freddie and Mariah, but continued to act as if she wasn't paying attention. Several guys approached her for a lap dance or a date upstairs, but she quietly sent them on their way. Hearing the names Angel and Antoine had her full attention.

"The police are looking for my baby. All I have to do is go report that she's being held against her will in here, and they'll shut this place down. Angel is only a minor. You're breaking all type of laws."

Freddie ordered a bottle of VSOP and two glasses. "I get it now. This is a shakedown."

"I'm not trying to shake you down. I'm just talking about a business proposal where I'll pay you to get Angel back."

Freddie's eyes lit up. "How much we talkin' here?"

"I don't know…three thousand."

Freddie laughed hysterically. "Are you serious. Starr can make double 'dat in one night. Did you look at yo' daughter's body? She a goldmine 'round here."

Mariah poured her a shot of VSOP and gulped it down. "Listen, I really need to take my daughter back home."

When Freddie poured herself a drink, she looked up and finally noticed Remy watching her in the mirror. "If you don't get yo' nosey ass up them steps and make me some money, I'ma fuckin' break yo' neck!" Freddie shouted, turning toward Remy.

"Fuck both of y'all cruddy bitches,' Remy said under her breath. She grabbed the closest guy to her and offered him a chance to role play upstairs. The guy didn't hesitate to accept, as they walked off.

"Damn, you don't fuck around do you?" Mariah asked.

Freddie tossed back her shot. "Not when it comes to my money. I don't give a shit 'bout none of these bitches."

"Not even Angel…I mean Starr?"

Freddie smiled. "I found Starr…I mean Angel's ass near South Beach where I normally find all these girls. Her pussy can be replaced wit' another young girl who don' ran away. Shit, I normally make weekly trips out there to find new talent anyway."

"So, how much for her?" Mariah asked.

"Why the fuck do you want her back so bad anyway? From the way the shit looked to me everybody in the damn club know she don't fuck wit' you."

Mariah took another shot. "Like I said, Angel ran away from her father because he abuses her, so I think she'll just be better off with me. I could care less how much she doesn't like me. I'm still her mother. Now, we need to get her out of here before he finds her."

Hearing Mariah talk about abuse instantly made Freddie think about her own father, who'd sexually abused her for years. For once, someone had finally hit a soft spot in Freddie's heart. "Look, just give me four thousand, and she can go."

Mariah's face beamed. "Deal. So, can I can go upstairs and get her now?"

Freddie poured them one last shot. They held up the glasses, clanked them together and swallowed. "Oh, hell no. If I'm lettin' her ass go for 'dat amount, she can't leave until she makes me a lil' bit more money. Come back and get her tomorrow night. She'll be ready by then, and don't forget my loot."

They sealed the deal by shaking hands.

As Mariah walked out the club a few minutes later, she thought her plan was finally going to even the score with Antoine. "I can't believe I'm getting ready to pay four grand to kidnap my own fucking daughter," she said to herself. "Oh well, it doesn't even matter. If taking Angel away from his ass for good, doesn't get back at Antoine then I don't know what will." When Mariah finally reached her truck she smiled. *Besides, I'm gonna make sure that little bitch pays for talking to me like that.*

CHAPTER 25

A ntoine walked into the house exhausted. He'd been out all day running errands, and signing the new lease on his 2600 square foot space for Five Star Therapy. Owning his own rehab and physical therapy center was something he'd dreamed about forever, and now it was finally a reality. However, despite his recent accomplishment, he found himself in a major slump. As hard as Antoine tried, the fact that he didn't have anybody to share the good news with bothered him constantly, and coming home to an empty house was not something he looked forward to. He missed the nights of hearing Angel sing along to almost every song on her iPOD or making love to Lady B. Those nights were special, which he obviously took for granted, and nights he wanted so desperately to have back.

Antoine walked into the family room, and immediately went over to the bar. Taking a shot of Hennessy was more of a habit than anything else lately, and the only thing that seemed to get his mind off things. Hunger never seemed to be in the picture. Once taking the shot to the head, Antoine slumped into his favorite chair before picking up the remote to flip through the channels. Another annoying habit he'd picked up over the past few days.

Antoine put his legs up on the coffee table and kicked off his shoes when the doorbell sounded. "Who the hell can that be," he said to himself. Antoine slowly got up and walked over to the door. When he opened it, a UPS delivery man stood in the doorway.

"I have a delivery for Angel Moore," the delivery man said.

Antoine didn't have the heart to tell the stranger that Angel was missing, and that he had no idea whether she was living or dead. "I'll sign for it," he replied, in a low tone.

After signing on the brown electronic type clipboard, Antoine took the small package and told the delivery guy to have a nice day. He closed the door then went back to the family room to retrieve the same spot on his chair. As Antoine inspected the package, he looked for a return address, but there wasn't any.

"I should respect her privacy, but since she's not here, I might as well see what it is," Antoine said, opening the package. As soon as he saw the big pink box with the words Victoria's Secret on top, he became furious. "Who the fuck would send her some underwear through the mail?" Antoine removed the top of the box to find a matching bra and thong set. As he held the skimpy items in the air a white envelope fell on the floor.

Shit, I've gone this far, I might as well open the damn letter. Antoine was floored when he opened the card, and began to read.

What's up my beautiful Angel?

Where have you been hiding yourself? Haven't heard from you in a while, so I hope you're not mad at me. If not, I was hoping that the next time we get together, you would be sweet enough to wear these for me. I love it when you parade around the room in little items like this just before you do all those freaky things I can't live without.

You know, I'm finally ready to leave my wife so we can spend all our time together. I hope the age difference won't be too much for me. Besides, nineteen years is not that bad (smile). Anyway, I hope you like the gift. Keep sucking on this thing like you do, and I'll shower you with any and everything you want. Please call me, I miss you.

Your Lover 4 Life

At this point, Antoine was beyond furious. He ripped up the card in tiny little pieces and threw it all over the floor, then picked up the thongs and ripped them apart with one pull. He was about to destroy the bra when he heard the sounds of high heel shoes walking on the titled floor. Antoine was shocked when he turned around and saw Lady B coming toward him.

Damn, I forgot to take my house key from her ass the other night. "You've got some nerve showing up and just walking into my house like that. Why didn't you call first?"

"Baby I need you to listen. Please give me a minute to talk to you. I'm so sorry about everything that happened," Lady B said, entering the family room.

"You've got to be kidding. Your ass lied to me. I shared things with you that I would've never done with another woman, and you played me. Get the fuck out and this time leave my key!"

Lady B didn't move. "I'm not leaving here without you hearing my side."

Antoine stared at Lady B, who looked sexy and powerful in her stylish business suit. He was so confused and really didn't know what to do. Part of him wanted to throw her lying-ass out, but the other part needed to hear what she had to say.

"You have every right to be upset. It's true. I started this with the sole purpose of keeping an eye on you for Mariah. But I swear to you…all that changed when I started spending time with you. I love you."

Antoine looked at her like she was stupid. "Yeah…whatever."

"It's true. Antoine, I've had feelings for you ever since we were in college."

"Then why didn't you ever tell me?" Antoine asked.

"Because…you were such a playa in school. I didn't want to get hurt like so many other girls, hell like Mariah. There were so many girls in my dorm and around the campus that you dogged. I just didn't want to become another notch on your long list of accomplishments."

Antoine made a hissing sound. "You're only saying all this because I caught your ass in a lie. A busted woman would say anything."

"You gotta believe me. I was getting ready to tell Mariah that it was over because I didn't feel right being her little watch dog anymore. I was going to tell you everything, I swear. There's so much that you still don't know."

Antoine rubbed his head. "What don't I know? I know it all. You and that no good bitch were using me like your own personal puppet. You pulled my strings while she sat back and laughed, but I won't be that little dummy anymore, so just get out!"

Tears started to stroll down Lady B's face. "You have to trust me. My love for you is real. It feels like my heart was snatched out my chest. I know now that my life won't be anything without you in it." Lady B walked over to Antoine, but he pushed her away.

He didn't want to hear anymore of her lies. Antoine jumped up and stormed toward the front door, hoping Lady B would follow, and she did just that. She looked like a lost puppy the way she held her head down. She also kept begging for him to stop and listen as he opened the door.

"So, did your job really transfer you back down here?" Antoine asked.

"No, I moved back to Miami when I lost my job in New York. I ran into Mariah at the mall after coming from an interview one day, and that's when she offered me money to spy on you. Being that I'd been out of a job for months, I accepted her offer.

However, I didn't expect my feelings for you to come back after all these years."

Antoine sighed. "So, how did you know I was at the Starbucks that day?"

"I didn't. I went to your job looking for you, and that crazy receptionist told me you weren't working, so I went to go get some coffee. I guess it was just a coincidence."

Even though Antoine was glad Lady B was finally being honest, he was still upset that she'd played him for a fool. "For the last time, get your lying-ass out my house, bitch."

The moment Antoine called her out of her name, Lady B's entire attitude changed. "You know what, I think because you're so pissed off at me that you've completely forgotten that you fucked Mariah when your ass was supposed to be my man."

For once, Antoine didn't seem to have a comeback. The tables had suddenly turned. "Yeah, what do you have to say about that shit? Now that I think about it, you lied to me too. You told me you were out drinking with Terrell that night, and actually you were somewhere screwing Mariah. How are you gonna question my loyalty when you don't have any yourself?" Lady B continued.

This time Antoine lowered his head. He knew everything Lady B said was right. How could he be mad at her for something he'd done himself? "You're right. I've been so mad at you that I blocked out my own faults," he responded. Antoine closed the door, then placed his hands over his face. "I'm so sorry to call you that. I just wanted the truth."

Lady B was determined to get everything out. "You want the truth. Okay, here's some truth. Angel is not really your daughter."

Antoine lowered his hands. "What did you just say?"

"I'm sorry Antoine, but Angel is not your daughter."

A cold stare came over Antoine's face, and he became glassy

eyed. He didn't know how to respond. He backed up against the wall and slid to the floor.

Lady B walked over to Antoine and got down on her knees. "I should've told you, but I knew it would destroy you if I did. With all the stuff going on with Angel's disappearance, I couldn't bring myself to tell you the truth."

"How long have you known?" Antoine asked. "Did Mariah just recently tell you?"

Lady B shook her head. "No. I've known since college."

Antoine couldn't believe what was happening. As if his life couldn't get any worse, the child who he'd struggled to raise over the past twelve years, wasn't even his own flesh and blood. It felt like his heart had been ripped out of his chest.

I must've done some fucked up shit in my life to deserve this. "Well, can you tell me one more thing 'cause I gotta know. Do you know who her father is?"

Lady B froze. She paused for a moment trying her best to figure out a way to say it. She stared into Antoine's watery eyes for what seemed like forever before finally getting up the nerve to blurt out the name. "Terrell."

CHAPTER 26

Terrell's name echoed inside Antoine's head over and over. His world had stopped. He didn't know whether to believe Lady B at first, but the more he thought about it, everything made sense. Antoine began to think about all the sneaky and uncomfortable glances the two had made whenever in each other's presence. He also thought about how Terrell used to talk about Mariah when he got drunk back in school. Antoine had obviously ignored everything until that very moment.

"I can't believe this. Why would Terrell do something like that? How could he allow this to happen?" Antoine finally said. "How did you know all this and I didn't? I mean I thought you hated Mariah back in school, and I know you didn't really talk to Terrell."

Lady B rubbed his head. "Mariah and I were best friends in college until she tried to sleep with my boyfriend, and that's when we had that big fight. But before that, Mariah had already told me that she and Terrell were gonna get you back for fucking his old girlfriend."

Antoine cracked a slight smile. "I can understand Mariah being mad, but not Terrell. We shared tons of women. Which one were they talking about?"

"Nina," Lady B informed. "When Mariah found out you cheated on her, she was furious, so to get back at you she slept with your boy. Her dumb-ass just so happened to get pregnant in the process."

I wonder why that girl hates using rubbers, Lady B thought.

Antoine covered his face with his hands again. He was almost in a full blown daze. "I did feel bad after I slept with Nina. I knew Terrell was in love with her, and I didn't even bother to respect that," Antoine mumbled. "You definitely reap what you sow."

"So, can I ask you something?" Lady B asked.

"Yeah, go ahead."

"Do you think you gave Mariah Chlamydia?"

He lowered his hands. "Yeah. I just found out yesterday when I went to the doctor. I should've gone a long time ago though, because I've been pissing out fire for weeks," Antoine admitted. "The crazy thing is, I've had sex with so many women, I don't know who could've given it to me."

Antoine's cell phone began to vibrate before Lady B could make a comment. He ignored it the first time as thoughts of how his life was spiraling out of control consumed his mind, but then the phone vibrated again. Annoyed by the caller's persistence, Antoine looked at the number but didn't recognize it, so he ignored it again. However, the phone continued to vibrate until Antoine finally gave in.

He pushed the button on the side of his phone. Whoever it was obviously wanted to talk real bad. "Who the fuck is this?"

"Umm…is this Antoine Moore, the trainer?" the woman's voice asked.

"Oh, yes. I'm sorry for the way I answered the phone. That was highly unprofessional. What can I do for you?"

"Well, you gave me your card the other night at Freddie's Penthouse. I was the woman with you upstairs."

Antoine took a second to think. *Shit, I hope she doesn't wanna talk about that now with Lady B right here.* "Oh yeah, I remember.

245

Right now is not a good time for me to talk though. Can I call you back when I get a free moment? I need to check my calendar. I'm sure I'll have a session available real soon."

"I'm not calling you about working out. I have some important news that you need to hear," Remy stated.

"What's your name again?"

"My name is Remy. Listen, I was downstairs at the club last night when I overheard this conversation with my boss and this woman. They were going back and forth about a price for one of our girls named, Starr."

"Oh, I heard a lot about that girl. Shit, I heard she got major talent," Antoine tried to smile. "But what does that have to do with me?"

Lady B seemed to be a bit annoyed by the conversation.

"Well, because I remember how you kept talking about your missing daughter when you were here. So after hearing them last night talk about a missing girl named Angel, I put everything together. Starr is your daughter, Angel," Remy stated.

Antoine's heart began to race. "Are you serious?"

"Yes, I am. Your daughter has been working at the Penthouse for a while now. She even lives with us in an apartment up in Little Haiti."

Antoine felt relieved, but was upset that his daughter had resulted to becoming a prostitute, and was now living in the hood. "Who is this *us* you're talking about?"

"Me, two other girls, and my boss, Freddie."

Antoine immediately pictured Freddie from the night he and Terrell went to the Penthouse. He couldn't believe his daughter had gotten involved with the female pimp. "Wait until I get my hands on Freddie's ass? Now that's two people who need to be dealt with."

"Who's the second person?"

246

"Never mind that. What should I do?"

"You need to come get your daughter. Like I said, some lady was talking to Freddie last night about paying her a lot of money to take Starr…I mean Angel away. If you ever want to see your little girl again, you better come to the club tonight."

"Who was this woman you're talking about?"

"I'm not sure who she was, but they looked a lot alike."

It didn't take a rocket scientist to figure out, the person Remy was referring to was Mariah. *Now that's three people who need to be dealt with.*

"Where's Angel at now? Can I talk to her?" Antoine asked.

"She's not with me. Freddie took her to get her hair and nails done before the club opens. Since this is Angel's last night, Freddie wants her to look good, so she can be with as many men as possible."

Antoine was furious. "What time should I be there?"

Remy paused. She peeked through the curtains when she heard the loud music coming from Freddie's truck. "Look, that's Freddie so I gotta go. We're on our way to the club now, so just get there whenever you can."

Antoine shut his phone when the line went dead and put it back in his belt clip. He stood to his feet, and ran upstairs to find his gun, never saying a word to Lady B.

"I love you Antoine," she belted, as he passed her.

When Antoine didn't respond, she dropped her head and slowly walked out the house.

Once upstairs, Antoine dialed Terrell's number but didn't get an answer. He didn't want to tell Terrell what was going on by leaving a message, so he hung up once his voicemail came on. This was information that needed to be delivered in person. Feeling the need to look gangsta, Antoine put on a pair of black jeans, a black sweat shirt and some black Nike boots. After grabbing his . 45 caliber Glock, he inserted the ten round clip into the handle.

Antoine got down on his knees, and began to pray to God for strength. It was definitely going to be needed for what he was about to do. Once his prayer ended, he jumped up, stuck the gun in his waist and headed downstairs. He stopped when he noticed that Lady B had left his house key on the last step.

"Everything that's gone wrong in my life is because of me and my past. I swear that from this moment on, I'm going to change my ways and remove all the negative people from my life... starting with Terrell and Mariah. Both of them motherfuckas are good as dead," Antoine said as he walked out the door.

CHAPTER 27

Terrell sat in the parking lot at Freddie's Penthouse listening to Usher's song *Seduction*, on the radio, which was definitely helping him get in the mood. "I hope Starr's pussy is all that it's cracked up to be," Terrell said, stroking his dick. He wanted to get his first nut out the way, so he would be a stallion during the second round. If Starr was as good as her reputation, he didn't have time for any one minute man episodes. He pictured himself smacking her ass and watching it jiggle back and forth until the needles suddenly built up in his feet.

"Ahh," Terrell moaned, as his dick exploded cum into the tan wash cloth he held in his hand. Even though he enjoyed jerking off, he had to prevent anything from squirting all over his leather seats. Terrell's car was truly his most cherished possession.

After carefully placing the wash cloth on the floor, Terrell placed his dick back into his pants then took out a bottle of hand sanitizer from his glove compartment. He squirted the clear gel into his palm before rubbing his hands together. Once that was done, he zipped up his pants, and looked at himself in his rearview mirror. He looked at his teeth thoroughly to see if any food had been left behind, then gave himself a quick breath test.

"That area could use a little bit of help," he said, popping several tic-tacs in his mouth. After making one last adjustment to his shirt, he finally opened up the car door. Terrell jumped out, barely able to withhold the anticipation, activated the alarm, and quickly headed toward the club.

Luckily the bouncers didn't make him wait in line very long, and once they let him through, Terrell didn't waste any time making his way inside. He walked straight up to Freddie, who was cursing out the bartender about a drink, she'd just screwed up, and tapped her on the shoulder.

"Do you remember me? I got the right amount this time," he said, patting his pocket.

Freddie turned around. "I remember you. Yeah, I hope you got all yo' shit 'cuz I don't have time to deal wit' broke-ass niggas. The pussy up in here is just like my liquor. If you want the top shelf shit, yo' ass gotta pay extra."

Terrell reached into his pocket and pulled out a stack of money tied with a rubber band. "Here's a thousand. This girl better have pussy that belongs on the damn roof. Fuck the top shelf."

"Actually you picked a night when my prized possession is in great demand, so I'm chargin' fifteen hundred to two grand to be wit' her."

Terrell looked crushed. "Come on Freddie. Don't do this shit."

Freddie laughed. "Damn, she ain't crack, muthafucka."

"I know, but it's just that I been looking forward to this."

"I'll tell you what, since this is Starr's last night here at the Penthouse, I'll let yo' ass slide this time. You can be wit' her, but you gotta bring me the rest of my fuckin' money tomorrow. You know what to expect if I don't get it." Freddie cracked her knuckles on her left hand.

Seeing that this was his only option, Terrell agreed. "Bet."

"Oh, one more thing, her time is precious tonight, so I'm not sure how long you'll have wit' her."

Terrell thought about it for a second. *I've been waiting to hit this pussy for so long, I could care less.* "As long as I cum, I should be fine."

"Take a seat at the bar. I'll go upstairs to get Starr ready for you. Have yo' money ready when I come back." Freddie turned to the bartender. "Give him two drinks on the house, and don't fuck up this time."

Terrell sat at the bar and watched as Freddie marched up the steps toward the Sex Kingdom. He ordered his usual Hennessy and Coke, but decided to add a shot of Remy on the side to switch it up this time. He was nodding his head to the beat of the music, when a sexy waitress walked up to the bar. Terrell began to flirt as she waited for the bartender to complete her order. He still had a few dollars in his pocket and thought a lap dance would ease some tension, but the waitress quickly brushed him off.

"Forget you then, trick," Terrell shouted, as she walked away. He pulled out his cell phone, and decided to call Antoine. He couldn't wait to inform his friend what he was about to get into.

"Just the man I wanted to talk to," Antoine answered. "I've been looking for your ass. Where you at?"

Terrell was so excited he didn't even recognize the hostility in Antoine's voice. "Man, you're not going to believe where I am. I'm sitting at Freddie's Penthouse waiting for that bitch, Starr to come downstairs. Now you know I'm going to knock the dust off that pussy."

Antoine was enraged hearing Terrell talk about Angel like that. "Well make sure you don't leave before I get there."

"Man I ain't going anywhere until after I get my nut. Oh, by the way what happened to your punk-ass the other night? Don't tell me the hoe was too much for your old ass to handle."

"I'll be there in a minute." CLICK.

"Damn, that nigga just hung up on me. He definitely needs some pussy."

"Baby you want a dance?"a soft voice whispered into his ear.

Terrell turned around to find Sandi playing with her nipples. "Hell yeah. I could use an appetizer before the main course," Terrell replied.

Just about the same time Terrell was being humored with one of Sandi's famous lap dances, Mariah walked through the double doors of the club like she was on a mission. She checked the time on her Chanel watch, and realized that she was about three hours early. Mariah and Freddie had come to an agreement to let Angel work the majority of the night, but Mariah had a gut feeling that something was going to go wrong. Her new plan was to offer Freddie more money to let Angel go a little earlier, so they could leave town as soon as possible. The sooner she got Angel out of Miami the better. That way, Antoine would never find her.

Mariah looked around the club, but couldn't find Freddie. She did however spot Terrell at the bar rubbing Sandi's ass and smiling like he'd just won the lottery. He was unaware that Mariah was a few feet away watching him like a hawk, but when he finally raised his head a few moments later, they immediately locked eyes. The expression on both of their faces said the exact same thing. *What the hell are you doing in here?*

Terrell quickly turned his head, hoping Mariah would get the hint, and leave him alone. However, it didn't work because when he glanced around the untamed wig Sandi wore, Mariah was sitting on the stool next to him. He leaned back and ran his right hand over his face.

"If you want a dance, I'll be finish with him once the song goes off," Sandi said to Mariah.

"Oh, take your time. I'm enjoying just sitting here watching you work this loser," Mariah replied.

Terrell sucked his teeth then pushed Sandi from between his legs. After pulling out a twenty dollar bill from his pocket, Terrell kissed her hand and thanked her for the wonderful job. He looked at Mariah hesitantly as Sandi took her fee, and walked away. She was between another customer's legs, seconds later.

"What are you doing here?" Mariah asked. "Are you following me?" She seemed very paranoid.

Terrell shook his head. "Why the fuck would I follow you? I'm a guy who likes pussy, and this is a titty bar, so you do the math." Terrell leaned closer to Mariah. "I think the better question is what are you doing here?"

"I'm done with dick. I'm a pussy licker now," she joked.

Mariah's response seemed to be more than Terrell could handle. His mind raced trying to figure out if she was serious. He grabbed his shot of Remy that had obviously been sitting there for a while, and tossed it back.

"I wouldn't be surprised if you were. I always thought you and Lady B should've been lipstick lesbians and shit. By the way, that's fucked up what y'all did to Ant."

"Well, he started it. He should've never done that child support shit. Now my marriage is all fucked up because of his ass."

Terrell smirked. "Don't blame Antoine because you're a trifling-ass mother. You should've taken care of your seed."

Mariah looked like she wanted to slap him. "Fuck you, Terrell. Don't be passing judgment on me asshole, especially since you've never taken care of your daughter either."

"Why would I take care of her? Even though the baby was mine, you chose Antoine as the father, remember? After you had Angel, you told me to stay the fuck away, so that's what I did."

"Still, you saw how Antoine struggled to raise her. You should've been a man, and stepped in or at least helped him out."

Terrell laughed. "And mess up me and Ant's relationship by telling him the truth? I don't think so. I was pissed when he fucked Nina, but not enough to claim Angel at that point. So now, you need to stay the fuck away from me."

Suddenly Freddie tapped Terrell on his shoulder. "Hey money man, here she is," Freddie said. "Starr's gonna make sure her pussy is worth yo' fifteen hundred tonight."

When Terrell and Mariah turned around and looked at Freddie, they couldn't believe their eyes. Angel looked like a runway model from the ton of makeup and expensive looking dress she wore. Angel was just as shocked.

"You nasty motherfucka! You're here to fuck your daughter," Mariah shouted.

Terrell was beyond speechless.

"What the fuck are you talking about Mariah? He's not my father," Angel replied. She placed her hands on her hips like she demanded answers.

"I can't believe you. How could you stoop so fucking low, Terrell? She's your blood. I always knew you were a piece of shit, but this takes the cake," Mariah said ignoring Angel.

"Are you crazy? I had no idea the new girl was Angel. I would never do any shit like that," Terrell replied.

"Can somebody fucking answer me? What's going on?" Angel asked. At that point, she could've cared less if Freddie was going to be mad from the way she acted.

"I don't care about none of this shit. All I know is 'dat somebody better hand over my money or both of y'all can get the fuck out." Freddie jumped in the middle of the chaos. She looked back and forth between Mariah and Terrell.

"Antoine's my father. I don't know why you just said Terrell was," Angel continued.

"I'm sorry Angel. I should've told you this from the very beginning, but Antoine is not your biological father. Terrell is."

The customers and dancers in the club were now engaged in watching the live soap opera unfolding in front of them. They stood around wondering what bomb shell would be dropped next.

"So, you just go around fucking everybody, huh?" Angel looked at Mariah with rage in her eyes. "You're such a fucking hoe."

Mariah jumped up off the stool, and lunged at Angel, but Freddie blocked her path. "Wait a fuckin' minute, bitch. You better kept yo' hands to yo' self up in my spot." She looked at Terrell. "Father or not, are you still tryin' to fuck or what? I got other people waitin' for this pussy."

"You're one crazy broad, cross-dresser, or whatever the fuck you are. This is some serious shit we're talking here."

Freddie just shrugged her shoulders. As the drama continued, no one ever noticed Antoine walk into the club. With all the yelling that was going on at the bar, he turned his head in that direction, and the first person he spotted was Terrell. Antoine moved as quiet as a mouse trying not to make eye contact with his former friend. The closer he got to the bar, he finally saw Mariah, and the one person who he thought he'd lost...his daughter. However, their reunion would have to wait because he had business to take care of.

Terrell turned his head when he felt Antoine coming closer, but all that did was make Antoine's right fist connect flush with Terrell's cheek bone.

The impact made Terrell hit the floor instantly. Antoine began to stomp every part of Terrell's body, then quickly pulled out the gun from his waist. At that point, all hell broke loose. Freddie yelled for the bouncers, and they all rushed Antoine at the same time, causing the gun to fall out of his hands. As Antoine and Freddie started to scuffle, Angel jumped on Freddie's back like a raging bullfighter.

"Get the fuck off my father bitch!" Angel screamed. She fought Freddie hard, scratching her in the face with deep scrapes into her skin.

A serious club brawl broke out within minutes. Punches were flying, people were yelling, and the sounds of bottles breaking rang out through the club as the intensity of the fight grew.

From all the noise going on downstairs, even Remy and Crystal came out their private rooms to see what was going on. When they saw Angel being knocked around by Freddie, Remy was the first to run down the steps with Crystal not far behind. When they got downstairs, each of them tried to pull Freddie off, but nothing seemed to work. Even Mariah threw a few punches to Freddie's body trying to rescue her daughter for the first time.

The fight had everyone's attention, and customers moved to better spots to watch the mayhem. That is, until loud gunshots were fired into the ceiling which caused everyone to come to a complete halt. Screams could be heard all over the club. When everyone looked in the direction of the gunfire, Cutty was standing in front of the door with a black semi-automatic Tec-9. He looked like Rambo himself the way he held the assault weapon in his hand.

"Freddie, where the fuck are you? Stand your ass up!" Cutty shouted. He looked around at all the people who were taking cover under whatever they could. "Freddie, did you fucking hear me?"

She slowly stood to her feet. "Cutty, what the hell are you doin'? Please put the gun down."

"Bitch, you set me up, so now it's payback time. That's what I'm doing."

Freddie looked puzzled. "What are you talkin' about? Set you up how?"

"Don't play dumb. I'm sure you know what your bitch-ass bouncers did to me in that motel?"

"I swear, I have no idea what you talkin' 'bout. You my best VIP, why would I set you up?" Freddie looked over at Angel. "So, 'dat's why I ain't heard from him. What the fuck happened over there that night?"

Cutty looked at Angel who was balled up on the floor. "I ain't finished with you either."

A loud noise on the opposite side of the club caused Cutty to turn his head in that direction. However, this also allowed one of the bouncers to grab Antoine's gun that had fallen a few inches away from him. Cutty stumbled back seconds after the bouncer pulled the trigger twice. One bullet landed into his left shoulder.

Cutty caught his balance and immediately started firing round after round. At the same time, another bouncer managed to slip his gun from his ankle holster. Three people were busting off like the fireworks on the Fourth of July. Cutty's Tec-9 with a 30 clip was being put to work. He unloaded every last bullet.

Moments later, when all the clips finally ran out and the echoes from the firing silenced, people started to rise and check themselves for gunshots.

"Oh my God!" Angel screamed, when she finally stood up and saw Antoine lying on the floor under a pool of blood.

She ran over and dropped to her knees next to Antoine. "Daddy hold on. You're gonna be alright." She looked frantically around the club. "Somebody call an ambulance."

"I'm...okay," Antoine managed to moan.

When both Crystal and Sandi rose to their feet, they walked over to Remy who'd gotten shot in her arm, but seemed okay. They then made their way over to Freddie, whose lifeless body laid on the floor. Even though her eyes were wide open, she was dead. The gunshot wound in her right temple oozed with blood. Mariah, Cutty and a bouncer were also dead.

Whoever wasn't wounded scrambled to get out the club as soon as possible. When the paramedics and the police arrived a few minutes later, there was barely anyone left. A few of the EMT's immediately ran over to Antoine and applied pressure to the bullet wound in his abdomen.

"Is he gonna be okay?" Angel cried.

"We need you to move Miss, so we can work on him," one of the paramedic's responded. He used a pair of scissors to cut open Antoine's shirt as Angel rose to her feet.

At that moment, Terrell tried to make his way over to Antoine, but Angel wasn't having it. "Get the hell away from him," Angel said, pushing Terrell away with all her strength. "You obviously caused all this shit."

"Angel..." Antoine called.

She turned around and kneeled down by her father's side. "I'm right here daddy." She looked up at Terrell to make sure he'd heard what she said.

"I don't...care...what anybody...says, you're my...daughter. Always will...be."

"I know daddy."

"I love…you. I'm…so… sorry I let…you down."

Tears began to rush toward Angel's chin. "I love you too, daddy but don't talk anymore. You need to save your energy."

Antoine paused for a brief moment, but decided to continue. "Promise…me you…won't let…sex ruin your… life. Promise… me that." Antoine coughed up blood before Angel could answer.

"We need to get him to the hospital," the paramedic ordered. "He's losing too much blood."

Antoine's chest moved up and down, as the blood continued to pour out. Seconds later, his body didn't move at all. The paramedics had seen it all before. The massive amount of blood loss, had taken Antoine's life.

Angel's screams pierced everyone's ears. "Daddy, wake up!" She moved one of the paramedic's hands out the way, and shook Antoine's shoulders. "Daddy, get up. I promise. Do you hear me, I said I promise."

There was no response. Angel continued to shake her father's shoulders, but eventually stopped. The tears made her vision blurry. Angel used her hand to close Antoine's eyes, then lowered her body to place a kiss on his forehead. The only person who'd ever truly loved her was gone.

Angel stood up, and quickly made her way toward the front doors of the club. She had to get out. Despite Terrell constantly calling her name, she never looked back. Angel worked her magic and convinced a police officer to let her go outside for some air, and after letting her through, she took off running as soon as her feet hit the pavement. Angel wasn't sure where she was headed, but she vowed to keep the promise to her father forever.

"This book will definitely have you
holding onto your daughters..."
-Tonya Ridley, Author of Talk of the Town

Daddy's House

BY AZAREL

Essence Magazine Best Selling Author of Bruised 2

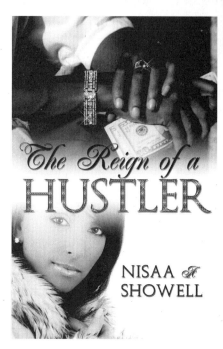

As a young girl Karen Whitaker dreamed of becoming rich and famous, promising to buy her mother that huge house on the hill with a Rolls Royce parked in the driveway. Her desire for material things turns into a grown woman's obsession with money, power and sex. Now of age, Karen possesses the brains of a scholar, beauty of a diamond, and a body that a Coca-Cola bottle would envy. She knows how to get what she wants even if it means taking advantage of those who trust her most. Greed and passion for tantalizing sex throttles her into compromising situations that may destroy her career and crumble her picture perfect relationship with a multi-millionaire. Take a journey into her intriguing story as demons from her past strike to unravel her fairytale life thread by thread. In the end, will she escape her dark clouds or be exposed as one money-hungry, conniving vixen?

Visit Nicolette Online @
www.myspace.com/paperdollthebook

Available At Borders, Waldenbooks and Independent Bookstores Nationwide

Quinnzel has led anything but a charmed life. After shattering his knee in high school and ruining a chance at a college scholarship, his brother finances Quinnzel's way through school. But everything has a price. After graduating at the top of his class from Georgetown, Quinnzel takes his business degree and uses it to run his brother's drug dealing operation.

Imani Heaven Best is everything Supreme has been looking for. She is Beyonce, Oprah, and Eve rolled up into one. Her business savvy, as well as her street smarts, makes her wifey material and she has his nose totally open. After losing her first love to the streets, Imani is not really feeling another ride down heartache lane. But there is just something about that man they call Supreme.

Experience thug life and gangsta lovin' as a steamy connection ensues between two effervescently brilliant identities in this pictorial tale of raw urban hooks.

Distributed by: Afrikan World Books, Ingram, Baker and Taylor, Life Changing Books. and Amazon

ORDER FORM

MAIL TO:
PO Box 423
Brandywine, MD 20613
301-362-6508

FAX TO:
301-579-9913

Ship to:	
Address:	
City & State:	Zip:
Attention:	

Date:
Phone:
E-mail:

Make all checks and money orders payable to: **Life Changing Books**

Qty.	ISBN	Title	Release Date		Price
	0-9741394-0-8	A Life To Remember by Azarel	Aug-03	$	15.00
	0-9741394-1-6	Double Life by Tyrone Wallace	Nov-04	$	15.00
	0-9741394-5-9	Nothin Personal by Tyrone Wallace	Jul-06	$	15.00
	0-9741394-2-4	Bruised by Azarel	Jul-05	$	15.00
	0-9741394-7-5	Bruised 2: The Ultimate Revenge by Azarel	Oct-06	$	15.00
	0-9741394-3-2	Secrets of a Housewife by J. Tremble	Feb-06	$	15.00
	0-9724003-5-4	I Shoulda Seen It Comin by Danette Majette	Jan-06	$	15.00
	0-9741394-4-0	The Take Over by Tonya Ridley	Apr-06	$	15.00
	0-9741394-6-7	The Millionaire Mistress by Tiphani	Nov-06	$	15.00
	1-934230-99-5	More Secrets More Lies by J. Tremble	Feb-07	$	15.00
	1-934230-98-7	Young Assassin by Mike G.	Mar-07	$	15.00
	1-934230-95-2	A Private Affair by Mike Warren	May-07	$	15.00
	1-934230-94-4	All That Glitters by Ericka M. Williams	Jul-07	$	15.00
	1-934230-93-6	Deep by Danette Majette	Jul-07	$	15.00
	1-934230-96-0	Flexin & Sexin by K'wan, Anna J. & Others	Jun-07	$	15.00
	1-934230-92-8	Talk of the Town by Tonya Ridley	Jul-07	$	15.00
	1-934230-89-8	Still a Mistress by Tiphani	Nov-07	$	15.00
	1-934230-91-X	Daddy's House by Azarel	Nov-07	$	15.00
	1-934230-87-1-	Reign of a Hustler by Nissa A. Showell	Jan-08	$	15.00
	1-934230-86-3	Something He Can Feel by Marissa Montelih	Feb-08	$	15.00
	1-934230-88-X	Naughty Little Angel by J. Tremble	Feb-08	$	15.00
	0-9741394-9-1	Teenage Bluez	Jan-06	$	10.99
	0-9741394-8-3	Teenage Bluez II	Dec-06	$	10.99
			Total for Books	$	
			Shipping Charges (add $4.25 for 1-4 books*)	$	
			Total Enclosed (add lines)	$	

* Prison Orders- Please allow up to three (3) weeks
for delivery.

For credit card orders and orders over 25 books, please
contact us at orders@lifechaningbooks.net
(Cheaper rates for COD orders)

*Shipping and Handling of 5-10 books is $6.25, please
contact us if your order is more than 10 books. (301)362-
6508

Black and Nobel

1411 W. Erie Ave.
Philadelphia, Pa. 19140
215-965-1559

Wholesale   **Retail**

African Shea Butter
Books
We Ship To Prisons

blacknoble1@yahoo.com

Marketing and Promotions

www.BlackandNobel.com
www.myspace.com/blackandnobelbooks.com
Major Credit Cards